TROUBLE WITH TIME

EDITED BY DAVID LAWRENCE MORRIS, CAROL
MCCONNELL AND ROBERT ALLEN LUPTON

THREE COUSINS PUBLISHING

ISBN 13   9798340138279
ISBN 10   8340138279

The publisher is not responsible for websites (or their
content) that are not owned by the publisher.

This book is dedicated to everyone who thought that if only they could go back in time and do it over, things would turn out better. Well, maybe they would and maybe they wouldn't. For most people, the first thing they'd do, if they could go back in time, would be to punch themselves right in the face.

THE

TROUBLE

WITH

TIME

AN ANTHOLOGY

Anthologies by Three Cousins Press

Are You A Robot?

Witch Wizard Warlock

Table of Contents

SADDLESAUR

By Campbell Blaine

We didn't always ride dinosaurs. It all started eleven years ago. It was a Friday. I remember because it was the day before my twelfth birthday. Davy had gotten into a fight with two of the Welch brothers at school and whipped them both. He said they'd made fun of President Franklin Pierce. I didn't think Davy cared much about the President, but he'd fight a fencepost if it was in his way.

Our sister, Carolyn, was feeding the chickens, and Davy and I were doing the afternoon milking in the barn. Carolyn ran into the barn and yelled. "Bobby get the shotgun. Davy, saddle the horses. Two flying lizards done stole a rooster and a hen. I aim to get 'em back."

Davy kept milking. "Probably hawks. Lizards don't fly much."

She hit him in the back of his head with a raw egg. He jumped up, stepped in his milk bucket, and kicked over his stool. He ran his hand behind his head and looked at his yolk-drenched fingers. "You hit me with an egg."

"As hard as I could. Get the horses saddled. Bobby, get the gun. I've got more eggs."

Davy and I looked at each other. I shrugged and nodded. We were always inclined to do whatever Carolyn wanted and I'd never seen a flying lizard. Truth be told, there wasn't much new that happened on a cattle ranch about fifty miles southwest of Santa Fe. I grabbed my single-shot 410 and a pocket full of shells and helped Davy saddle our horses.

"Carolyn, we should tell Mom where we're going," said Davy and he climbed on his horse.

"Don't know where we is go'in. Them lizards flew toward the mountains."

I was the oldest, not the smartest, but the oldest. "I'll tell her." I rode to the open kitchen window and shouted, "Mom, two flying lizards stole some chickens. We're gonna chase 'em down and kill 'em."

She sat a wild blackberry pie on the window ledge. "That's nice dear. Don't shoot any of the cattle. Dinner's at sundown."

1

Carolyn took the lead. I didn't expect no flying lizards, but when you're twelve and live on a remote ranch, you take adventure when you find it.

She pointed at a bird in the distance. "That's one of em."

Davy sneered, "Just a buzzard."

"I've still got eggs. Follow me."

We didn't have to follow her very far. The spec got larger. It was flying toward us. A second spec joined the first one.

"Bobby, you get off your horse and get that shotgun ready."

I did. One shell in the chamber and one clenched in my teeth for a quick reload. I put my Stetson on the saddle horn and waited. The specs got closer. They had wings, but they didn't flap them like eagles or hawks. They didn't soar like buzzards. The closer they came, the lower they flew.

"I'll be damned," said Billy. Those are lizards. No, wait. They're dinosaurs. I read about them in school. A guy named Owen in England came up with the name a couple years ago. They're sposed to be all dead."

The two lizards swooped down to inspect us. Brownish colored with long thin faces, they screeched like a hog stuck in a barrel hoop. I'd like to say that I was brave and aimed carefully. Carolyn screamed shoot and I closed my eyes and fired.

One of the creatures was dead on the ground and the other one flew toward the mountains. Davy and I walked to the dead one. I poked it with the shotgun barrel. It was twice as big as an eagle and its feet had sharp talons. I'd shot away half its face.

"Leave it, it's dead. It'll be here when we come back. I'm after the live one, "shouted Carolyn. She spun her horse, Queenie, around and galloped away.

Good brothers take care of their sister and 'sides, she was meaner'n either of us, so we mounted up and chased the terry dac'l thing across the grassland.

We came to the base of the Jemez Mountains. Carolyn pointed. "Cave! It flew into that cave."

Chasing a flying dinosaur into a cave doesn't seem like all that good an idea looking back, but children are children. So armed with a single shot 410, three knives, half a dozen raw eggs, and good intentions, we entered the cave. We didn't have a carbide lantern or nothing else to see by, but the cave looked strangely lighted inside.

2

The floor near the entrance was covered in footprints that no cow or human had made. "Gonna kill it," said Carolyn.

We entered the cave. Cold moisture formed on my arms. After a few feet, a white mist filled the air. Carolyn sniffed it. "Fog, just fog. Going in."

I lost all sense of direction inside the fog and was thankful when after only a dozen steps it ended. I must have gotten completely turned around because the cave mouth was right in front of me. The three of us walked to the entrance.

The world was different. Our horses were gone and so were the grasslands. It was a lush tropical jungle. Giant trees, tall grasses, and huge flowers. Bees were the size of robins. A web as large as a house glistened with moisture in the hot sun. I touched a strand and a dog-sized spider scampered into the treetops. A flying lizard bigger than a bull flew lazily above us. Snakes as long as a fence line climbed vines bigger around than a full-grown hog. Davy stared. "I don't think we're in New Mexico anymore."

I was for leaving that second, but Carolyn wouldn't hear of it. "Got the shotgun loaded. Let's find a flying lizard nest."

Bravado and revenge aside, the three of us stayed near the cave mouth. At the base of a large conifer tree, we did find a nest with three huge eggs. The skull of what appeared by its teeth to be a giant rodent snuggled the eggs. Suddenly a screech like a freight train interrupted our inspection.

A bluish-green dinosaur twice as big as a horse spit a dead hairy animal out and screamed louder. It stood on two legs and its front arms were smaller than mine. It turned its square-jawed head to the side so it could see us better. Droll and blood dripped between teeth the size of Bowie knives.

"Be still," I said. "It can sense motion."

The creature took two steps toward us. Carolyn picked up an egg and whispered, "It can hear, too, Time to run. Bring the eggs, leave the skull."

I grabbed an egg and chased Carolyn into the cave. Davy was right behind me. I thought I felt dinosaur breath on my neck, but it didn't catch me. We charged into the disorientating fog and in a few steps staggered outside the cave. Our tethered horses were happily eating the foliage they could reach.

Carolyn said, "Hand me the egg. Aim the shotgun at the fog and be ready."

I grumbled and gave her the egg. "You're not the boss of me."

I put a round of double ought buckshot into mama dinosaur's gaping mouth, reloaded, and fired again. I reloaded and waited, but nothing came after us. Carolyn loaded all three eggs into her saddlebags. "Someone that's not you has to be the boss of you. Let's get home. Supper's waiting.

We hid the eggs under the straw in the barn. They hatched a week later into perfect little replicas of mama dinosaur, the one I'd shot. They were like little baby ducks with sharp teeth. By that, I mean that the babies did what baby ducks do, they decided that the first things they saw were their mothers. That would be Carolyn, Davy, and me, Bobby.

The only book we had at our house was the Bible and we picked names from that. Shadrach, Meshach, and Jezebel. Carolyn insisted her lizard was a girl. I mentioned that Jezebel was an evil woman. Carolyn touched one of Jezebel's sharp teeth and said, "I hope so."

Carolyn was meaner than both of us.

We didn't know what to feed 'em, but it was clear that they didn't want corn or potatoes. With teeth like they had, they had to be meat eaters. While we were trying to figure that out, Shadrach dashed across the floor faster than a roadrunner and snapped up a rat. Jezebel took it away from him.

I said, "Looks like they'll feed themselves for now. No doubt about it. Jezebel's a girl, sure enough."

Davy petted Meshach. "Rats are good, but when they get bigger, they'll go after the chickens, the pigs, and the cattle. Dad won't like that."

"We'll teach them not to. Plenty of rabbits, coyotes, and such out there. The Jemez is full of deer and elk. They won't go hungry."

Mom and Dad found out about the lizards in less than two days. Dad noticed the rats were gone and mom caught Meshach stealing a crabapple pie. Carolyn convinced Mom and Dad that we were training the trio to be guard lizards. Dad agreed to give it a try. "First rooster that dies or a single cow goes missing and I'm making new belts and boots."

We bonded with our dinosaurs better than I ever expected. Truthfully, I thought they'd eat us when they grew big enough. We

4

didn't have any rats or mice. Coyotes stayed out of the henhouse, and we never lost a calf to wolves. The trio had the run of the ranch and even Dad admitted that they earned their keep.

They grew quickly. On Saturday, Davy got the bright idea that he could ride Meshach like a horse. Amazingly, Meshach loved it. The problem was that Meshach was at least three times faster than a horse. His gait was smooth, which was quite surprising since he only had two legs. Davy couldn't hold on. Carolyn and I had to try and soon we were racing around the ranch like a small Mongol horde, except for falling off every little whipstitch. I pointed out that Mongols don't fall off.

Dad watched us for a couple days. Bring 'em in the workshop. I'll modify some saddles."

It was easier said than done, but soon enough we had functional rigs. Shadrach and Meshach took right to wearing saddles. Jezebel wasn't too happy about it at first, but Carolyn wore her down. Carolyn always got her way.

We ran the cattle from dinosaur back for the next few years, right through the War Between the States. The cattle were a mite skittish at first, but they got used to it. Like I said, we never lost a single head to a predator. The time gate or past portal in the cave was still there and it still worked. Carolyn insisted on calling it the past portal. She'd read Charles Dickens's *A Christmas Carol* too many times and insisted that Scrooge visited the past in the future. (I'm confused. Is it 'from the future?' If so, why?

Once a week or so, some dinosaur or other creature wandered out of the cave. They were mostly hungry when they arrived. Oversized wolves, fast lizards the size of turkeys with teeth like razors, striped pigs, and deer with horns to kill you are a few examples. Without exception, the visitors provided food for our mounts. Sometimes we hunted on lizard back, but mostly we let them roam the ranch.

The war didn't bother us much out west of Santa Fe. Not much happened on our side of Fort Union. We only had one single incident. A lot of outlaw groups pretended to be soldiers, Rebs or Yanks, it don't matter. Outlaws is outlaws. Quantrill's Raiders, the James Gang, the Mason Henry Boys in California, and the Jayhawkers are some of the ones folks remember. The Canter Gang is hardly remembered. They sprung up in Oklahoma Territory and worked

5

their way toward California. They skipped Santa Fe, too well defended.

A dozen of 'em rode up to our house early one morning. They circled the yard, trampling chickens and firing into the air. Mom came outside with a rifle and I aimed my 410 out a window. Dad stood on the porch, axe in hand. Davy and Carolyn stood quietly at the water pump.

"What's all the fuss about?"

"War. Country's at war. I'm Captain Canter, Gary Dean Canter. I'll need to commandeer your horses, weapons, and food for my men. Any gold you've got is ours, too. We don't take kindly to those who fight for the wrong side."

"Captain, you didn't ask what side were on, nor did you say what side you're fighting for. I don't see no uniform."

"Don't sass me. Twelve guns is all the uniform I need. I believe we'll take the women as well, to be cooks and such."

Dad scowled, but answered politely. "I see. Kids, we need to do what the Captain says. We don't want anyone getting hurt. Carolyn, would you and Davy bring out the three best horses. That'll be Shadrach, Meshach, and Jezebel.'

Carolyn nodded and ran into the barn.

The Captain dismounted, winked at his men, and followed Carolyn toward the barn. Dad yelled at Davy, "Help your sister!"

Davy dropped the water bucket and raced into the barn. The Captain turned back toward the house and pointed at me. "Youngster, I see you in the window. You'd best put down that scattergun and join your parents outside. I won't ask twice."

I thought about it, but before I made a decision, the barn doors burst open. Jezebel leapt into the barnyard. Carolyn was on her back. Davy and Meshach were right behind her. Shadrach, saddled and looking for me, jumped over both of them and landed right on top of Captain Canter. My reptilian steed held him down with one clawed foot and screamed in his face. Meshach and Jezebel screamed with him.

Horses what never been around giant screaming lizards don't react well to the experience. The raiders' horses panicked, milled about, and threw several of their riders and trampled them underfoot. Not a shot was fired. It's hard to shoot from rearing horseback and even harder to aim when trying to protect your head from iron-shod hooves.

Carolyn guided Jezebel to one of the remaining mounted raiders and her beast plucked him almost gently from the saddle and bit him in half. Carolyn shouted, "I'm nobody's damn cook. Kill them! Kill them all!"

Shadrach bent down and took off Captain Canter's head. He swallowed it without chewing. He left the bleeding body in the barnyard dirt and ran to me. I mounted and we joined the melee. One raider spun his horse around and fought for control. He held the reins with one hand and a Colt pistol in the other. He shot at Carolyn on every spin.

Shadrach and I bumped 'em and when a two-ton lizard hits a man on horseback, the lizard wins. Shadrach caught the man on the first bounce and ripped him into pieces. He turned on the horse and Carolyn shouted, "Not the horses! Don't hurt the horses."

Three of the raiders managed to stay mounted, regained control, and rode, as they say, hell-bent for leather, toward Santa Fe. Mom shot one of them with her rifle. Davy and Meshach chased after them, Davy waving his Stetson overhead in celebration of the moment.

Carolyn dismounted and removed Jezebel's saddle. I did the same. Mom and Dad helped us round up the horses. I got a wheelbarrow and shovel from the barn and started to clean up what was left of Captain Canter. Dad put his hand on my arm. "Leave it be, Bobby. Our lizards will eat most of them. At sundown, we'll let the pigs out. No need to clean nothing, the pigs'll eat what's left 'fore sunrise."

Davy arrived about midday on horseback and led a second horse. His shirt was torn and he had a black eye. "I left Meshach to clean up. He seemed a mite peckish after the fight."

Dad said, "You've got a black eye."

"I do. Didn't want Meshach to have all the fun. Two raiders, one for me and one for him. We bumped mine off his horse and chased him for a bit to wear him down. He fought better than I expected. Fear does that I hear. Anyway, he had a good hat. I've got their guns, horses, and their gear. Meshach will be along soon enough."

7

We kept the rifles and the ammunition, but Dad sold the horses to the Army at Fort Union. We didn't bother anyone for the rest of the war and nobody bothered us.

I married Anna Lee. Her family was traveling west on the Santa Fe trail and she decided she'd traveled enough. Davy and Carolyn got married as well. They both married into the Welch family. One of the boys was killed in the War and Carolyn married the other. Davy married their sister, Lindy.

Dad passed away around 1870 and Mom the year after that. Anna Lee and I moved into the house. We built two more homes on the ranch. We never considered moving away, after all, we ride dinosaurs. Can't say that our spouses were overly comfortable with that, but if cattle could learn to tolerate our big lizards, family can't be expected to do any less.

The only incident that I remember was when Carolyn's husband, Stephen, was deathly afraid of Jezebel, something I completely understood. At Sunday dinner he said, "That girl lizard looks at me like I'm her next meal. I don't like her. I think we should put her down."

Carolyn dropped the plate of fried chicken on the table. "She said the same thing about you."

Stephen said, "So, which of us is it going to be."

"Don't have to be either one of you. I can control Jezebel. You control yourself. I will remind you that she's been here longer than you. She's trying to decide if you belong or if you're just visiting. Frankly, I'm trying to decide the same thing."

We never found out how that conflict would have turned out. Creatures big and small, but not too big to come through the cave, wandered from the past into our world every week or so. Our lizards fed well on the visitors.

Davy rode into the barnyard one morning. "Meshach and I checked on the north herd. Four of the cattle are dead."

"Shot?" I asked.

"No wolves, maybe. But maybe big wolves. Could be something from the cave, I mean from the past portal."

Carolyn said, "Let's check it out."

We mounted our dinosaurs. Carolyn kissed Stephen. "Don't know how long we'll be gone today. Something's killing cattle. Take care of things here. We haven't fed the horses."

8

"Be safe. I'll feed the horses after I fix breakfast."

"Horses before people. Love you."

Buzzards led us to the dead cattle. I inspected the site and didn't even need to pretend to be a better tracker than I am. "Not wolves. These prints aren't canine, they're cats. Biggest I've ever seen. Bigger than bobcats, bigger than mountain lions."

Carolyn put one booted foot in a paw print. "Mountain lion is about as big as cats come."

"I hear that Africa's got really big lions and tigers from India are huge."

"Davy, we ain't in India, nor the Congo."

We circled the mutilated cattle in wider circles. The footprints came from the mountains. "From the cave," I said. "Look at the trail. Some big cats have come through the cave."

Davy wheeled Meshach around. "Let's go to the cave and kill them before they kill more cattle."

Carolyn said, "We'll go to the cave later. Right now, I'm more interested in where they went than where they came from."

A wider search turned up blood-flecked paw prints leading in the general direction of our ranch houses. To this day, I don't know how we missed them. We should have passed each other. We followed their trail. It meandered a bit, but the crushed grass and footprints in the arroyos made it easy to follow. At the edge of one arroyo, still damp from the recent rains, I counted footprints as best I could. "Seven, I count seven, maybe a couple more. I didn't know that mountain lions hunt in packs."

"They don't," said Davy. "But I read the African ones live in groups called prides."

That's when we heard gunfire from the ranch. Two quick shots, a three count, and a third shot. Our signal for help. We didn't say a word, we just took off for the ranch. Jezebel was faster than Shadrach and Meshach, so Carolyn got there first, but Davy and I were right behind her.

The cats were as big as cows and colored brown with yellow and orange stripes. Their teeth were a foot long if they were an inch. Two of them were on the roof. Three stood on the porch, growling and pawing at the roughly hewn door. Stephen fired out of a small window at them, but they treated the bullets like we treat horseflies, annoyance, and nothing more. I'd counted seven, there should be

9

two more, but I'd worry about them later, the house and our families came first.

Jezebel snatched one of the cats by its haunches and dragged it off the porch. She stomped it with one claw and held it down. A cat jumped off the roof onto Jezebel's head and scrambled up her neck toward Carolyn. I fired my Winchester four times into the beast, but it never even reacted. Carolyn slid down Jezebel's tail and ran toward Davy and Meshach.

The cat chased her. One of the cats at the doorway ran toward me. Shadrach and I braced for battle. Stephen blasted out the front door firing at the cat chasing Carolyn. The second cat leaped off the roof and charged Meshach and Davy.

Stephen failed to realize there had been three cats on the front porch and he stood less than an arm's length from one of them. Jezebel stepped toward the porch to help him, but Carolyn screamed. Jezebel hesitated for the briefest second. She couldn't save Stephen and Carolyn both and she chose Carolyn. She turned and was on the fanged cat in seconds.

Shadrach and I had our own beast to fight and so did Davy. After Shadrach stomped our cat into the dirt, I hurried to the porch. Stephen was dead and so was the cat. When we had the chance to inspect things later, we found the barrel in the cat's mouth and five bullets in its brain. Stephen kept firing while the cat ripped his guts out. A far braver man than I gave him credit for.

You can't help the dead so I whistled for Shadrach and remounted. I always felt safer on his back than anywhere in the world. I called to Anna Lee. She stuck her head out the kitchen window. "Me and Lindy is fine. So are the kids. Are all them things dead?"

"No, stay inside. I think there are two more." And there were.

I have to give the cats credit. They didn't have not an ounce of quit in 'em. The other two, no doubt attracted by all the commotion found us, we didn't have to find them. They just attacked the second they saw us. Didn't give no mind to fighting dinosaurs four times bigger than them, they just waded right in. Reminded me of that Charge of the Light Brigade battle in Europe about twenty years ago. Bravery and stupidity aren't the same thing. Sometimes it's hard to tell the difference.

The last two cats didn't last a minute. Jezebel snatched one right out of the air and bit it in half. Shadrach and Meshach played wishbone with the other one. Meshach won.

We buried Stephen the next day. Things were pretty tough on Carolyn, but she had two kids to take care of. The day after the burial, she sent the kids outside after breakfast. "The five of us have to talk. The past portal is still open and up to now, I've been fine with that. It's just been another source of food for Jezebel and the boys. We have to close it. We have to think about Anna Lee, Lindy, and the kids. I've got the two boys, Bobby and Anna Lee have little Maybelle, and Davy and Lindy have the twins, Roland and Frank."

"We lost Stephen and I don't want to lose anyone else. It's time to close it. We've got plenty of gunpowder. Let's blow it up."

It's hard to get five adults to agree on what day it is, but that wasn't a problem. Linda and Anna Lee were for closing the portal and men who have some sense, tend to agree with their wives, and remember, Carolyn was the toughest one of us all.

The hard part was our dinosaurs. The wives wanted us to send them back through the portal and Carolyn was inclined to agree with 'em, but said that she thought they'd grown too big to fit. "If they can't fit inside, I'll be damned if I'm gonna kill 'em. I'll take all three of 'em and my kids and run off to Canada or Hell, whichever one I find first."

We didn't decide about our dinosaurs that morning, but we spent the day loading saddlebags with black powder and the next morning we rode out to the cave. We did take three horses with us so we would have to walk back if, well you know, if.

At the cave mouth, we packed black powder all around, but mostly at the top of the opening. There wasn't any question about sending Shadrach, Meshach, and Jezebel through the cave, they'd grown far too big. That left the question of what to do.

Davy stammered. "Carolyn, I know you said you'd take them and your kids and run away. I hope you don't still feel that way. We have to keep our children safe."

"Ain't a single one of our mounts ever hurt a soul but what we told 'em to do it. I think our kids are plenty safe. But, to answer your question, No, Davy, I'm not running away and no one is dying today especially not our dinosaurs. Things have changed since yesterday"

I didn't meet her eyes when I spoke, I'm ashamed to admit. "What could have possibly changed?"

11

Jezebel laid eight eggs in the barn. That's a dinosaur each for our kids and one each for your wives. They'll be safe enough when they have their own dinosaur to ride."

"You said eight eggs."

"I did. The other thing that's changed is that I'm pregnant. Egg eight is for my baby."

We lit the fuse and collapsed the cave mouth. We never told anyone how to find it.

In due time the eggs hatched and Carolyn gave birth to Maximillian, her son. We made sure that each baby dinosaur imprinted on one of our family. Within five years they all could ride, even Carolyn's five-year-old. He and Samson are fearless.

No, we didn't always ride dinosaurs. But we do now.

Campbell Blaine is a graduate of MSU, having worked her way through college as an exotic dancer. She currently teaches Honors English at a small regional university in northern Ohio. She writes romance novels, bodice rippers if the truth be told, under several names, including her Barbarian Lover series, which includes "Vandal Vigor," "My Viking Master," Celtic Captive," and "Saxon Slave." She dabbles in science fiction, fantasy, and horror. If you attended the costume contests at science fiction conventions, you've seen her costumed as different characters from the classic works of Thomas Burnett Swann. She wears some clothing in most of the contests.

THE WITCH IN THE WOODS

by Alyson Faye

Ellie sat, cross-legged in the tent telling one of her stories, whilst outside the rain pattered on the canvas. Tiggy, Maz, and Albie, her best friends, stared at her, expectantly. Albie chewing gum, Tiggy the end of her blonde plait, whilst Maz, the coolest of the group, fake-smoked a cigarette pinched off his mum.

Ellie knew she had them in the palm of her hand, hanging off her every word. "The creature crawled out of the bushes, drool dripping from its jaws, eyes ablaze above a long black snout. It was the witch's 'familiar'. In the firelight Marina danced naked, singing in tongues, tossing her long raven-black hair.

'Come Belin! Come Traxor! Come forth and do my bidding,' Ellie, speaking as Marina, deepened her voice.

"Beneath the earth, something was forcing its way . . ." Tiggy gasped and clutched at Albie, who jumped, swallowing his gum. Ellie smirked. ". . . a claw thrust from the ground, followed by a furry foreleg, then another, as Traxor rose from his grave. The two death-hounds snuffled at the witch's skirts, nibbling at the human meat roasting on the spit over the fire, and then sat, ready to do her bidding."

Maz stubbed out the unlit tab. "Don't believe it. Not that bit bout cooking humans."

Ellie turned on him, scorn in her voice. "Oh, right. So, when those two teenagers went missing twenty years ago in these woods, where'd you think they ended up?" She pointed down at the ground. "And they're still here."

Maz shook his head. "Bet they just ran away."

Albie began to sob quietly. "I don't want the witch to get me." He was the youngest at nine-years-old and the most gullible.

Tiggy gave him a hug. "Don't worry, Albie, we'll keep you safe."

The group huddled inside their den; a construct of second-hand curtains, poles, and a tarpaulin. Inside Ellie had decorated it with feathery, colourful dreamcatchers, homemade paper lanterns, and leftover tinsel.

The sun was setting over the fields, and the shadows of the trees consumed the ground. There was a chill in the air. An animal, larger than a fox, rustled behind the den, making them jump. Tiggy shivered, pulling her fleece around her.

"OK gang, time to go home. Let's tidy up." Ellie announced.

The kids sorted their stuff, packed rucksacks, and hiked over the fields to their respective homes. Inadvertently, they'd left behind a single dreamcatcher and a strand of neon-pink tinsel.

The dreamcatcher spun faster, a blur of colours, as something latched onto it, a force awoken by Ellie's words and emotions, creating a bridge inside the den between past and present. The name of the witch had been uttered aloud, for the first time in centuries. There was power in the speaking of names.

Ellie tossed in bed, unable to sleep, her mind busy as a motorway at rush hour. At last, she got up and logged onto her laptop. She clicked onto the news site where she'd first read the story about the missing teenagers.

The headline from 1997 blared:

TWO TEENS MISSING
WOODS SEARCHED.

Beneath the byline, the piece named the runaways as Isabel Martinson, aged 16, and Harry Byne, aged 17. They were pupils at Gilstead Secondary School.

The police had searched Milner Woods. They'd found signs of a camp-site, cigarette ends plus a hair scrunchy, which Isabel's mum had hysterically identified as her daughter's. They never found the two runaways though, not then, nor since. The teens had vanished into the woods one warm evening in June 1997; it was as though the forest had swallowed them.

Ellie sat back in her chair. She loved Milner Woods - its tracks, trails, and unexpected nooks, the ruins of the mansion buried under decades of undergrowth, the derelict cellars, the occasional blessed glimpse of a fine-boned deer in flight, the remains of the wide carriage path, the bird boxes and, most of all, what it represented - freedom from home and school routines.

It was her mum's neighbour, Mrs. Albertson, who'd first told Ellie the story of the witch in the woods. "Marina, the locals called her. I'm going back a few hundred years now, luv. Some said she was the

14

cast-off mistress of the local lord of Milner Manor, others that she was a Romany traveler whose family had died of plague, but others whispered," (Mrs. Albertson lowered her voice and winked) ". . . she was a 'pure blood', a seer."

Ellie was fascinated. "One day I'd like to live in the woods, Mrs. A. and be free."

Mrs. Albertson laughed. "Aye, well it's not a bad life, lass. Fresh air, cooking over a fire, catching your own fish and meat, and no husband to worry about nor kiddies mithering you. In a way, Marina was freer than most women of that time. But she was also an outcast. It would be a dangerous, hard life too. Any roads, I've got a book here, somewheres, about her. Here it is. You can borrow it."

Ellie reached out and stroked the spine of the cloth-backed book. The golden letters on the spine read, '*Local Lore and Myths: Witches and Warlocks*'. She flipped the foxed pages. They fell open at a well-thumbed page depicting a black and white sketch of a wild-haired figure crouching amongst the trees, almost camouflaged by them, as if she was merging with the trunks. She was peering at a burning firepit above which an animal roasted on a spit. Next to the pit, lounged a pair of black, short-haired hounds. The caption read, '*Marina of Milner Woods and her Hounds, Traxor and Belin.*'

It was Marina's face that drew Ellie's gaze. Despite the long, unkempt hair and ragged clothing, the witch's face was beautiful, with high cheekbones, and wide lips. Ellie would have sworn the unknown artist had drawn from life. This was a woman a lord would lust after or could be a 'pure blood' with magic in her veins.

Ellie traced her finger over the face, gently stroking it. Her head nodded, as she drowsed.

In Milner Woods, near the children's den, under the full moon, something was stirring, and stumbling around. Something human, for it made too much noise to be an animal. Then it coughed and swore.

"Dammit, where's me bottle? Oh, there you are, darlin'. Come to Daddy."

The man swigged from a green bottle right down to the dregs, before tossing it into the shrubbery. An animal cried out, as though injured. The man rubbed his nose, spat on the ground, and then crawled into Ellie's den, draping the tinsel around himself, whilst singing, 'I wish me a Merry Christmas', then collapsing, falling into a drunken sleep.

The woods waited as if holding its green-scented breath. The moon shone on the den and its bone-ivory rays touched the dreamcatcher, which stirred above the sleeping man's head, although there was no breeze. The purple and green feathers twirled, moonbeams glinted off the gold sequins as it whirled faster and faster, and a doorway appeared in the air, limned by an altogether more ancient and weary moonlight.

The man slept on, oblivious.

A hand reached out of the shimmering, moonlit portal and stroked his stubbly cheek. He sighed. The hand was followed by an arm, and then the rest of the figure appeared.

It was a woman - petite, wiry, with waist-length black hair. She hovered just above the tarpaulin, her figure outlined in a pearly light. She allowed her bare feet to land on the ground. She bent and sniffed the man, wrinkling her face, and then ducked outside. Two low-slung shadows sloped out of the greenery; silent, feral.

"My beloveds. Traxor." She fondled the larger hound's velvet ears. The beast whimpered with joy. "Belin, come to your mistress." The second hound padded over to her, licked her hand, and sat at her feet; bony haunches splayed. In the moonlight, the hounds were two dark shadows. "How I have missed you during my long sleep."

She gazed around at the woods, somewhat changed to her eyes, but achingly familiar too. "I hear you," she whispered to the animals of the night. She turned back to the sleeping man. "You, wake from your slumber!"

The man stirred, muttered then stood up, wobbling. He turned towards the woman's outstretched hand.

"Come with me."

The strange couple stepped back through the moonlit doorway, shadowed by the two hounds. The doorway sealed over and the dreamcatcher ceased spinning, just as the moon went behind a cloud.

The disappearance of Jimmy Lonsdale, the village's former postman, who'd fallen on hard times, was all anyone was talking about the next day. Some of his clothes and a graveyard of beer cans had been found in Ellie's den, so the police cordoned off the area and then placed Milner Woods off-limits, just as they had done in 1997.

Ellie and her friends were devastated. In one stroke they had lost their den, the freedom to go to the woods, and instead gained a raft of curfews and boundaries.

"That could have been you," each one of the children's parents told them. They forgot about all the picnics and hikes their families had safely enjoyed in the woods over the years.

"Do you think aliens abducted him?" whispered Ellie, during a secret FaceTime session with Tiggy.

Tiggy scoffed, "Don't be daft, Ellie."

There were rumours amongst the dog-walking community of pets running terrified from something in the woods, hearing howling at dusk, and a sense of being stalked. Milner Woods gradually emptied of human traffic, leaving it to the rule of others.

It was Ellie, who decided over the long, tedious summer holidays, during which a mini-heatwave baked the village, that she'd had enough of the curfew. Jimmy Lonsdale's disappearance had been two months ago, and she wanted to reclaim the woods.

She didn't consult her parents, but one day ventured further afield, calling for Maz then Tiggy (not Albie – for he was permanently cloistered at home happy with the bribe of a new X-Box).

There were, too, the liquid attractions of the stream which meandered through the woods, in parts deep enough to paddle and lie down in.

Ellie called for Maz, found him in, and the teens hiked to Milner Woods, rucksacks loaded with drinks, sweets, and sandwiches. Beneath the cool, leafy canopy of the trees Ellie jogged, hopped over fallen logs, and breathed in the green-scented air.

"I'm a nymph. I'm a sprite!" she yelled.

"Sprite?" Maz replied. "So, you're a fizzy drink, are you?"

Hooting with laughter they walked to one of their favourite spots by the stream, shielded from view. Only an inquisitive dog might find them.

Or a hound . . . out hunting.

Ellie took off her trainers and plunged her bare feet into the water. "This is bliss."

Maz did the same and the pair paddled and splash-kicked each other until they were soaked. Afterwards, they lay on the sunbaked earth, drying off.

Maz lifted his head, sleepy-eyed, sun-drugged. "Did you hear that, Ellie?"

"Nah, what?"

"A noise, like a growl?" Maz's eyes closed. "I'm so tired, Els. Gonna take a nap, wake me up . . ."

Ellie lay staring up at the canopy, watching fingers of sunlight poke through, showing up the dancing motes and insects. She smelled something feral and earthy nearby and closed her eyes, squeezing them tight to get rid of sun-dazzles.

She sensed they were no longer alone, and sat up, looking around. In front of her stood a woman, wild-haired, in ragged clothing, flanked by two massive hounds. She had the bluest eyes Ellie had ever seen. Her mouth was wide, her cheekbones high. Once she had been beautiful.

Ellie knew her face. "Hello, Marina."

The air around the witch shimmered, swirling with dust, spores, insects, and pure energy. The hounds watched their mistress, their pink-as-ham tongues lolling, slobber dripping to the earth.

"Which one is Traxor?" asked Ellie.

The witch stepped forward, reaching out her finger she stroked Ellie's face, then licked it as though tasting the girl. Ellie sat still, hardly daring to breathe.

"How old be ye, girl-child?" Her voice creaked, as if with lack of use.

"Sixteen, just."

"Old enough to wed, old enough to bed," the witch laughed, but did not sound amused.

Ellie shook her head. "No, I am not."

At her feet, Maz slept on, open-mouthed, snoring.

"Have you put a spell on him?"

The witch glanced at Maz, as though he was of no consequence. The trees seemed to be listening. The silence suggested the animals and birds were on pause, as though the witch had stopped time.

"Walk with me," Marina said.

It was not a request, and Ellie felt compelled to obey.

18

"I will show you my woods, and my world." The hounds loped beside her, silent, graceful. "Belin boasts the white plume on his chest."

"They are handsome dogs." Ellie tried hard not to think of the powerful jaws with the brutal canines, and how easily they could rip and tear flesh.

Did they eat Jimmy Lonsdale? The thought skittered into her head unbidden.

Around her the woodland landscape was changing, the layers peeling away, trees shortening, clumps of bushes thinning then vanishing. They walked past what would have been the ruins of Milner House, the nineteenth-century mansion, a mill owner's folly, but there was no masonry, for it had not yet been built.

They were moving backward in time, Ellie guessed, perhaps hundreds of years. The distant phone masts, the queues of skeletal metal poles, all had disappeared from the skyline, and the air smelt cleaner.

The sunlight was fading, and Ellie looking up, saw a swollen-bellied, yellow moon hanging low in the sky. It was not a moon she was familiar with, but rather an alien moon from a different age. She shivered in the chilly air, feeling under-dressed in shorts and a T-shirt.

They walked until they emerged into a moon-dappled glade, where Ellie was surprised to see a small but well-made wooden hut. There was a firepit and a spit where an animal had been spiked and was roasting. The air was rich with the aroma of the meat. Ellie's stomach rumbled.

"How long have you lived here?" she asked.

Marina paused, head cocked on one side, hawk-like. "Four winters." She held up a hand displaying four fingers. Ellie noticed the top of the ring finger was missing.

"Four? Wow, that's er -" Ellie didn't know what to say, it seemed an eternity to her.

The dogs lay down on either side of the firepit, eyeing the roast, but making no move to grab the flesh. Marina beckoned Ellie into the wooden hut, as she followed, she ducked down for the door frame was lower than she was used to, she followed. Inside was just the one room, which contained a narrow, single bed, a wooden stool, and a woven basket filled with clay dishes. Lying on a wooden shelf near the bed were, to her surprise, a handful of hand-stitched books.

"Books?" She itched to go and look at them. Marina nodded her permission.

Ellie picked one up, its thick vellum pages smelt divine and she ran her fingers over them, enjoying the texture. '*Historie of Herbes and Potiones,*' she read out loud. Inside there were detailed sketches of plants, with notes in a curving script, Marina's hand, and lists of ingredients for making drinks and potions for 'rheumatics, for dropsy, for impotence, (Ellie blushed) for fever . . . for rashes . . .'

"You're a –" Ellie searched for the right word, ". . . healer?"

Marina nodded. "Healer. Yes. They come to me." She waved her hand at the door. "The women and children from the village. They come for help when there is nowhere else to go." She patted her stomach and Ellie understood – help for unwanted pregnancies.

"I saw a picture of you in a book once," Ellie offered. "I knew then you were real. Who drew you?"

Marina pushed back her waist-length wiry hair. "He did." She tossed her head towards the west. "From the manor. The son. My lover. Here in the woods, we walked, swam, laughed together. He drew me and his two hunting hounds. We were so – free."

Free, the word echoed, resonated. Ellie could almost taste it.

"But we were followed, spied upon, betrayed. By the other son. His own brother. Jealous, so jealous. He wanted me too." Marina's eyes clouded over. "They came one day. His brother and his men. They came with steel and fire, slashed my lover's throat, buried him nearby, and left me his hounds to remember him by. Laughing, they rode off. I was too weak then to stop them. Too young." She frowned, "I have learned much since then."

Ellie swore she could hear the crash of hooves through the undergrowth, smell the horses' sweat, and the coppery tang of the lover's spilt blood. She looked around, and realized Marina was conjuring up these sensory effects, for there was nothing to be seen but the moonlit glade through the door, and the inside of the hut.

Marina rocked from side to side, threw back her head, and howled in grief. The two hounds got up and began pacing, agitated, whimpering, tails down. Ellie felt helpless in the face of such raw grief and anger. Instinctively she reached out a hand to stroke the woman's skinny arm.

20

At the contact, Marina's eyes refocused on Ellie. "Come Traxor, Belin. Come to me." The hounds rushed to her side, she nestled in their fur. Several minutes passed before Marina spoke again. This time, more calmly. "Come sit with me by the fire, girl, and share my meal."

Ellie did not know how long they sat watching the wild pig roast, tossing scraps to the hounds, eating, talking, drinking mead, and staring up at the stars. Marina knew the names of them all, 'The Bear', and of course, 'The Dog'.

Ellie ate and drank until her stomach bulged and sleep took her, while Marina sat beside her, stroking her hair, singing a melody in her deep voice.

'Lavender's blue, dilly dilly, lavender's green . . .'

Ellie didn't care if everything she was feeling and seeing wasn't real or if it was magic – she just wanted – to stay – here – forever.

Wishes have power.

As she slept Marina drew arcane shapes in the dirt with a stick and laid out bowls of water to capture the moon's rays.

Maz woke suddenly. His sleep had been filled with nightmares of huge dogs and a wild-haired woman. "Ellie, I said to wake me up . . ."

Looking around he realized he was alone. The only sign of Ellie was her footprints in the mud.

Ghost prints, he shivered at the thought.

"Where are you, Els?"

He sat down, hunching up, hugging his knees. He didn't feel alone; there was something out there watching him.

Ellie woke the next day at dawn beneath a rough woollen blanket. Marina was nowhere in sight, but the two hounds eyed her across the ashes of the fire pit. Ellie felt content, at peace. She breathed in the sweet mulchy-scented air and stretched.

Time to go home. She headed to the edge of the glade.

Behind her the two hounds began to growl, quiet and low, stalking her. A sudden blur of movement on her right and left and Traxor stood full-on blocking the path ahead with Belin at his heels. The dogs' amber eyes were wide, fixed on her, teeth bared; fear gripped

21

Ellie. She took a couple of tentative steps back towards the fire pit and the hut. The hounds ceased growling and relaxed.

OK, so what now? Keep calm, Ellie.

Marina came into sight, carrying a basket overflowing with plants, smiling at her. She looked happier. "Good 'morrow, girl, how dost thee?"

"I would like to thank you – er – ye – for your kindness, Marina, but it's time I was leaving now. My family will be worried." She wondered how long she'd been away – did time pass differently here? Had she been gone weeks? Or even months?

Marina smiled again, but this time Ellie didn't see any warmth or joy in it. "You be home now, girl-child. Here with me. I wish to teach you my ways. You will live here with me as my apprentice."

Ellie stepped up to confront, to argue. Traxor rose at once, haunches rippling with muscle. Teeth bared; yellowing canines visible. There were red strands dangling from them.

"I *have* to leave. You'd . . . don't understand." Ellie stuttered.

Marina shrugged. "It was you who called to me, girl, through your dreams, your storytelling, your wishes. You left me the dreamcatcher and I used it to enter your time. I found you because you wanted me to. You came willingly with me. I did not kidnap you. You desired to be free. To live as I do."

Ellie listened, horrified. Everything Marina was saying was true, in a fashion. She had been fascinated by the book, by the sketch. Yes, she loved camping in the woods and telling stories but it was a game, satisfying her love of history and nature. Now all these good things were being twisted by Marina into something darker and sinister.

"It was an accident leaving the dreamcatcher behind. And you, you were just a story in a book." Ellie didn't mean to give offense, but Marina turned on her in fury, throwing a pan at her head, which narrowly missed.

I have to be careful. Keep calm. I mustn't make her angry.

Ellie swallowed her upset, managed a weak smile, and threw out her hands in apparent acceptance. "Let me help you. Can you teach me about those plants? I want to learn."

Marina stared, blue eyes still suspicious, then nodded. "Come sit with me, girl."

Ellie obeyed. The dogs stayed close, corralling her.

###

So the pattern of the next few days was set, with Ellie, waking, washing in the stream, accompanied by Belin, reading and cooking with Marina, and receiving lessons in herbal medicines, botany, and biology. Ellie was never hungry or thirsty but, she was always frightened and lonely. Sometimes on their forays into the woods together, Marina would point out badgers' setts, and deer tracks, and Ellie witnessed the full brutality of Milner Woods and nature. At night she slept on the hut's floor beside Marina, with the dogs guarding the doorway. She saw no other human. She began to despair of ever escaping.

On the seventh day, Ellie was tending to the fire, when she heard children's voices shouting and laughing not far away. Marina was absent, with Belin, on her daily plant-gathering trip, and Ellie had earlier mixed a sleeping draught and hand-fed it to Traxor. The hound lay snoring.

Fear made Ellie sweat and her stomach cramp, but she headed into the woods, praying to recognize the route she had walked with Marina just a week ago, though it seemed more like a lifetime. The ferns were now taller than her, and the greenery had exploded into a living, viscous mantle that bristled, seeming to grab at her limbs.

She had not gone far when she glimpsed up ahead a shallow dip and the heads of four children bobbing around a handful of grave mounds, marked with wooden crosses. The two boys wore tunics. They'd grabbed the wooden crosses as 'swords', and were running about, play-fighting. The two girls wore ankle-length grey shifts, whilst their hair fell loose to their waists. The boys ran after the girls, pretending to chase them, and when they caught them, stole a kiss. After a few minutes, they tossed the crosses away and ran off into the greenery, which consumed them in moments.

Ellie sidled cautiously towards the dell, drawn by curiosity and a driving compulsion to replace the crosses on the graves. Something itched at the back of her skull. She picked up the first cross, and read, '*Isabel, died winter, 1701*'. The name tugged at her memory, irritating but persistent. It came to her in a burst of recall: - Isabel Martinson, the Gilstead pupil who 'ran away' into the woods with her boyfriend in 1997.

Ellie plunged the cross upright into the dirt and picked up the other one. *Henry, died spring 1703*. Could this be Harry Byne, the

23

other missing teen? She recognized Marina's handwriting burned into the wood.

One mound was fresher, recently dug. With no wooden cross.

Jimmy Lonsdale? Ellie guessed.

Not runaways then but time travelers, abductees and prisoners, or perhaps companions for a lonely woman? Would this be her own fate too?

The thick, interlocking greenery behind the graves ripped apart, and Marina emerged, with Belin, snarling, at her side. Marina's own face was fiery-cheeked," You will never leave me!"

Ellie had only one thought in her head - *run!*

She leapt to her feet, still holding Henry's death marker in her hand, and raced away from Marina, hurling herself into the mass of greenery twisting and weaving between the trunks, scraping her hands on the gnarly bark, but not stopping.

Behind her she heard Belin's panting, gaining on her and Marina's screeching, but fainter. Ellie knew she had no choice, it was her or the hound. She stopped, planting her spine against a tree trunk, she turned and holding out the sharp end of the wooden cross, pointed it at the approaching hound - hoping the animal's forward momentum would drive it onto the stake.

Belin leapt towards her, slavering jaws wide open, hair standing erect along his spine. Ellie screamed, but shoved the cross, point outwards, at the dog's broad chest. She felt the dog's weight judder up her arm, she closed her eyes but heard its yowls of agony as he impaled himself. The weight of the corpse dragged her arm downwards; it landed with a wet thud.

Ellie turned and fled further into the guts of the woods, whipped by branches, and tripped by rocks, the very greenery determined to brutalize her. She plunged on, straining to hear a whisper of running water.

Sweat poured off her, her hair blinded her, blood trickled into her eyes from a gash on her scalp, but she ran on. She thought she caught the sound of someone calling her name, not a woman's voice, but a male.

"Maz? Maz, is that you?" Ellie gasped, but her voice was weedy. He would not hear her.

The smell in the air turned peaty, damper, the ferns grew lusher, the ground mushier. She heard the rush of running water – she was so near.

The sun seemed to disappear, she felt its heat fade from her skin, and looking up Ellie saw the sky darkening, as though a storm was approaching, but instead, to her amazement, the moon rose, so swift it was as if it had been pulled up by a cord. It hung bulging and oddly humpbacked, as though distorted by its early appearance, leaching all colour from the woods, turning the trees' outlines into an army of grey silhouettes.

What's happening? How's this possible?

Ellie turned to run on, but stopped dead, for in her path, hovering above her – was Marina. The witch was naked, her skin a chilly alabaster in the moonlight, her eyes moonstones.

She draws her power from the moon.

Marina spread out her arms and the branches reached over to grasp her hands, whilst her long, dark hair floated above her head and the trees' canopy bent to weave their twigs into her tresses. Leaves drifted down to dress her, vines looped around her ankles. She was becoming part of the woods, merging as one with it.

Ellie gazed up at Marina. "You *are* a witch."

"I am so much more than that, girl-child. You could learn my magic. Let me teach you. Stay with me, please." Marina's voice was the wind in the branches.

Ellie shook her head. The trees rippled and the air filled with spores.

"You are mine. You wished for it. You called to me." Crystalline tears rolled down Marina's cheeks, turning to petals, drifting in a flurry of pink and white. "I am so - *lonely."*

Ellie's insides contracted. It would be so easy to stay, she could feel the pull of the magic. It throbbed within her, a note of alien power. She breathed in. Focused her mind and thought of home.

"You have to let me go."

She felt tendrils of ivy grip her ankles, glimpsed more roots slithering across the ground towards her, like obscene brown snakes, ivy bracelets handcuffed her wrists. Marina's green army was taking her captive.

"Please, Marina, let me go home."

Behind her, so near, was the trickling stream.

25

"Ellie?" It was Maz's voice. "Where are you?"

His voice broke Marina's concentration, her head swiveled. In that moment Ellie tore at the ivy shackles and threw herself across the last barrier of bushes, pitching face-first into the stream.

Maz gawped at her. "You're back! I've been so worried, Els."

"She's coming for me." Ellie looked over her shoulder, saw the bushes shake, heard the twigs snap, but no one appeared.

"Who?" Maz was bewildered.

A fragile-limbed doe stepped out into the moonlight. Her coat gleamed silver. The woods fell silent, nothing moved.

Ellie stared into the blue eyes of the doe; a single tear formed. Then with a flick of the tail, Marina disappeared – back to her own time.

Aly lives in the UK, with her family and rescue-Labrador, Roxy and one-eyed pirate kitten, Ewey McPhewey. She is a tutor, editor, mum, dog-walker, wild water swimmer and avid film buff.

Her fiction/poetry has been published widely - in Space and Time #141, Bridgets Gate Press' Were-Tales', 'Musings' and 'Daughter of Sarpedon', by Perpetual Motion in 'Night Frights 2', on 'The Casket of Fictional Delights', (and as audio downloads), Coffin Bell, various Sirens Call ezines, World of Myth, Unsettling Press' 'Still of Night,' and Northern Life magazine.

Her stories can be downloaded on various podcasts, including her 'Night of the Rider' as part of the Gothic showcase - After the Gloaming - a production of Dissonance Media and The Other Stories.
https://shows.acast.com/after-the-gloaming/episodes/night-of-the-rider
Her author bibliography is over at Amazon :-
https://www.amazon.co.uk/stores/Alyson-Faye/author/B01NBYSLRT

THE SEAHORSE

By Shebat Legion

The Ocean watches as I sit on the wave-touched beach, occasionally slapping at sand fleas, and I remember when I was young and fought the sea god and won. We made a bargain that day. Only I, a foolish mortal, expect it to be honored. I hope, nothing more, for I hold doubt in my heart, but, of this much, I am certain, magic is real, time is an illusion, and Herne rides with his hounds, sounding his horn as he hunts the souls of the lost.

I tense as I hear a sound from beyond the blue line, "Sally," it seems to call, but it is only a seabird. I know what the voice of the Ocean sounds like; who better?

Beside me is a music box and the Seahorse, old now, with most of its garish paint covered in vinyl patches; it was a wonder that I could inflate the cursed thing all these years later. But Stacy kept the Seahorse in good shape; maybe she knew what I planned and could see into the future.

Perhaps she, too, made a bargain that day.

Time is slippery, especially when you are old, as I am now. As the waves grow stronger, catching at my ankles, I hear that voice from beyond the blue line. It is the same day; I am that child once more. Like many children who grow up beachside, my friend Stacy, a petite seven-year-old, and I, a robust ten-year-old, had something in common: we could not swim. One could not count the crude dog paddle accomplished in the many hotel pools after the tourists had gone, leaving nothing but their echoes behind – the odd earring, a pair of stylish sunglasses worn by me with a grand sense of possession. Nor could one count our odd, graceless dance in the Ocean proper: floating, hopping, and body-surfing the waves as they came through.

A true child of my generation, I grew up with unequaled freedom, left to my devices, and expected home by dinner, not sooner. That day, I spent time on the beach with my new friend. We had a can of soda, some licorice, a towel, and my blue blow-up floatation ring covered in pictures of smiling dolphins and starfish, its proud, inflated bobbing head that of a leering seahorse.

It was low tide, and for those who do not know what this means, the Ocean that touches the beach is shallow, and one can walk for quite some time before the water gets deeper, farther still, before it reaches a proper depth. During first-quarter or third-quarter moon phases, gravitational forces of the sun and moon counteract each other, resulting in lower tidal ranges known as "neap tides." We didn't call it this, nor did we even know that the term existed, but we were warned about its power, something we ignored as we walked further out toward the blue line in the distance that signals where the tame Ocean ends and the true Ocean begins.

The lifeguard, occupied with a straggling of female admirers, did not blow a cautionary whistle. So, with the avarice of youth, we plunged ever forward until our feet could no longer touch the sandy floor. And we floated, grinning at each other, while the gulls flew overhead, and the gentle swells rose and fell, and unaware to us, the ebb tide caught, snatching the Seahorse and carrying us far into the deep until we could barely make out the sight of the shore.

The sky seemed to darken as we discovered our predicament. The ebb is no friend to swimmers, and it was only then that we understood the warnings. I clung to the side of the ring, Stacy inside the ring, her arms draped over it.

Our scared eyes met, and Stacy began to cry.

This is where the true story begins. Or, depending on how you look at it, how it didn't.

I ordered Stacy to stop wailing, and with one hand clutching the Seahorse, I began an awkward sideways crawl, pushing through the water with my free hand and kicking my legs as hard as I could to swim us back to safety.

They say the god's attention is attained by a sacrifice or a glorious battle. I never considered abandoning my friend, not then, although the trip back to shore would have been easier without her. But, If it had been a battle the gods enjoyed watching, it would have been a battle I gave them to watch that day.

For every inch I made against the tide, I was swept further backward, and it became apparent that my attempt to swim us in was only accomplishing exhaustion. I squinted at the shore, waving my arm and shouting. Stacy lent her voice, and I could hear the terror. Only then did I accept that we were alone; she and I were unnoticed without rescue. We had only ourselves, or rather, we had me.

"Stacy," I addressed her, clinging as she was, small and terrified against the smiling Seahorse whose grin seemed to mock our plight. "Stacy, I want you to float on your tummy and kick as hard as possible. Okay?"

She only nodded and turned, briefly losing her grip on the tube, then sputtering up like a top.

"Ready?"

She nodded again and began to kick her legs furiously while I held on at the back, pushed at the Seahorse with both arms, and kicked with my legs simultaneously.

We seemed to make some progress this way, and it is possible we would have made it if the clouds hadn't moved in for a sudden storm. The raindrops made the Seahorse's surface slippery, and the wind did not favor us. Stacy's hair clung to her like wet seaweed, and her eyes were exhausted. I felt before I saw my friend lose her grip and slip beneath the surface.

"No," I screamed.

I grabbed beneath the waves without letting go of the Seahorse and caught her by her hair, yanking her upward, the motion pulling me down until my head was beneath the water, never losing my grip on the Seahorse. Finally, my toes found a place to cling to slippery rocks, my face barely clearing the surface.

It was then that I heard the voice for the first time.

"Child," the voice sighed. "letting go is easy; drowning is peaceful. Let her go. Save yourself."

Stacy coughed and threw up ocean water as I held us there. The Ocean pushed at us, and rain fell, blinding us both.

"No," I grunted. "Never."

Stacy looked at me, and I could see how tired she was. I smiled and then coughed as a small wave slapped me in the face. Then, forcing my toes to let go of our temporary refuge, I kicked with my legs, not asking anything of Stacy, only that she hold on. I made some progress this way but felt myself tire as the wind picked up and the rain fell ever harder, working against me, and if I didn't yet understand that it was a battle in the truest sense, I was soon to know, when I heard the voice again, laughing at my efforts.

"Child," the Ocean whispered, "you fight hard; this is true. But you are a tiny fish, and I am vast. You cannot defeat me."

I did not know whom I addressed, but I shouted, "Shut up! I will defeat you, and I'm not a fish!"

"A tiny fish," the voice chuckled.

I think it is easier for a child to accept such things, that an ocean can speak, that it is alive. Yes, I accepted these facts entirely and without question. I still do, all these years later.

Stacy called over the rain, "who are you talking to?"

"Stacy," I yelled, "I want you to sing me a song."

"A song? What song?"

"Any song!"

And Stacy began to sing, and while the rain tried to drown out the tune, I did catch most of it.

Yellow bird. At home in a banana tree.

Yellow bird. You sit all alone like me.

As if angered by my friend's innocent tune, the wind picked up in a sudden gust, and a wave slapped me so hard that I momentarily lost grip of the Seahorse and sank beneath the water, my hands grasping at air. A hand caught mine, and I struggled to the surface, clinging to my friend's arm, gasping for breath as the ebb caught us again.

I held onto the Seahorse, kicking hard and scraping my feet on a sudden rock; I caught at it with my toes, and I panted and gasped and felt Stacy patting my arm, even while she sobbed.

"We are going to die."

"No, we won't," I asserted, "would I do that to you?"

Even if it were true, I would never have admitted it, not to her. She was as much my sister as my best friend; sometimes, she was even my child, and I was loyal to a fault. I still am. I feel sorry for you if you have never had a friend like that.

"I have an idea," I said.

Taking a deep breath, I let myself sink; toes braced against whatever rock I could find, digging into the cold sand when there was none, my head beneath the water. I walked, my arms above my head, firmly grasping the Seahorse and dragging it with me, only stopping when I needed to breathe.

Stacy stared at me with an expression of worry, song forgotten. 'It's okay," I gasped while gulping air. "Keep singing!"

30

Did your lady friend leave the nest again?
That is very sad, makes me feel so bad.
I dragged us along, one step at a time.
"Wave! Wave!" Stacy screamed.

I felt it before I saw it, a gathering of energy pushing us upward until we felt like we were hanging in the sky.

"Hold on," I yelled. "Wrap your legs around the Seahorse; hold on to me!"

Like monkeys, we clung to the Seahorse and each other. And I realized something as I felt my young friend's hands clutching me, even as I clutched the inflatable tube.

I was Stacy's Seahorse.

Again and again, the waves pounded us, and was it my imagination that I saw a face in the water peering at us in curiosity?

Time stopped.

You might ask me if it was only terror or imagination that made me think this, but I tell you, it is true.

The Ocean stopped moving, and the wave that threatened us paused. I looked around wildly, caught in the sudden, still water.

"Little fish, I admire you," said the Ocean.

I looked at my friend, who appeared lifeless, and I shook her arm, "Stacy," I called, "wake up."

"She cannot hear you, little fish. We are in a place in between."

"In between what?"

"Between time, "laughed the Ocean.

"Why," I asked.

"Because I can," replied the ocean

"If you can do that, help us get to shore," I demanded.

"Brave little fish, to command a god," the Ocean breathed. "Have I not said I admire you? I do. And so, I offer you a trade for your life, even though it doesn't matter how long or short it might be."

"What trade?"

"Let go of the smaller fish, and you will make it to shore safely. I cannot promise that you will both survive else. Herne rides tonight, child, do you not hear?"

I heard the sound of a horse's hooves and the bay of hounds, but I shook my head.

"Herne?"

"They do not teach of Herne to little fish?" The Ocean asked. When I shook my head again, the Ocean sighed, sounding like a wave on the shore.

"I know things that I could tell you, but I won't, but if you knew them, oh, little fish ... "The Ocean laughed and laughed, but to my ears, it sounded sorrowful. Or so it seemed to me. All children know things. They don't know how they know, but they do, and I was no exception.

"I will never let her go," I swore.

"But you will, little fish, trust me in this. Then, now, there is no difference, not to me."

"I don't understand," I whimpered, the strength suddenly leaving me, but the still water held me fast, and I did not sink.

"No, you cannot understand, a little fish like you, for you do not live forever as I do. This thing that you measure is an illusion. Only eternity is real, and it, too, means nothing."

"Shut up," I yelled, tired, hungry, thirsty, a mortal without understanding, a child who only wanted to go home.

"I remind you that there is peace; let the hunter have his due, and you can go home," the Ocean tempted. "You do her no real favor, this friend of yours. I say this, and it is true."

I think about what the Ocean said, all the years to come, over and over, as Stacy sickened, first with a palsy that left her back twisted, and her walking with braces, and then, later, her heart failure and its many subsequent operations. Also, I seemed cursed with success for everything Stacy suffered, yet I could not enjoy it as I watched my friend endure trial after trial. And yet, for all of the pain, she bravely pushed through life, and it was only once, in her deepest moment of despair, after the death of her husband, did she swear at me, pushing me away, and saying, "you should have let me die."

But I did not know these things then, and I can't say that my choice would have been any different.

"No!" I shouted, my decision made. It would be us together, whatever the consequences.

"Selfish, "accused the Ocean.

"Selfish? To not want my friend to die?"

"Selfish, I say. You think only of what you cannot live without."

I didn't understand; how could I? But I screamed at the face I thought I saw peering at me from inside the water and cursed it, using every swear word I had at my disposal.

The Ocean laughed and laughed, and it was terrifying to see; its eyes were the white of sea foam, and its mouth held the teeth of the shark.

The Seahorse neighed wildly, pulling at its reins.

The Ocean chuckled finally," I say this only because you have caught my attention and amused me. If you ever change your mind, let me know."

"Deal," I yelled, not knowing what I agreed to.

Suddenly, the Ocean let me go, and the water moved once more,

The waves brought us closer to shore, and we kicked and screamed as they pulled us back to the deep, over and over again. Between each wave, I let myself sink beneath the water, my face covered completely, hands on the Seahorse, dragging it closer to the beach with every agonizing step.

"Child," the Ocean sang, startling me. I thought our conversation was over, but it still tempted me. "You must be tired. Never forget that I offered peace."

"Don't you care that we are only kids?" I wept. " This isn't fair!" My lungs felt as if they were bleeding, and I could not feel my hands at all.

"I am nature, child. Nature is not fair. Nature is."

"You are a bastard!" It was the most offensive word that I knew.

The clear voice of my friend sang to me, only interrupted by the occasional cough.

Yellow bird, up high in banana tree, yellow bird, you sit all alone like me.

Oh, Stacy, did you know? Did you hear? You never told me, not once, not ever. Did you hear the bargain that I made? Did you understand it? I never did, or understood too late, that I only saved myself by saving you.

You can fly away, in the sky away, you more lucky than me.

Another wave hit us, then another, but still, I struggled, my rage giving me strength.

I think about how the waves are the Ocean's breath, with its long inhalations and exhalations. And how a ten-year-old girl dragged her friend in an inner tube across the ocean floor to safety during a sudden storm. And I think about time and how it ceased to matter, for I cannot tell you how long we were out there or how long it took us to crawl to shore. It could have been hours, days, or even weeks. Time had no meaning; only the battle mattered.

The rain ceased suddenly, as tropical storms are wont to do, and I struggled on. It became mechanical, a deep breath, grasping the Seahorse firmly, arms above my head as I sank beneath the water so that my feet could touch the rocks, using them to push us closer to the shore.

The waves continued, but not as powerfully. With renewed confidence, I dragged us ever closer to safety.

Then, the cramp hit.

I yelped, swallowing saltwater as I did, as a wave bade us rise once again into the sky. The pain made me grit my teeth so hard that my jaw hurt for weeks after.

"Why?" I screamed at the Ocean, "why are you so cruel?"

"I am not cruel, child. I am what I am."

"Give us a break?" I pleaded, even as I hung to the Seahorse, doubled over, unable to straighten long enough to resume our bid for freedom. I wept as I watched us lose the ground I had fought so hard to gain and howled again in rage.

The Ocean chuckled, "such an angry little fish."

Then I heard Stacy's sweet voice.

Yellow bird, at home in banana tree.

Yellow bird, you sit all alone like me.

I joined in, shouting the words like a challenge.

Did your lady friend leave the nest again?

That is very sad, make me feel so bad.

I slowly uncurled—the cramp easing, singing along with Stacy.

You can fly away, in the sky away, you more lucky than me!

I don't know how many times we sang that song, but that last line became the one we shouted.

You can fly away!

In the sky away!

The words became a magic spell—our way of telling the Ocean what for. Over and over, we chanted the song, my feet sometimes failing to grasp a rock and us losing ground, but me always finding another second wind to find the energy to propel us forward. It seemed as if Stacy had also discovered some core of inner strength, and she kicked like a frog without being prompted, the two of us working as a unit, us against the Ocean, the only witness, the sky and the occasional sea bird.

The Ocean was silent, but I felt it watching us all the same, waiting for us to fail, not because it wanted us to, maybe, but because it was what it was: a force of nature, and nature isn't fair.

If I knew nothing else, that much I learned that day.

Bit by bit, we made progress, belting out the song over and over as we did. And, although we never spoke of it afterward, I know in my heart that we survived when it was almost certain we couldn't. We didn't have the words as children, and as adults, we chose not to use them.

Stacey and I remained friends for the rest of our lives. Perhaps our shared survival played a key, or maybe it was simply a strong friendship. But I remember the only time that Stacy broached the subject, having just put her husband to his final rest, her sorrow hanging heavy like a shroud.

"You should have let me die; you should have let me go, "Stacy wept. I held her as best as I could without hurting her pained and twisted body. She always marveled that she had found love, whereas I was only surprised that it had taken as long to find her.

"Do you think about it at all?" Stacey asked out of nowhere, and she could have been talking about anything, except that I knew, and she knew that I did.

"Yes," I answered. Just that.

"I always wondered ..." Her voice trailed off, and I raised an enquiring eyebrow. But then, a well-meaning acquaintance walked toward us with offered tissues and condolences. We never did get back to the conversation. I often wondered about that moment long after she was gone, long after I could ask.

Because I never did.

Maybe I didn't want to know.

And later, as I sit on the chair in Stacy's peaceful hospice room, my eyes droop, and I am dreaming. In my dream, I hold Stacy's hand as the Ocean pulls her away from me, and her hand slips from its grip on the Seahorse, which bucks and neighs in a frenzy.

"Don't let go," I scream, but she does, and I let her. I let her go. Her face sinks beneath the water, eyes watching me until she is gone.

And, I am weeping, but I don't know for whom.

"Selfish," says the Ocean.

"Selfish," says the Seahorse.

My eyes fly open to see Stacy watching me from her bed. I tremble as I walk toward her, my eyes begging her for forgiveness.

Stacy, what did the Ocean offer you in trade? And did you say yes?

When I went to help close her house after she passed, her daughters urged me to take what I wished, saying also that there was a box with my name on it. I lifted the Seahorse, which was wrapped in a protective material. I wasn't surprised to see it. I think I would have been surprised if I hadn't. I set it aside, giving it an awkward pat, not amazed that Stacy had saved it. The only other thing in the container was a small porcelain music box decorated with a branch, some leaves, a small nest, and a little yellow bird. My hand shook as I wound it up, tears sliding down my cheek as the song, nay, the spell, from all those years ago tinkled into life, and I almost dropped it. I caught it in time, holding it close, wrapping it carefully in its tissue, and taking it home, but I never played it again.

The story could end here, with me on a hired boat. It could end with me opening the latch of the urn and letting Stacy's ashes drift onto the water as she asked me to do. It could end with me holding the music box and getting ready to pitch it overboard, screaming in anger at things gone, pain suffered, and choices made.

But, in the end, I couldn't let go of the music box, which let out a single note, as if agreeing that I had finally made the right choice.

I get up slowly, my body having waged many battles in its time, age only one of them. I tuck the Seahorse beneath my arm and stroke its freshly inflated head. Then, I pick up the music box with my free hand and walk toward the waiting Ocean.

Before I enter the water, I wind up the music box and leave it on the beach to play its haunting tune.

"Remember me?" I whisper to the Ocean, and if it's a challenge, it is, or maybe it is an acceptance, or perhaps something else entirely.

I am what I am.

I kick at a wave, willing the Ocean to speak, and then laugh when it doesn't. Of course, it doesn't. Gods only listen to heroes.

I set out, conserving my strength. The tide was high, and the deep water found me quickly. I held onto the Seahorse and let the Ocean carry me away. When I judged I was deep enough, I began to swim back to shore, but a wave took me, as I expected to, to deeper water.

It is the same day, except I am alone—except I'm not. The Ocean watches in silence as, head below the surface, I walk back to shore, step by step, dragging the Seahorse with me.

I am old, as I have said, and my strength is not what it was; I begin to struggle, thinking the Ocean may be immortal and maybe a god, but it lies.

Then it speaks.

"Little fish, why have you come?"

I hold on to the Seahorse, panting. "You offered me something once." "I did."

"We had a deal."

"We did."

"I'm back to take you up on it."

"Such a bold little fish," the Ocean laughs, but a wave catches me up, flinging me into the sky, and I am back. Stacy is holding on, and I am letting her go.

The two little girls run into the Ocean during a low tide. The older girl holds an inflatable seahorse, its face garishly painted and its smile pointed at the sun. The lifeguard blows his cautionary whistle, but the two girls run further until the lifeguard blows again, more insistently, and they hear themselves called through the bullhorn to return to the beach. Grinning and caught, they turn back to shore and safety. The younger girl is scolded by a parent who grabs her by the arm and takes her home. The older girl is not expected anywhere and watches as her new friend leaves, forgetting to ask her name. She calls out, but the girl is too far away now to hear. Shrugging, the older girl sinks to her knees on the sand to build a sandcastle, but a shimmer of colour catches her eye, and she looks into the distance beyond the blue line. She rises to her feet, one hand shielding her eyes to see more clearly,

And a little girl drowns, her eyes staring up at her best friend as she sinks beneath the water.

But it is only the dance of light on the surface, and a wave washes in, briefly lifting the Seahorse from the sand and then retreating. The girl feels the clouds cover the sun, and she shivers.

The hooves of the hunter sound against a frozen sky. The Seahorse screams, pulling on its reins, as Herne blows his horn.

As if in a daze, the girl steps into the water, feeling its cold hands close around her ankles, but the Seahorse, raised from its nest by the tide, bumps her shin. Its eyes stare into hers, burning.

And she runs home alone, weeping, for what she can never say.

The Seahorse is quiet as the Ocean lifts it, carrying it far beyond the blue line, where the tame Ocean ends and the wild Ocean begins.

Shebat Legion is an award-winning, best-selling, consummate storyteller/producer/publisher whose quirky tales have appeared in numerous anthologies of various genres, and offerings of her work have been archived on the moon via The Lunar Codex associated with NASA.

FINE, EVERYTHING'S FINE!

By Carol McConnell

Kindergarten was child's play. All of my teachers loved me, I was their darling. I did everything first. I read, wrote, and learned my numbers first. I could even color in the lines and sing on key.

I expected to breeze into first grade as "Harrett the Wunderkind". But, on the first day, HE transferred in from another school. Apparently, his father was a physicist and his mother was some sort of computer genius. At first, I thought he might offer me a bit of companionship as the reigning smart kid. You know; be the Methos to my Amanda, the chocolate to my peanut butter. That is until I realized that he was dead set on winning everything. He would smirk and say, "There Can be Only One." As though he were the only Highlander fan, the nerve of him. I had a serious dislike for the obnoxious twerp. The teachers seemed thrilled to have both of us in the same class, as though it was a feather in the school's cap. Schools that cater to brilliant kids seem to take themselves way too seriously. After all, they didn't make us smart.

###

That first day of second grade, I jumped off the school bus and checked the mailbox before running down the long dirt drive to my house. I slammed the front door and stomped into the house. When Mom asked what was wrong, I yelled, "I'm fine, everything is fine." I was way too upset even to remember to grab my cookie from the counter, let alone the milk. She shrugged and kept sewing her latest project.

Gregory Bonfield McKenna had just become my mortal enemy. He's been my nemesis ever since the first grade, but this last stunt was too much. He dared to brag about learning trigonometry. Did he think he was the only one who could graph a sine wave? He was a jerk. I had been waiting for the perfect moment to show off my math skills and he'd beaten me to the punch. Oh, it was on!

That was years ago and we've battled it out for first place in every competition ever since. He'd win the state spelling bee one year, and the next, I would win. He won the talent shows, but I swept the historical diorama competitions.

My mom is a historical costume designer and set artist and my dad is an all-around "old things guy". He's part Paleontologist, Archeologist and Geologist. I've learned to love the past through both of them. My dioramas were spectacular. They gave excellent advice. Greg excelled in every class except for anything to do with the past. He'd sneer at me and mock my fossil collection. He didn't think that any of that old dead stuff mattered. But I loved my trilobites and mammoth teeth, I was fascinated with the changes that time had brought to our state of Wyoming. We have some of the best fossil hunting in the world right outside our door. He would insist, "The past is past, look to the future."

Ironically, time passed as it inevitably does and we found ourselves in the 8th grade. Sage Valley Junior High School was a magnet school for gifted and talented kids. We were its two stars, (Go Eagles!). Our animosity had continued to grow and this year the competition had reached a fevered pitch. More than once the principal had cautioned us that the school preferred that we cooperate rather than compete. My thought was always the same, if they didn't want us to compete then why keep score? Greg would just smirk and not say a thing. I was ahead by two points in paleontology and he had me by four in our physics class. I had argued against those points. He had gone to a physics lecture given by his dad and received five extra credit points. I didn't think that was fair, no one else in class had the opportunity to earn extra points. Which meant he was winning overall, top of the class, valedictorian, and the one and only.

Our school science fair was in March. It was followed in April by the county fair. Each school could have as many as three entries at the county level, so we both had a chance. The winners at the county level would battle it out at the state fair, in August. The state winner would be flown to the capital to see their science entry displayed in the Capital building. I desperately wanted to win, I'd never been on a plane. This was our first chance to make an impression on a grand scale. It was a real prize; the winner's work would be there for everyone to see and marvel over.

I could already imagine my project displayed in the lobby of the west wing of the Capitol building. Where all 30 state senators would stop and gaze at my brilliant display. It would hold their rapt attention until next September when the next winning project would arrive. No doubt many of them would petition to make mine a permanent exhibit. Winning was a whopping big deal and could lead to all kinds of scholarships and stuff.

I had big plans, I intended to really kick Greg's butt. But in the first week of February, I came down with COVID-19, followed immediately by chickenpox. I was as miserable as a girl can be. I didn't think that I'd make it to the science fair, I was out for weeks. But a few days before the big event I started feeling better. According to the doctor, I was no longer contagious and was cleared to go back to school and incidentally the competition.

I was fine. Only I wasn't, I was still tired and pale and I hadn't done anything on my project. I had a few days, but between catching up with my missed schoolwork and being completely exhausted, I couldn't get going on my experiment, I kept procrastinating, which isn't like me at all. Finally, it dawned on me that I only had a day left. I knew it was too late to pull together what I had initially planned, but perhaps not too late to still enter something. I spent all afternoon thinking and came up with something fast, easy, and brilliant, or so I thought. I had asked myself the crucial question, "What is it that everyone accepts as a given that is wrong and how could I disprove it?" That would do fine, just fine. Still feeling not quite myself, I imagined that proving that water does not conduct electricity would fit the bill and surely earn me at least a second-place ribbon, enough to get to the county fair. After all, who knew what would happen? I set up my experiment, I had a shiny white plastic stand and data boards explaining that it is the particulates in water that transmit electricity, not the water itself. I had wires going to a light bulb powered by a battery and each wire had to be placed in the water by the observer, to prove or disprove my hypothesis. I even had a clever little button system to dunk the wires. I thought my project being interactive would make it interesting and I'd gain extra points. I didn't think it would take first, after all, it was a throw-it-together project and not up to my usual exemplary level of work. But adults are always impressed when a kid points out the glaringly obvious. As I put the finishing touches on, I fantasized that I had an outside shot at winning county, just as long as Greg didn't pull a rabbit out of his hat.

###

I entered the gym and saw my competition. Beans growing in jars, baking soda balloon experiments, eggs in vinegar to soften their shells, homegrown crystals, baking soda & vinegar volcanos. It was all run-of-the-mill stuff. One kid had built a SimCity and had been expanding it for a year into a metropolis. That was pretty cool, except it wasn't a science experiment as much as game-playing, but who knows, maybe the judges would count city planning as a social science? Would that even count? I've seen them do some weird stuff when judging contests. I felt pretty smug and began to plan where to hang my blue ribbon and contemplate what I'd do along the same lines next year. I hummed as I set everything up in my booth space.

Then I noticed Greg bringing his project in. He carefully carried a small box and was followed by two men wheeling in a crate filled with stuff. My heart sank. Yup, he was going to outdo me for sure.

I watched with interest as they set everything up under his direction. You could see the smugness. Oh... I think I hate him even more. If only he hadn't gotten so cute over the last few years. One look from him and I'd get weak in the knees. (Nope, not going there, never mind, I'm fine.)

Finally, he had it all assembled. He placed whatever he had in the small box last, gently easing it into place. Then he covered it all with a large, dark blue, satin sheet. Interestingly, it looked like he planned to unveil his experiment like a magician. He was going to make a big show of it, yup, he was going to pull a rabbit out of his butt. Adults love that kind of theater. They think it's so cute when kids show off. What a creep! How egotistical and brilliant of him. I had to admit, that being sick had dulled my edge. I had underestimated him, again. This would be the last time.

The moment came to show the judges my experiment. I explained it and asked for a volunteer to press the buttons and dip the wire ends into the purified water and the salt water. Greg stepped right up and volunteered. I expected some sort of nastiness but he was complimentary about my experiment. Why, he was even nice, I smelled a trap. I sulked and showed off my experiment, resenting that I didn't have as much theater as he was about to create.

Crowds had already gathered at his booth in anticipation. Most of the judges made their way to him as quickly as they could without completely running past the lesser entries. You could see the anticipation on their faces. Soon enough, they stood in front of his experiment. I have to admit I had wandered over to stand with the rest of the crowd. I had pushed and elbowed my way to the front. If he failed, I wanted a good view. The first thing he did was ask for a volunteer and he looked directly at me. What could I do? I couldn't not reciprocate in front of the judges. So, I stepped forward, raised my hand, and gave the crowd a big smile. All the while staring at his covered experiment, wondering what I was getting myself into.

He called for attention and dramatically whipped the cloth from his experiment. It was an odd-looking thing, there seemed to be boxes within boxes. Some could be seen through but were not plexiglass. Others were dark like smoked glass and at the center of it all was a small spinning light that looked, for all the world, just like the illustrations of an atom with its protons, electrons, and neutrons whirling around it. The entire thing glimmered. There seemed to be an opalescence along some edges and light flashed from others. I wondered aloud, "Fiber optics?" he curled his upper lip and all but snarled, "Pleeease."

He turned to the judges and in his most annoying and imperious voice announced, "Ladies and Gentlemen I give you time travel". I laughed out loud and so did many others. But I could see he was serious. I began looking more closely at his nest of boxes. It was then that I realized that some boxes had sides that sheared off and were missing while other boxes intersected each other at odd angles. Some of the edges were blurred as if they weren't in focus. I couldn't see how it could not collapse in on itself, but it didn't. Was I looking at something that existed in other dimensions, or times? Now that I was paying attention it hummed, ever so softly and ever so quietly. I was a bit afraid. I had volunteered and there was no getting out of it now.

He began babbling on, he never explained his hypothesis except to tell everyone how much smarter he was than Einstein. He said Einstein had it all wrong, that time didn't work as he said it did, and that it was easy when you knew the truth. He claimed that light was a function of time. That his new understanding of physics and the nature of the universe would revolutionize the world. I could see the condescending smiles on some of the judges, but others were buying it. Some already had their phones out and were filming for posterity. He droned on and on, saying nothing and declaring himself the architect of the glorious future we were about to witness the birth of. It was ridiculous. He held up a small book with pages askew, held together with a rubber band, and said everything in his theory was in the book, along with his new calculus necessary for understanding time travel. He said he'd gotten the idea while watching a Highlander episode flashback and began to wonder what law of physics made immortality possible. What would the math for it look like, what was wrong with our current time theory? Because immortality was a sort of time travel, wasn't it? Then he explained that the second thing that had led to his brilliant discovery was his father's lecture. (You know, the lecture he'd gotten extra credit for.) As he sat in the audience, only half listening, he'd thought about light and acceleration and how their relationship would have to be reassessed as defined by his new theories. Everything we currently thought was wrong and with his new understanding of the true universal laws, physical time travel would become a possibility as a function of the 6th derivative of his new immortality calculus, and kaboom, it all came together. That's when the design for the "Array", as he called it, came into his mind fully complete, all he'd had to do was write it down and develop the proofs. Continuing, he commented on his brilliance and speculated that he alone was in a position to have lined up all the dots to make this discovery. He'd had an epiphany concerning his stellar intellect. All the adults chuckled about the Highlander comment and his newfound humility, they found him adorably precocious. Oh, Brother! He claimed to have run experiments at home with his pet hamster and they had worked and the rodent was fine.

Great, fine, now I'm his lab rat. I wanted to run, but I would never give him the satisfaction. I thought of fading into the crowd, and then I saw my experiment across the way. Two of the judges were standing in front of it gesturing. Maybe I still had a chance? I really couldn't see how. I looked at my sad little experiment. Why, it wasn't science at all. It was just exploiting a little-known fact. Just because people were ignorant didn't make my plastic box with buttons and lightbulbs anything new. I swallowed hard, pasted a big smile on my face, and said to Greg, "OK, enough pontification let's get on with the show. What do you need me to do?" I could see that all but the two judges loitering by my project were paying rapt attention. I had to make the best of it. Greg said, "OK, Harry, (I hated that nickname, and he, darn well, knew it.) I need you to put your left hand on top of this box and your right inside of this other one, directly below and to the left." I didn't see how my hand would go inside the box, because it seemed to have a solid side, but it did. As I stood there, he began to explain what was going to happen. According to him, the boxes would begin to glow and continue to hum, then at the right moment, he would touch spots mirroring my hands to complete the circuit, and the box and I would both disappear. Huh? What? Oh no you don't, I tried to remove my hands and found that I couldn't. He gave me an evil grin and said, "Once in place, you can't remove your hands until the trip has been initiated. But don't worry you won't end up in Salem being burned as a witch. You'll stay right here in Eastern Wyoming, on this exact spot. You'll simply slip into the past before this school was built. I'm still working on a way to calibrate exactly how far back you'll go," he said with a wicked grin. Sometimes I'm not sure if I hate him or admire him. I didn't believe him for a moment, he was too thorough not to know exactly when he was sending me. He continued, speaking directly to me, "You can look around for about three or four minutes. You'll notice that the "CA", which is short for Cubic Array, will begin getting bright, shortly you'll be returned here. Don't worry about arriving in the past, buried under the ground or suspended hundreds of feet in the air." My mouth dropped open, Huh? Well, shit, I hadn't until he'd said that. He continued; "the array will maintain its exact comparative distance from the ground below it. The return is an automatic boomerang effect. One caution thought; you can't take your hand out of the box, or off the top. If you do, you will be out of sync and it will return without you."

As you might have already surmised, I was dubious. But what's the worst that could happen? If it worked, I'd make history and be the world's first time traveler. I'd lose first place in the science fair, but so what? On the other hand, maybe it would blow up. That was worth being concerned about. Which led me to wonder how it was powered, I didn't see any plugs or cords. At the exact same moment that this occurred to me, one of the judges voiced the same question. Greg explained that there was power all around us but we hadn't developed the physics to capture it, until, of course, now. I felt sick. The jerk had discovered time travel and limitless free power, what next; World Peace? The boxes were glowing and humming. He turned and nodded to the judges and asked the crowd, "Ready?" I was about to shout, "WAIT!" when he slapped the bottom cube and stuck his hand in opposite mine. I had time to suck in one startled breath when my stomach lurched and I was violently ill. After vomiting I looked around and realized I wasn't in the school gym anymore.

An educated guess told me that I had gone back considerably. All around me were great waving fields of grass. The air held an ozone tang to it. I wasn't sure if it was always that way or if my appearance had caused it. This must be the Cenozoic, perhaps the Pliocene or the Miocene epochs because that's when the great grasslands began to spread. I had traveled somewhere in the neighborhood of 5 to 7 million years back into prehistory. I could see megafauna in the distance. They were too far away to accurately identify but I suspected they were Mammoths, I thought I could see tusks. How I wished they'd come closer, I wanted to see what they were. Knowing if they were Mammoths or Mastodons would give a clue as to how far back I'd traveled. I was fascinated by everything, I wanted to touch the plants and explore. So much so that I almost broke the connection with the box. I was suddenly riddled with terror. It had been sheer luck that I hadn't pulled my hands free upon arrival. I felt all the hairs rise on my skin at the thought of being trapped here, I tasted metal and thought I'd be sick again. Thankfully, I had remembered just in time. I became aware that the array was beginning to gently hum and glow. Then I realized it was getting brighter, how could the minutes be up already? It seemed as though I had only just arrived. I nearly dislocated my neck trying to see everything at once. I noticed the grasses and seeds. I desperately wanted to reach out and gather some to take back but I didn't dare. I could see footprints and dung in the dirt at my feet. I really couldn't wait until Greg and I could refine his design so that travelers could walk around and study what historians and paleontologists have only fantasized about. I was already formulating my arguments for why he should allow me to be his lab assistant. We had always been rivals, but this, this was too big for petty squabbles. I'd be his go-for if it got me onto the time team. I rubbed my shoes in the dirt, hoping to wedge dung, grass seeds, and microorganisms into the tread of my shoes.

###

I was back in the school, and this time I vomited on the principal's shoes. Fabulous... just what I needed. Who knew there was anything left in my stomach?

Everyone grabbed at me and shouted at the same time. The teachers and judges were all in an uproar, everyone arguing and carrying on. When they realized I was OK they simply turned and continued their arguing. My paleontology teacher looked at me and raised an eyebrow. He was the only adult paying any attention to us kids anymore. I looked at the bottom of my shoes, nothing. I shook my head and he took off after the others. They had all continued to walk away arguing about who to call first, and how much this would mean to the school. Whether or not the school owned part of the patient or if the discovery was all Greg's? They just weren't paying any attention to us kids anymore. Adults, go figure?

Greg stood to the side with a smug smirk on his face. (I swear it's going to freeze that way.) He asked how far back I thought I'd gone. I gave him my best estimate. He grinned and said, "Let's do it again." He reached out and turned boxes, the configuration was different, and I could almost sense the difference that his movement had made. I was dying to get a look at his book. He said, "Put your hands back in when and where I tell you, I'm going this time." I said that I needed to wipe my mouth first, I stepped over to the nearby snack bar and grabbed a handful of napkins. On the way back, I noticed his book sitting on the seat of his chair at the front of his booth. I casually laid my vomit-smeared napkins on top of it, covering it completely. I wasn't sure why I had done it, I didn't have a plan, but maybe while he was gone, I could get a peek at it. There was something familiar about the way the cubes intersected. I knew if I could see the formulas, I'd have a good chance of figuring it all out. After all, He's smart but I've always been smarter. I took my place opposite him. He stood where I had been with his hands already in, I hesitated, and he said, "The one on this side always travels." He continued, "Like your experiment, you need another contaminant, if your will, a person in this case, to establish the time field. Oddly enough our two experiments show that our minds were both going in the same direction. Beginning with proving that what everyone believes, just isn't so." I looked at him quizzically, he smiled with real warmth and said, "I'll explain when I get back." Shyly he added, "You look really pretty today." I blushed and instead of saying anything I stuck my hands in place and he and the boxes vanished.

Go figure, all the adults sucked air at the same time and rushed back to scream at me for being reckless with HIS life. That didn't last long. They quickly got back to bickering over how much Greg's invention was worth, and who would collect the noble prize and academic credit. Fine! I'm a bit indignant, but not so much that I forget to sneak the book off the chair, take it back to my booth, and stuff it into my packing box. If I get caught, I'll say I was protecting it while he was gone.

I waited and waited for what seemed like forever. Exactly 3.5 minutes later, the machine returned. Greg did not. The machine was filled with water that poured out all over the table and floor. The whirling center flickered out as it arrived; it was dead and I suppose Greg was too. No one can hold their breath that long. As near as I can tell he sent himself further back, a lot further.

I rolled my eyes, realizing that, of course, he'd have to beat me by an order of magnitude. I almost laughed; I'd underestimated him yet again. At a guess, I'd say he went almost 500 million years back to the Ordovician period when Wyoming was submerged in a shallow sea. Poor Greg, if only he'd studied Wyoming's past, he would have understood the significance of our ancient Geology, and might not have drowned as a result.

A sudden insight occurred to me, temporal studies were going to be a very diverse field, encompassing all manner of studies. Historians, paleontologists, geologists, archeologists, blacksmiths, and period costume designers were going to be in demand. My parents were going to have more work than they could handle.

Anyhow, I got a second-place ribbon, and Greg got first, posthumously, of course. However, my experiment represented the county at the state fair and won second place in the state. So, there is that. I lost to a kid who raised bees and tracked their pollination habits to improve honey yield. You can't beat bugs…

We were all really sad at the memorial and everyone cried, especially Greg's mother. But with him and his book both missing, everyone sort of tried to pretend that the whole thing had never happened. What was left of his cubes was given to the physics club.

They didn't look so interesting without their power source; they were just some scraps of wire and glass and not much more. I mean, we had no proof that it had worked, and who would believe that a Jr. High School student could do what so many other, more brilliant academic minds, had failed to do? All of the video footage could have been faked and people were already arguing about it online. There was no reason not to let the physics club fiddle around with the remains and see if they could make heads or tails of the dilapidated mess.

It all made me wonder how many times time travel had been invented and lost, all due to the inventors' over-inflated egos. Still, my heart skipped a beat when he smiled at me, I'll miss him. Maybe I'll get some scuba gear and go back for him before he drowns? I wonder if that would work? Would it create a new timeline…? Interesting questions. But first I'll have to do some research and develop a way to break the connection with the array without being stranded. That's going to take time, why I might even be old, like 20 or something, before I've worked out how to rescue him. Time isn't on his side, I mean, he's cute and all, but what does a 20-year-old want with an eighth-grader?

Later that afternoon, when I got home from the memorial, Mom asked how my day went, I grabbed a cookie and said, "Fine, everything's fine, I'm joining the physics club." She barely looked up from her sewing as I left the room. I went upstairs to my room, closed the door, and retrieved the little black book from its hiding place under my mattress. I shoved the remains of the cookie in my mouth, snapped off the rubber band, and flopped down on my bed to read.

Carol hates doing these things. She can talk your ear off, but not about herself. When asked to submit a biography she's always stumped. According to her, her life has not been amazing, it's rather ordinary. Does it make a difference that she's snow skied since she was three or that she raced off-road in my twenties and thirties? She's an excellent cook and has written cookbooks, only a few of which are completed because she keeps adding to them. Will you enjoy the story more, if you know she spent much of my childhood in Germany? Will you see into the depths of her soul by hearing that she dug for rocks and fossils over much of the southwest? Does anyone care about that stuff? Finally, she's left with the glaringly obvious truth, "I'm me, I wrote it, let it speak for itself." But if you insist on having a mental image of here, she's a short, white-haired, Grandmother who has had a lifelong affair with reading and is now flirting with writing.

FISH FRY

By Kelly Piner

Joyce lay hidden far away behind the corn stalks where the autumn sun warmed her body. Her private place, it was here that she daydreamed about school dances, summer vacations, and possibly cheerleading tryouts in a couple years. Plus, with any luck, she'd talk her mother into letting her have one of the new kittens born down the road in the Taylor's barn. She took a deep breath and inhaled the air coming from the house next door. It smelled of burnt charcoals and seafood.

As she savored the memory of smoked bluefish, her favorite, her dad came outside through the screen door. "Joyce?" he called.

"I'm here, Dad." She climbed to her feet and ran back to the house.

"Your mother and Jeffrey just phoned. The team made it to the hotel. They'll rest up before dinner."

She tried to catch her breath. "What time is Jeffrey's game tomorrow?"

"Noon. They'll be home before seven."

"OK. I'm hungry."

"I'll start dinner as soon as Bill and Joyce get here. I'm just sorry that your mother and Jeffrey couldn't be here to see them. Who knows when they'll be back?"

"Jeffrey can't miss a football game."

Her father laughed. "Not if your mother has anything to do with it. Afraid she's building him up for a big letdown."

"Mama said he's good enough to play in college."

"We'll see about that. Come inside and help me get started."

Dressed in jeans and a brown wool sweater, Joyce followed him into their country kitchen. The kitchen reminded Joyce of her grandmother, who had died last year. She'd left Joyce's father the house, and Joyce could still smell the fresh ginger her grandmother would grind for cookies.

From the refrigerator, her dad removed a large bag overflowing with bluefish that he had gotten free at Davis Seafood, where he worked. He also sometimes caught fresh fish himself, at Atlantic Beach, over twenty miles away. Her family went there most

51

weekends when her father didn't have to work and accompanied him in his small trawler.

Today, Joyce hoped her dad would let her help clean the fish. When she'd asked in the past, he'd always said that she was too young.

Outside, he slipped on a pair of black rubber gloves and used a long boning knife to scale each one.

"Can I help? Please."

"Just don't tell your mother. She'd skin me alive." He removed his gloves and placed them on Joyce's tiny hands. "Remember, this knife is very sharp. Hold the fish low, away from your body."

Joyce gripped the fish by the tail and slid the knife across its scales. The scales covered the ground and shimmered like fresh snowflakes. This was so much fun that she thought maybe she could get a job at Davis Seafood and work alongside her dad.

"That's right. Steady."

When Joyce had cleaned both sides, she asked, "Can I chop off the head?" "

"No. That's the best part of the fish."

She could never get used to it, the dead eyes staring up at her from her plate.

After they'd cleaned the last fish, her dad tossed them into a large bucket filled with ice.

"What's Mama and Jeffrey having for dinner, fish?"

"I seriously doubt it. Sizzler Steakhouse is my guess."

"I'd rather have fish."

"That's my girl."

Away from her mother's watchful eye, her father never scolded her and didn't care what she did, as long as she didn't burn down the house.

"Let's get those steamer bags ready. That's Uncle Bill's favorite part."

Bill wasn't really her uncle, but her father's best friend. According to Bill, Joyce's father had saved his life during the war. She couldn't remember which war. Joyce's mom had said more than once that the Dahls were rich, and sometimes, when the overdue bills arrived, she said, "Too bad you didn't follow in Bill's footsteps, Jerry."

Inside the kitchen, Joyce stuffed bags with clams, sweet potatoes, and chicken breasts, which her dad then tossed into a large steamer pot.

Her father pressed his index finger to his lips when he pulled a can of beer from the refrigerator.

Joyce giggled. "I'll never tell." Her mother disapproved of alcohol so her dad's only break was when she went out of town. Her mom bossed everyone around and always got her way. But Joyce's dad told her not to be too hard on her. "Remember, your grandfather was killed by a drunken driver when your mother was just a little girl. She's had a rough life."

With his tall, lanky body and full beard, Joyce's dad reminded her of Abraham Lincoln. Kind and gentle, he stood nearly 6'5" and Joyce took after him. Already, she was the tallest girl in her fifth-grade class, with plenty of growing ahead of her.

It had been over a year since Joyce had seen Bill and Betty. They lived clear over on the other end of the state, near the mountains. Aunt Betty always gave Joyce a gift. Last year, she had gotten a butterfly necklace that her mom let her wear to church each Sunday. This year Joyce longed for a pair of earrings for her newly pierced ears.

Joyce was sitting outside, flipping through a children's magazine and sipping lemonade, when a shiny red car pulled into the driveway. It was the largest vehicle she'd ever seen and seemed to stretch a mile long. She raced up to it.

Bill and Betty climbed out and smiled. Betty wore a full red shimmery skirt and a white blouse with a lace collar. Her jet-black curls were arranged on top of her head, and to Joyce, she looked just like Elizabeth Taylor. "Come give your Aunt Betty a hug."

As Joyce approached her, she hesitated. There was something different about Betty, maybe her eyes?

Her dad and Bill embraced. "It's been too long, my friend." Her dad stepped back. "Whew! Where'd you get the fancy wheels?"

"Just came off the showroom floor. Brand new 1969 Impala with all the extras."

Joyce was glad her mother wasn't here to see this. She'd been complaining about the family's old Ford that spent more time at the garage than it did in their own backyard.

"Not hard to do when you own the dealership," Joyce's father said.

53

Everyone laughed.

"Can I get you a beer?"

Bill smiled. "You know it, Jerry."

"Betty?"

"Make mine a lemonade."

Everyone sat at the large cedar picnic table with the red gingham cloth.

Joyce sat perfectly still. There was something different about Bill too, his voice? It sounded too deep, almost like when she'd turn down the speed of her records. Had something taken over his body, like in a recent horror movie she'd seen? Joyce watched his entire face for signs of change. A knot tugged at her stomach, just as it had when she'd hugged Aunt Betty.

She turned to her dad to see if he had noticed anything, but he was just his happy self, talking about old times.

Joyce's dad and Bill discussed boring topics like politics and a recent prison riot. When they cracked another beer and walked to the barbecue, Joyce moved next to Betty, who wore a golden fish brooch with green eyes pinned to her blouse.

"Would you like to touch it?" Betty asked.

Joyce nodded and could feel her heart pounding as she tentatively moved toward it. When she tapped it with her index finger, the fish's body wriggled. She jerked her hand back.

Betty laughed. "You didn't know it was alive, did you?"

"Alive?" Joyce didn't understand how a brooch could be alive. Maybe it was a special fish for rich people?

"Watch out, Joyce," her father said. "It could bite you." By now, he and Bill were on their third beer.

When Joyce had worked up the courage, she asked, "Did you bring me a present?"

"Joyce!" her dad yelled. "That's not polite."

Joyce's face flushed hot and she lowered her head.

"Don't worry about it, Jerry. You should know that I always bring a gift for my only godchild. Betty opened her purse and removed a yellow box. "Be careful when you open it. It's delicate."

Joyce took the box and looked at her father.

"What do you say?"

"Thank you." When she heard something moving around, she held the box next to her ear. "What is it?"

54

Betty smiled. "You'll just have to open it."

Joyce carefully removed the yellow bow and opened the lid. "Ahhhhh!" Inside lay another golden fish brooch, this one with sapphire-blue eyes. It wriggled around, just like Betty's.

Joyce didn't speak at first.

Her father leaned over. "Let's see what you got. Oh my! That's a very special gift for such a little girl. Betty, you're spoiling her."

"What good is money if I can't spoil the people I love?"

"Can I put it on, Daddy?"

"Let Aunt Betty help you. Remember, it's alive."

Joyce still didn't understand how a pin could be alive.

Betty pinned it to Joyce's wool sweater.

"Do I have to feed it?"

Betty took Joyce's hand and leaned in close. "We'll talk about that later."

Joyce felt all grown up, wearing a fancy brooch that was alive.

"When are we going to eat?" Bill asked. "I'm starving."

Jerry set out a platter of crispy fried bluefish on the picnic table alongside the steamed bags, chips, and a platter of brownies. "Let's eat!"

Bill raised his finger in the air. "First, let's join hands."

Joyce's family only said grace on Sundays, after church, but she took Betty's hand. Instead of the warmth that Joyce had expected, of one hand in another, clasping Betty's hand caused Joyce's body to go cold, as if she had ice in her blood.

"Let's bow our heads," Bill said. "Hail, Odin, god of wisdom and inspiration! Grant me the gift of your knowledge and guide me on the path of your warrior. Allow me to safely take this family back home. Amen."

When Joyce looked up, her dad smirked. "What's with the Odin prayer? Are you trying to reconnect with your pagan roots?"

"It's all part of my mission, my surprise."

Joyce lit up. "I like surprises."

"Your mission?" her dad asked.

"You'll see."

Following the prayer, Joyce filled her plate with as much food as it would hold. She was poking at the fish head with her fork when she said, "This fish looks like Mama. It has the same color eyes."

Her dad looked over and chuckled. "A little."

Joyce was munching on chips when she felt something nibbling at her shoulder. "Ouch!"

"What's wrong, honey?"

"Something bit me."

"Let me have a look." Jerry peered over the top of his glasses. "You're bleeding."

"Bleeding?" Betty said. She pulled back Joyce's sweater from her shoulder. "Something did bite her."

"It was the fish pin," Joyce said.

Jerry shook his head. "It's a brooch. A brooch can't bite."

Joyce tapped the fish's tail and it wriggled.

Betty took Joyce's hand. "Come inside and let me clean that wound."

When they returned, Jerry and Bill were eating brownies and chugging down more beers.

"Are you okay, honey?" Jerry asked.

Joyce nodded. "I took off the pin."

"Joyce, that brooch didn't bite you. Aunt Betty put a lot of thought into your gift."

"You said it was alive."

"We were joking, that's all."

Bill cleared his throat. "Before it's pitch dark, let's go out to the Jarrett Bay."

"Why the bay?" Jerry asked. "Those woods get awful dark at night."

"You'll see," he said.

Joyce tugged at her dad's shirt. "It's the surprise, daddy." Maybe they'd take turns telling ghost stories or even take a boat ride under the full moon.

"Hmmm. Now you've piqued my curiosity. I'll get the flashlight."

Moments later, even with the flashlight, the heavy autumn foliage made it nearly impossible to see more than a foot ahead. In the distance, a coyote howled.

Joyce grabbed her father's hand. "Will it get us?"

"No, sweetheart. He is as afraid of us as we are of him."

Newly fallen leaves crunched under Joyce's sneakers. Soon, they passed the old cemetery containing only a handful of graves, a family plot. The dates on the headstones date back to 1804. The names had faded long ago. Once, she and Jeffrey had shone a flashlight into a crumbly grave, and Jeffrey claimed to have seen a child's skull. She had never told Jeffrey, but she had felt as if she were looking down into her own grave. That was the last time Joyce had visited the small plot.

When they finally reached Jarrett Bay, Bill and Betty stood off to the side, whispering.

When Joyce looked up into her father's face, his eyes were glazed over, the way they were the day he had found his father dead on the bathroom floor. Joyce didn't really understand it, but everyone said that her dad had the gift of second sight, just like his father before him. He somehow knew things before they happened.

Joyce longed for her mother and Jerry. She couldn't shake a vague sense of dread.

"I want Mama and Jeffrey."

Her father's voice was barely audible. "I'm sorry, but they're gone."

There was something in his voice, the way he said "gone" that frightened her.

Bill shone the flashlight onto the edge of the sound, exposing a large school of fish. "This is your new family, Joyce."

"The fish?"

"Yes, the fish."

Her father's body went stiff and he neither spoke nor moved.

Bill walked out into the water and raised his arms to the sky. "I praise and honor you. I thank you for your blessings. Poseidon, friend of the sailor, the fisherman, and of those who find their livelihood on the sea. Poseidon, have mercy on the children of men, still and subdue the wrathful Earth."

Joyce didn't understand the strange words. She only knew that the excitement she'd felt earlier had transformed into something that she did not quite understand.

Betty outstretched her arms. "Come, Joyce."

Joyce tightened her grip on her father's arm. In the glow of the full moon, Betty's face looked distorted, like in the funhouse mirrors at the carnival.

"Daddy, I'm scared. I don't want to go."

"Do as Aunt Betty says."

To Joyce, it felt like hours since dinner. She did as told, and Betty led her by the hands into the creek until Joyce stood waist-deep.

"I'm scared."

"Nothing to be afraid of. This is the surprise."

Now, Bill looked up into the sky and spoke a strange language, as if performing some ancient ritual that Joyce had recently seen in an old movie about the Vikings.

A school of fish jumped from the water and sailed through the air.

Joyce's last memory was of fish gnawing and feeding on her flesh as Aunt Betty led her through the black water to a small fishing trawler.

"Joyce. Joyce!"

The ailing woman looked up from the gutting station where she'd been cleaning fish since 7 am. "Yes, Kenneth."

"Customers are lined up at the register. Take a break and wait on them. I have important calls to make."

Why was it that her supervisor always disappeared just when things got busy? "Of course," she said, and slipped off her heavy rubber gloves, exposing arthritic hands, gnarled from too many years of shucking oysters and filleting fish. She'd lost track of how long she'd been here. But just like her father, she had worked at Davis Seafood most of her adult life. She barely remembered her life before this.

Up front, a man and his young daughter stood at the counter.

"What can I get you?" Joyce asked.

The man gently nudged his daughter. "Betty, go ahead and tell the lady what you want." The child wore a fish brooch that wriggled when she moved. She couldn't have been more than eight or nine.

"We want three pounds of bluefish. Oh, leave the heads on."

"Three pounds? That's an awful lot of fish for such a little girl."

She smiled. "Yes, Ma'am. We're having a fish fry."

"Good for you. I love fish fries." The words nearly stuck in Joyce's throat.

Joyce placed a pile of dead-eyed fish on the scale and fought against the memory of her last fish fry. She hadn't known it would be the last time she'd see her father. *A tragic boating accident*, the authorities had called it; an entire party wiped out, except for Joyce. She remembered so little. What she did recall seemed like a bizarre, disjointed nightmare; she couldn't be sure if it was reality or the trauma of the whole evening, waking up in a hospital and learning that her mother and Jeffrey had been killed in a violent bus crash. Her father must have known it that night, the look in his eyes when he'd told her they were gone. He may also have known about his own fate.

Joyce rang up the fish and wrapped them in brown packing paper. She glanced once more at the fish brooch.

"Would you like to touch it? It's alive," the girl said. "I have to feed it later."

Joyce shook her head. "That's okay, honey. I don't want to scare it."

The man paid and led his daughter out into the parking lot where they climbed into a shiny red 1969 Impala.

Joyce's chest swelled from a sense of loss, a distant memory of a little girl playing in the cornfield, daydreaming about her future. Where had her life gone?

Joyce watched the man and child speed away. Then, she turned toward the long line of customers and forced a smile.

Kelly Piner is a Clinical Psychologist who in her free time, tends to feral cats and searches for Bigfoot in nearby forests. Her writing is inspired by Rod Serling's Twilight Zone. Most recently, Ms. Piner's story, "Euthanasia," was chosen as The Best of 2023 by After Dinner Conversation. Her short stories have appeared in Litro Magazine, Scarlet Leaf Review, Dragon Soul Press, The Last Girl's Club/Wicked News, Rebellion Lit Review, The Chamber Magazine, Drunken Pen Writing, Lit Shark Magazine, The Literary Hatchet, Weirdbook, Written Tales and others. Her stories have also appeared in multiple anthologies.

THE MAN WHO CONQUERERD TIME

By Chris L. Adams

A COMING AGE

"Well, Ahmel? What are we waiting for? Did this mechanical apparatus of yours work, or not?"

Gritting his teeth, Ahmel stared into the condescending scowl slithering down the long nose of Brimpo, financier and self-styled leader of the expedition. Before Ahmel could speak, however, his assistant, Fimfa, interposed, an undisguised strain of annoyance edging her voice.

"One need but glance out the nearest porthole to note the evident changes in our environment. Of course, the machine worked. We but await the atmospheric sampling to verify that it is safe—"

"Technological prattle! Our world is about to enter a catastrophic age of ice, laying to waste everything for which our society has strived for a million years, and you allow a water sample to stand in the way of opening that blasted hatch! Stand aside!"

"Brimpo, no!" Ahmel shouted. Before anyone could stop him, Brimpo slapped the lock upward to free the device and then spun the 8-armed wheel with another brutish smack of his large hands. The wheel spun smoothly and, with a *whoosh* of pent air pressure and bated breaths, the hatch popped open with an inrush of warm, moist air.

"There!" Brimpo beamed, inhaling deeply. "Fresh air, if a bit humid. But it's warm air! Not those frigid blasts that today drive ice particles through the streets of Zonthrovolis! But wait!" Brimpo's eyes narrowed. "I know we agreed to one-hundred-fifty million, but indeed, this air is far moister than I care for. I think an additional fifty million would be perfect. Yes, let us go back an additional fifty million years," he ordered, and with that, he slammed the hatch closed.

Ahmel's face flushed crimson. "You opened that hatch, potentially infusing the cabin with airborne toxicities for all you knew! Not to mention I was unable to verify our present time. I agreed to build this machine based on my understanding of the physics dictating that the possibility to break the time barrier exists, a truth that this machine bears out in reality. But I did so with the understanding that I would command this vessel and that I would dictate when *and if*

60

we disembark this machine! You put our lives at risk by opening that hatch, and you did so literally for nothing because you in the same instant changed your mind!"

"And I told you," Brimpo said coldly, eyes narrowing, "that I was the leader of this expedition. Remember who is paying for all of this and consider carefully what you say, and in what manner you say it."

"*Once we* exit the vessel you may have your dictates," Ahmel replied, "but not before." That last statement held a distinctly sharp edge, so he tempered it with a reasonable question, "So, now you wish to go to a different time. Why?"

"Because I seek the *perfect* time, Ahmel, one without the drifts of snow and ice inundating at this very moment a city at one time considered climatically perfect. And after all, it is the entire population of Zonthrovolis we propose moving to the new time. Now reset the machine." Brimpo's eyes were flinty, easily hard enough to deflect the icy stare directed at him by the machine's designer who turned to do as he was bid.

AHMEL

The second time traversal, traversing an additional fifty million years into the past, went smoothly, and this time Brimpo allowed them to follow safety protocols before opening the hatch. Standing by the traverser, Ahmel watched Fimfa as the girl crouched at the edge of a lake gathering samples. He was conflicted about her. She suffered from an extreme case of hero worship, and he happened to be the object of that infatuation. And it wasn't that he mistakenly assumed this. He knew it because she had confessed it to him. And this latest success, that of developing a machine capable of traversing time, had only driven her admiration to greater heights. It explained why she leaped to his defense after that first time traversal when that pompous moron, Brimpo, suggested the machine had failed to function.

When she entered his employ two years ago, she admitted that she had followed his work since she was but 5 when she briefly met him, and that she found him exemplary of everything she strived to be herself as a scientist. He told her he barely recalled the event while, in actuality, he did. For he had also followed her as she grew up on the grounds of the institute. When she was later unable to pay fully to attend, it did not matter as he had already paid for it, never telling her, and swearing all who knew to secrecy.

But more seriously, he had for the last year suspected her of being in love with him. The signs were palpable . . . the increased frequency of supposedly accidental touches, her body brushing him in the tight confines of the lab, her fingers touching his as, together, they adjusted the various equipment with which they worked. They were noticeable tell-tales, but they were not all. Most obvious were the many wide-eyed stares he often intercepted as she watched him work when he would notice that her eyes were moist with so much more than scientific zeal.

He let out his breath in a long sigh. She had come to him straight from the best university Zonthrovolis had to offer and begged him to take her as his apprentice. Even had he not followed her efforts since she was a child, her institutional scores alone would have sufficed, not to mention her pluck in coming to him as she had. Of course, he accepted her. She had worked tirelessly with him ever since on sundry projects, many of which were successful in great part because of Fimfa. He had not yet told her, but he intended to bequeath everything he owned to her.

But that was *all* he could bestow upon Fimfa.

He could not give her the one thing he knew she hoped for: his love. He cared far too much for her to condemn her to the fate haunting his heels. Not to mention the great age difference. No, he was not good enough for Fimfa, but more than that, he was unfit for her. No one was good enough for her, but he especially would not allow her to involve herself with a condemned old man fated to die a terrible death at the hands of an abysmal disease that, despite his scientific capabilities, he could neither stem nor cure.

No, the best thing he could give Fimfa was compassion that prompted him to encourage her to seek a man who was healthy and closer to her own age. Certainly, she should look elsewhere than to a decrepit old man who would soon become food for the simple invertebrates of their protein farms . . . the inescapable fate of all, true, but a fate that approached him with increasing rapidity.

"But I conquered time," he muttered to himself, tearing his eyes away from the girl.

"You did indeed," Brimpo assured him, grinning as he stopped beside the operator of the time-traverser.

Ahmel spun. "Brimpo! I was not aware you had snuck up behind me."

BRIMPO

Brimpo grinned down into the surprised face of Ahmel. He knew it to be an uncomfortable grin for those who were its recipients although he himself was unaware precisely of their reasons. Had he asked, he might have learned that it was because his was a grin in which they saw no real merriment, unless it was the deranged mirth of one who takes delight in the suffering and disquietude of others.

"It is lucky for you, then," Brimpo continued, "that we are here and not our old world from which we fled over a million years ago. For, as the histories have it, that world, spinning in some distant galaxy far from here, contained many deadly creatures that hunted our people nearly to extinction before we advanced technologically and turned the tables on them. Imagine one of *those* sneaking up on you! And then it was *we* who hunted *them*! And that's how it should be!" Brimpo laughed.

Brimpo suddenly noticed Fimfa, bending over as she scraped samples from a rocky deposit at her feet, all unknowing that Brimpo's lascivious gaze raked her from head to heel. Brimpo looked askance at Ahmel. "I must say, I honestly had not noticed, but she is rather a fetching girl, isn't she?" he commented. "She cuts quite a figure, for sure. You chose your assistant wisely, Ahmel."

"You cross a line, Brimpo!" Ahmel hissed. "Ours is a professional relationship; she is to be my successor."

"Ah, so?" Brimpo's grin deepened. "I've seen her look at you as though—well, I'll say no more!"

Ahmel saw that leering grin and instantly guessed his debased thoughts as perfectly as though the man had expressed them aloud. It was true that Brimpo was of the age that he felt Fimfa should look to in a possible mate rather than wasting her devotion upon a man nearly three times her age. Not to mention he was wealthy; the girl could fail utterly as a scientist yet never want for a thing for the remainder of her days.

Yet Ahmel would rather see her homeless and begging in the streets than become Brimpo's plaything. The likes of Brimpo would never perform the mating rites with a commoner like Fimfa, despite her multitudinous shining qualities. Rather, Brimpo would use her up then cast her aside, as he had no doubt cast others aside, saving his final joining rites, which dedicate the remainder of one's days to

63

a single mate, for one chosen from amongst the top tier of snobbish noble elites.

Brimpo had no idea that Ahmel was armed with anything remotely more dangerous than a test tube until he felt the slight poke of something pointy touching his belly. Looking down quickly, he saw that Ahmel held a trenching knife such as scientists use to excavate in the field aimed where a firm thrust would send it through a crucial organ. He had seen these tools at work, and so knew their capability of punching their way through tough deposits with ease. Making a passage through the soft tissue of his abdomen would be like passing a sharp knife through one of the tender, skeletonless creatures of the warm pools in Zonthrovolis of which he was fond when they were properly seasoned and grilled.

"This is your only warning," Ahmel hissed.

What might have happened next Brimpo would never know because Fimfa, having no clue as to what ensued behind her, called out, "Ahmel, come quickly! You should see this."

Brimpo glanced down as the scientist turned from him just in time to see the older man slip the digging knife back into its scabbard on the hip opposite that facing Fimfa, with the girl none the wiser. The act was performed quickly and smoothly, like an expert swordsman returning his blade to its scabbard.

"Well played, Ahmel," Brimpo said softly after the other quickly walked away, grinning again that grin of his that only reached one side of his mouth and in which his eyes declined to participate. "But somehow I seriously doubt you have the conviction to carry it out." Shrugging, he walked over to join the two scientists where they stood looking at something the girl had in a large beaker.

FIMFA

While the surreality of her position was not continually uppermost in Fimfa's mind nor was it lost upon the girl as she crouched before a glassy lake reflecting a beautiful, low-ceilinged sky, surrounded by pristine tropic forests, two hundred million years before her own time.

Fimfa's upbringing had been fairly normal so finding herself where she stood now was quite extraordinary. Her family were neither wealthy nor destitute, nor were they of the nobility nor of the affluent. If they were *of* anything, they were of mostly average stock and intelligence. As such, everyone with whom she was related were common laborers who worked for a living, most beginning at a young age. Fimfa began working at a younger age than all of them so she might afford the Science Institute of Zonthrovolis, the institute of choice for the city's elite. And the desire to attend an institute, when literally no one in her family had ever done so, would never have entered her mind but for the most minute of occurrences.

It was a memory she frequently revisited that she might not forget it, and whenever she pondered just how close it came to not happening her heart would race as if something still might prevent it, and her future be snatched away. She was but 5 when, upon seeing some trinket in the market, a small, inexpensive object such as a child might covet, she asked one of her sisters if she would purchase it for her. The girl had looked at Fimfa for a long moment, then sighed and purchased the silly bauble, a copper bracelet of braided wire. Later, this same sister and another of Fimfa's siblings were speaking when Fimfa overheard her admit that she had something that she had desired for herself but had to forego it to buy the trinket for Fimfa.

Fimfa went straight to her parents in the small kitchen where they were preparing an evening meal and told them she desired a job such as she might perform. They were a hard-working family, and both her parents beamed that such a work ethic had been instilled in the youngest of their offspring.

"I am working on a project for that university near the coast," her father said. "The other day, the director mentioned that if we knew anyone who needed work, they needed helpers to carry small parcels for instructors and courier messages across the grounds between buildings. I will take Fimfa with me tomorrow and see if they still have such a need."

They had indeed, and Fimfa began immediately, doing many small things and learning her way around the grounds. In a shorter time than she had guessed possible, she had earned enough to pay her sister back double what that silly bracelet had cost.

It had been Fimfa's desire for the bracelet—which she wore ever after as a reminder—that instilled in her a desire for employment, but it was another occurrence that fostered a desire to attend an institute such as that at which she labored. On this occasion, she was asked to quickly bear a message to the Great Hall where a speaker of some notoriety was shortly to teach a special class.

Fimfa was, for all her youthful naivete and petite stature, one of the fleetest couriers at the university, able to speed her way to her destinations with which she was by now quite conversant, earning her a great many tips from the wealthy students and faculty in addition to her daily wage. Set on this latest task, the fast little girl ran swiftly along the wooded paths and over the carefully maintained lawns, zigzagging between chatting students making their way hither and thither until she sped breathlessly into the science building, up marble stairs, down ornate halls, and through a certain side door until she came to the backstage area before which hung a beautiful dark blue curtain. She slipped almost invisibly between them at the precise point where stood the man at the rostrum who was to teach the class . . . and handed Ahmel the missive in the delivery of which Fimfa had been dispatched.

She could never quite put a finger on what it had been about Ahmel that caused her to linger after he smiled, accepted the message she carried, and thanked her. Was it the kindness in the man's eyes, or the soft modulations of his voice when he spoke? Whatever it was that had captivated her, she paused just long enough to cause him to ask, "Would you like to stay and listen, little one? I was just about to begin."

She had nodded, and smiling at her again, he had ushered her into a chair near the rostrum. For the next two hours she sat, ignoring the crowded auditorium, her eyes glued to this fascinating man who spoke eloquently and knowledgably, at times impassioned, at other times in hushed tones as he revealed the mysteries of a universe bright and glittering to Fimfa's young ears. By the end of those two hours, she knew what she wanted to do with her life.

It was fifteen years later before she entered the offices of the institute's admittance administrators with bags full of coin, having disdained to spend a single one on childish things from the instant she began working toward that moment. And it was enough, it seemed, to pay for the classes she wished to take, not knowing it was nowhere near enough, or that the balance would be paid by a benefactor of whom she was completely unaware.

SOMETHING ISN'T RIGHT

Ahmel walked quickly to where Fimfa stood beside the lake from which she had been taking water samples. In her beaker was not water but some freakish aberration, unlike anything he had ever seen. Ahmel felt his heart rate accelerate at the sight of it.

Continuing to stare at the organism in the beaker, he shook his head, "Something isn't right."

The girl also watched the creature as though hypnotized, somehow managing, "Yes, Ahmel, this means precisely what you are thinking. But how?"

Brimpo looked quickly from one to the other, his own expression reflecting the utter puzzlement he presently experienced. "Well?" he snapped after a moment. "Are you two walking talking brains going to leave me perplexed forever or do you intend to explain why this ... hideous thing ... is causing you to act so strangely?"

Ahmel, looking stunned, continued to gaze at the creature for a moment before turning toward Brimpo, his expression bleak. But instead of answering the question their financier had asked, he turned his face upward into a sky where a swollen red sun glared blindingly through the thick atmosphere.

"Will someone say something!" exploded Brimpo.

The shout jerked Ahmel's attention back to his employer. Frowning, he replied, "We were apparently wrong when we believed the declining temperatures signaled the coming of a permanent ice age. You may not know it, but this creature here is a far more complex lifeform than those of our time. As we progress backward through epochs, we expect to find organisms of simpler and simpler nature until all that exists are single-celled lifeforms swimming in the hot seas of a planet finally able to support life after having suffered terrific birthing pains where its surface was nothing but molten rock. Now do you understand?"

Brimpo knew he risked looking as imbecilic as, indeed, he was, but he said it anyway. "No. Now explain what this means and do so quickly."

"It means we have traveled *forward* in time, not *backward* as we intended. It means we are obviously beyond what we thought was an approaching, *permanent* ice condition, that the planet somehow threw itself out of that state and warmed up again. It means that life never became extinct as our scientists warned—yes, even I. It means that life endured, although that does not mean that *our* species survived those frigid temperatures. This creature," Ahmel continued, pointing at the beaker, "means we are now 250 million years in the *future*, not in the *past*."

FLEE, FIMFA, FLEE!

"What do we need to do," Brimpo asked, his eyes narrowing.

"Fimfa and I must try to understand what all this means. Are we safer to move our people into the future now that we know the coming ice age will not endure? Or do we return to our own time, revisit the calculations, reconfigure the time-traverser, and attempt to traverse in the correct direction to seek a temperate timeframe to which to transport the people? It won't cost too much more to reconfigure the machine.

"Unfortunately, the work must be done in the laboratory as we do not have the equipment here to refashion the necessary components. The preset equipment should function to return to our own time, however, so we aren't stuck here. I'm sorry. I know this machine cost a fortune, but no one is infallible, and in this case, my best effort has resulted in us finding ourselves in the wrong time. This new information upends things, Brimpo, surely you see that," Ahmel finished.

Ahmel felt Fimfa's eyes upon him but he ignored her questioning gaze. Nothing would induce him to reveal that it was primarily she who had written the calculations in question. The fact that the girl had checked them hundreds of times would not matter. He signed off on the work, and he would accept the blame.

Brimpo looked at Ahmel like he wished to brain him. "I will tell you what I see," Brimpo spat. "I see that you have cost me a fortune to develop a machine that doesn't work properly. You convinced me that this science of yours, and your ability to build a machine to exploit it, was a safe venture! Blast you, Ahmel!"

Ahmel looked stunned. "The machine *does* work, it just works backward. If you do not wish to invest the additional funds, we can help you seek supplementary stakeholders. People will want to invest in their own futures. I mean, their very lives are at stake!"

"You blithering fool! My funds are exhausted!" Brimpo screeched, his face turning purple. "You believed I was some idiotic philanthropist! This was never about 'saving our race'! This was about me regaining my lost wealth, wasted in gambling dens and bad ventures. All of that is immaterial! All that matters is that it is recovered. This was never going to be a free ride for the masses, you stupid simpleton! People were going to pay to escape their dooms . . . and they were going to pay dearly!"

Brimpo glared, staring with crazed eyes at the surrounding verdure, its beauty utterly lost on him. Out in the warm water, a long neck with a small head on the end of it abruptly broke the surface, interrupting the three on the shore. The head rose lazily two dozen feet into the air, a mouthful of underwater vegetation drooping from between its jaws as it slowly chewed. It was the largest creature either had ever seen. While it ate something large swimming just beneath the surface darted in quickly and exploded from the depths in a savage attack.

Powerful jaws sank into the soft flesh of the victim, chomping gruesomely into its neck. The predator just hung there, teeth clamped, as the stricken creature reactively straightened, rising even higher into the air, the action dragging its attacker partly out of the water. With a sickening rending sound, the flesh tore loose, and the hunter collapsed back into the lake. The herbivore staggered, blood gushing from its horrible wound. It fell, struggled to its feet again, and stumbled toward shore only to fall once more. The hunter tore into it again, this time from beneath the surface. The three on the bank knew this because the poor beast was knocked from its feet from the force of the strike before crying out in agonizing despair as it was dragged under.

"This future is not safe!" Fimfa cried, pointing at the foaming, blood-stained surface. "We cannot bring them here! Remember the histories! Our people were hunted nearly to extinction on our old world. If there are creatures like that in the water, imagine what lurks in the forest, perhaps watching us at this very moment!"

Brimpo seemed unfazed, however by what he had just witnessed, seeming detached somehow. "You have ruined me," he said, his voice calm. Casually, he picked up a driftwood stick and struck with it at a flower on a nearby bush, decapitating the bloom and leaving the stem twitching.

A dreadful sensation came to Ahmel. Quickly, he said to Fimfa, "Take that sample back to the traverser, Fimfa. It might be of use to our biologist friends back home."

69

Fimfa hesitated. "You both saw what just happened! We should all return to the machine together. This place frightens me."

"As well it should!" screamed Brimpo. He suddenly struck the older man across his shoulders. Stunned, Ahmel fell to the shore, started to rise, but was again struck from behind.

"She is right!" Brimpo cried. "No one will want to come here! Supplementary stakeholders, indeed! They would aid them to escape our frozen city for *free*!" And he struck Ahmel again, and again.

"Flee, Fimfa!" Ahmel shouted through teeth clenched in agony. "Get to the traverser!"

"Ahmel! No, I—"

Ahmel cried out as the stout piece of wood crashed agonizingly into his tortured flesh. "Run! Run!"

Tears poured down her face, and Fimfa ran.

Behind her, Ahmel rolled over onto all fours and clutched two handfuls of sandy soil. Rotating on his knees, he flung it into Brimpo's face. The man cried out and swung blindly with the stick. By chance, it hit Ahmel with a glancing blow on his head, nearly stunning him. Ahmel lurched to his feet and hurled himself at Brimpo, his hands instinctively clutching the man by his throat. At this proximity, the larger man was forced to drop his stick. They staggered down the short strand of beach onto a layer of rock protruding over the water.

At the traverser, a sobbing Fimfa watched the fight. Both men clutched one another by the throat now. The larger man drove Ahmel closer to the edge of the rocky shelf upon which they struggled. Back and back Brimpo drove the older man, Brimpo's eyes tightly closed for some reason that Fimfa did not understand, not having witnessed Ahmel throw the soil into the maniac's face. Back they staggered until the inevitable occurred and both men went over the edge, crashed into the water, and sank from sight.

Fimfa waited a long while, far longer, she knew, than either man could have survived underwater. Movement from the forest caught her attention. An immense creature over twenty feet tall, walking upright on massive hind legs, its slightly parted jaws stained with dried gore, emerged from between giant fern trees, coming to investigate the sound of battle. The sight of the monster caused a stab of instant, unmitigated horror to rip through her chest. With her heart shattered with grief and her face streaked in tears of remorse, Fimfa slammed the hatch on the traverser and started the sequence that would return her to her own time.

MODERN DAY

The dig was sprawling, having produced more fossils than any other in recent years. Madsen, a young Danish student who hoped to find a Tyrannosaurus or maybe even something unknown, whistled happily while he dug, alternately chipping, and then brushing the dirt away in the immense hole that was once a lake bottom during the Permian and Upper Triassic. His partner, Thompson, dropped into his hole abruptly, startling him.

"Find anything?" the young American asked.

"*Ingen.* . . I mean, no, not yet, Thompson," he replied in his accented English.

Thompson took up his own pick and brush and went to work nearby.

A few minutes later, something caught Madsen's eye. "Thompson, come see this." Madsen continued to work his pick gently, brushing the ancient soil aside with his brush. His partner joined him and together, using smaller tools, they unearthed what appeared to be a fossilized footprint.

Suddenly Thompson recognized the shape. "Is that a boot print? Wait a minute! A boot print in a two-hundred-million-year-old hole? Someone's pranking us, Madsen."

They expanded their search, finding a few fossils that one would expect from a hole so ancient which only added to their confusion. Every so often, Thompson would glance at the area with the boot print, marked now by a flag, and wonder. Nor were they alone. When the other paleontologists working the dig heard about the print, they became quite excited. Soon, many had joined them. It was Madsen, patiently scraping away in the same area that he had not vacated except to relieve himself when he would leave Thompson holding his spot, who found the intertwined, fossilized skeletons.

It was as if two men fought to the death in this very location. Each's hands were at the other's throat. They lay, side by side, for all the world as if they had struggled to their deaths, and then sank into the mud of this ancient lakebed. Madsen had made the find of a lifetime, and he became famous for it because the skulls, *both in the shape of Homo Sapiens,* did not exist in the fossil record at this date. At least . . . they shouldn't exist.

Yes, Madsen became quite famous for his discovery of the 250-million-year-old boot print and the entwined fossils of two men who should not exist. When asked about it in later years, he would often ponder and reply, "Why did these men fight? Who were they? Were they visitors from another world? Were they time travelers from the future? If only these old bones could talk!"

###Chris spent years playing guitar in various bands and during that time was more of a voracious reader than a writer. After his last band collapsed, he turned from writing songs to writing stories, including Dark Tides of Mars and its forthcoming sequel, Gauntlets of Mars.

In addition to writing, Chris also dabbles in painting; the cover art for his latest novel, A Savage from Atlantis, was created from one of his paintings. More information about Chris and his works can be found on his website, including links, a list of available stories, and other items of interest.

Chris resides in Southern West Virginia with his wife and daughter.

https://www.chrisladamsbizarretales.com/

THE HOLE IN THE HEDGE

By Rose Strickman

On a bright summer's day when I was ten, I kicked a ball through the hole in the hedge.

We had only just moved into the new house in Somerset. Mum and Dad sent me outside to play while they finished unpacking: "And don't spend all afternoon on your phone!" Sulkily, I slunk outside, where I began kicking the old orange ball around.

It was a beautiful day, the sun shining and the birds singing. The house had a large garden, overgrown from years of neglect. I kicked the ball through the rank, weedy grass, wondering what the garden used to look like back in its heyday. Mum said the subdivision had been built on the site of property that had been in our family for generations. The original house was all gone now, replaced by rows of near-identical units on a flat, quiet street. But this yard, with its ancient hedge, had remained, slotted into place behind one of the new houses. Gran had insisted on it when she sold the original property. She had also ensured that the family had the right to return to live in one of the subdivided units should one fall empty and the need arise.

That need had arisen for me and my parents. So here we were, back on the ancestral property, changed though it was.

I meandered across the yard, following my ball, coming ever closer to the preserved hedge that bordered the property. The hedge was an unbroken wall of bushes rising higher than a man's head, foamy white with blooms. It looked ancient and immovable, a monument to time.

I gave my ball an extra strong kick, sending it flying into the hedge. Where it disappeared.

I frowned, then approached the hedge. There was a hole in it, I saw, an archway just high enough for someone to crawl through. My ball had flown in through that hole.

I went to my hands and knees, peering through. There was a sort of tunnel of branches, green and shadowed. And at the other end, I saw a lush green expanse of lawn. The legs of a deck chair. And my ball, lolling in the grass.

73

I hesitated a moment. But I wanted my ball back. And surely our neighbor wouldn't mind if I just nipped in and grabbed it? I would be in their yard for only a few seconds.

And so, I crawled through the hole in the hedge.

Upon emerging into the neighbor's yard, I blinked hard, suddenly disoriented. It was still a bright summer's day, but the light seemed strange like the sun had moved an hour's worth of distance across the sky during the few seconds I was inside the hedge. The temperature had shifted too, growing cooler, and where before it had been a perfectly clear day, now fluffy white clouds drifted across the sky.

But what really caught my attention was the house. It wasn't yet another unit in our subdivision, built of brick and concrete and shingle. It was an ancient farmhouse of stone, sprawling and unplanned, organic as a mushroom. The splintery back door was painted blue, and lacy curtains fluttered in its diamond-paned windows.

I had lived in our new neighborhood for a week and had never seen this house before.

A strange hush lay over everything. I couldn't hear cars from the road anymore, but only birdsong and, far away, the rumble of a tractor. I looked around, nervous and uncertain, and saw, with a startled shock, that the yard of this house was enclosed by a hedge just like our own. Like ours, it rose higher than a man's head, starred with white flowers. Bees and butterflies buzzed and flapped around it. The grass, far from being rank and overgrown, was shaved to a neat shortness. Deck chairs stood around a wrought-iron table.

There came a crash, and I jumped, yelping. The back door had opened. A girl stood in the doorway.

She was about my age, dressed in pink shorts matched with a striped shirt that looked just slightly odd and out of style. Her golden-brown hair flowed wild and shaggy over her shoulders, and her hazel eyes stared at me with curiosity and surprise.

"Who're you?" she asked, voice clear, accent slightly unfamiliar.

I backed away. "Who're you?"

"I asked first." She crossed her arms. "And this is my house."

I could hardly argue with that. "Natalie Preston," I said. "I came to get my ball. I live next door." I pointed back to the hole in the hedge.

"Next door?" The girl stepped off the lintel, crossing the lawn on bare feet. "There is no house next door!"

"Yes, there is—look!" I jabbed hard at the hole in the hedge, through which I could see a patch of our weedy backyard.

The girl squinted at the hole. "Huh. There's never been a hole in our hedge before. Where'd that come from?"

"How should I know? It was there when I came out to play." Though, now that I thought about it, I was not at all sure about that. Had the hole already been there, or had it just appeared? "Anyway, you haven't said your name."

She turned, flashing me a bright, surprising grin. "Marion," she said. "People call me Marion." Her gaze traveled to my orange ball, still sitting in the grass. "Is that your ball?"

I nodded. She grinned again. "Well, Natalie, now that you're here, want to play football?"

I hesitated. Marion seemed harmless, but everything about this situation was strange, like the world was just slightly off-kilter.

"It's all right if you don't want to," said Marion quickly. But I could hear the disappointment in her voice. The loneliness.

I grinned. "All right, then."

"Brilliant!" cried Marion, so happy I was glad I'd taken pity. She raced over to the ball and kicked it over to me, so hard it flew past my head.

I chased after the ball, and we had a lovely game of impromptu football, kicking the ball back and forth, using deck chairs as goals.

At last, we slowed down, both panting. "Good game!" I said, with my hands braced on my knees.

"Yeah," Marion smiled. "Good game." Her gaze flicked down to my denim shorts. "Where'd you get those shorts?"

"Online."

"On...line?" Marion looked blank.

"Yeah—you know. Mummy got on the clothing website and bought them for me."

"Website?" Marion looked blanker still.

I stared. "Do you...not have Internet?"

"What's Internet?" Marion asked, mystified.

We stood and stared at one another. The lacy curtains fluttered in the breeze. The ancient house looked immovable, rooted in the earth, but I knew it hadn't been here before. The way the sun had moved...Marion's odd, old-fashioned clothing...

I may have only been ten years old, but I was not stupid.

"What year is it, Marion?" I said at last, slowly.

"1964," she said, so promptly I knew it couldn't be a lie.

I felt ready to faint. "Marion," I said, "where I come from, it's 2024."

"What?" Marion gaped at me, then whirled to gape at the hole in the hedge. "It...it must be some kind of time machine!" She ran to the hole, crouching down and peering through it eagerly. "I can't see anything."

"Really?" I came over, kneeling down and peering through. "I can see our yard. And our house. What do you see?"

Marion frowned. "Just...mist. Sort of blank mist." She hesitated, then slowly extended her hand into the hole. It stopped at around her wrist. "I can't push it any further. It's like there's a wall there."

I stuck my arm into the hole. It entered with no trouble. "I can put mine in."

"Try going through it." Marion sat back on her heels, watching with bright eyes.

"I don't—" I began before a bellow erupted from the house.

"Marion!" It was a man's voice, and he sounded furious.

Marion blanched, all the light draining from her face. "You need to go!" She rushed to grab my ball and shoved it into my arms. "Quick, before Dad catches you!"

Eyes glittering with fear and urgency, Marion half-shoved me into the hole in the hedge. I crawled hastily through the leafy tunnel, holding my ball in one hand, and emerged into our yard in 2024.

I heaved a sigh of relief at having gotten home again. I turned to look back through the hole. But it was gone, the hedge an unbroken wall of green.

I felt a bitter kick of disappointment. My amazing experience was over and I would never see Marion again.

***

But I was wrong. A few days later, the hole reappeared in the hedge.

I was alone in the yard once more, having been banished out from under my parents' feet. I simply stepped outside and there it was: the neat little archway at the end of the lawn, through which I could see Marion's garden.

I grinned. With a glance behind to make sure Mum wasn't looking, I dashed down to the end of the yard and once again crawled through the tunnel back in time.

It was a cloudy day in 1964, the windows of the farmhouse reflecting mirrored grayness. I stood, looking around uncertainly. "Marion?"

A pale face appeared in one of the lower windows. Marion grinned at me, then disappeared. The back door opened seconds later and she popped out, dressed in a velveteen skirt and button-up shirt this time. "Natalie! You came!"

"'Course I did," I said, grinning. "How's it going, Marion?"

Her smile faded. One hand rose, to cover her upper left arm. Two of her fingers were wrapped in bandages, tied together. "All right," she said quietly, then hastily changed the subject. "I didn't see the hole for days! I thought you were never coming back."

"I didn't see it at my end either. I guess it just comes and goes. Do you think you can go through it this time?"

She couldn't. We experimented some more, throwing various small objects at the hole, but they all bounced off, flying away. "I guess it only works going backward, not forwards," I said, peering in. I was reassured that I could still see my yard through the tunnel. I liked Marion, but I didn't want to be stuck in 1964 forever.

"So strange!" Marion bent over, inspecting the hole. Her left sleeve rode up, revealing dark bruises on her arm. "Like something out of Doctor Who."

"Do you have Doctor Who?"

"Oh, yeah! It's this great new telly program. Only just came out last year. It has time travel too." She glanced at me curiously. "Do you have Doctor Who?"

"Yeah, though I like Star Wars better. I watch it on my phone."

"On your...phone?" Marion laughed incredulously.

"Phones do all kinds of things in 2024," I bragged. "I'll bring mine next time and show you."

Marion frowned in confusion. "How can you watch telly on a phone?"

"Well, it has a sort of screen and..." I trailed off at the expression on Marion's face. "Look, I'll show you next time, all right?"

Marion shrugged. "Okay." She brightened. "But let me show you something right now!"

She grabbed my hand and hauled me toward the house. I glanced back over my shoulder, a little nervous about leaving behind the hole—what if it closed in our absence? — but followed Marion indoors. The interior of the house was strange, more so than the exterior. The structure of the house was obviously ancient, the stone floors worn with generations of feet, the walls covered in rough plaster, and the furniture was all old, heavy, and Victorian. I blinked, surprised at seeing so many Victorian tables, chairs, and ornaments in a single home, all of it obviously well-used. I supposed such furniture wasn't so ancient or so unusual in 1964 as it was in 2024.

Marion, oblivious to my discomfort, ran to a machine in the corner of the parlor. "Look! It's a record player! It plays music on these records." She flipped through a crate full of records. "Ah!" Taking the great vinyl disc out of its wrapper, she loaded it into the machine, awkward with her bandaged fingers, and put down the needle.

Familiar strains of music sounded, breathtakingly clear and loud to someone used to online music videos. "The Beatles!" I exclaimed.

"Oh, you know them!" Marion, already half-dancing, boogied up to me. "Aren't they brilliant?"

"My gran loves the Beatles!" I laughed and joined her in the dance.

We danced to record after record, giggling and singing along to the lyrics. "I want to hold your haaaannnd!" Marion sang, and threw a pillow at me. Laughing, I threw one back, and soon the historical living room was a whirlwind of cushions and near-hysterical little girls.

One of my cushions flew, hitting Marion on her bandaged fingers. "Ow!" She recoiled, holding them near her chest.

"Marion! Sorry!" I hurried over. "Are you okay?"

Tears of pain glittered in her eyes, but she nodded. "I'm fine. It just hit my fingers wrong, that's all."

"What happened to them?" I examined her bandages. They looked hasty and inexpert, like someone had wrapped them in an impatient hurry.

Instantly, Marion's face shuttered, all the light shut away, her expression blank. "I—I broke them," she whispered. "My own fault."

I frowned, opening my mouth to question her further. But then I felt it. The hole in the hedge. Calling me back, like a hook jerked suddenly in my stomach.

I froze. "I have to go back. The hole is closing."

78

"It is?" Still cradling her broken fingers, Marion cocked her head. "How can you tell?"

"I just can." I ran for the door, Marion behind me.

We dashed down the yard to the hole in the hedge. The hook pulled harder the closer I came to the hedge until it was all I could do to force myself to stop by the hole and give Marion one last hug, careful around her injury. "I'll come back, I promise. I'll show you my phone!"

"Okay!" Marion hugged me back and waved me goodbye with her good hand as I dropped to my hands and knees and crawled back to 2024.

I waited in an agony of suspense for the hole to reappear in the hedge. It took a few days, during which I kept my phone with me at all times, just in case, and kept a wary eye on my parents. Luckily, they were still busy with the move and setting up a new life and hadn't seemed to have noticed anything.

At last, one day when my parents had driven off and left me alone in the house, the hole reappeared, the neat archway in the hedge visible from the living room. Checking to ensure I still had my phone, I ran to the end of the garden and crawled through it.

Marion was there, lurking behind some bushes, as though she'd been waiting for me. "Natalie!" she whisper-yelled and gestured me over. Her eyes flicked warily to the stone farmhouse. The windows were open on this warm, sunny day in 1964, and music was drifting out. "You've got to be quiet," Marion hissed. "My dad's in today."

I came over to her hiding place as quietly as I could, glancing at the house. "You haven't told him about me or the hole, right?"

"'Course not," she said, as though it was an idiotic question. "You've got to be quiet this time, Natalie. I don't want him finding out about you!"

She spoke with such repressed passion, such anxious fervor in her eyes, that I did a double-take and peered at her more closely. Gone were her earlier high spirits; her face was strained and anxious, her gaze flickering constantly to the house. There were strange bruises on her neck and arms, bruises that hadn't been there last time. Her broken fingers were still bandaged, the wrapping grubby.

"Marion," I said hesitantly. "Are you...okay?"

"I'm fine!" Immediately, she hoisted up a smile. "We've just got to be quiet this time, okay? Did you bring that phone?"

I frowned, but got out my smartphone. Marion seemed to forget her worries in examining it, exclaiming over all the apps. There was no wi-fi in 1964, of course, so I couldn't display my phone's Internet capabilities, but I showed Marion my photos and the gaming apps. She laughed with joy and wonder over each one, and was even more delighted when I played the opening of Star Wars: A New Hope, which I'd downloaded. "This is amazing," she marveled. "Does everyone have a phone like this in 2024?"

"Pretty much," I said proudly. "Well, not babies. But most people do."

"How about flying cars?" Marion turned to me eagerly. "Everyone says we'll have flying cars and spaceships by the year 2000."

"No, no flying cars," I laughed. "And no spaceships, really, except rockets. But we all have computers and the Internet..."

Marion listened raptly while I tried to explain computers and the Internet, even as A New Hope kept playing. Then the quiet was shattered by a roar from the house.

"MARION! MY TEA!"

Marion leapt as if stung. "That's my dad!" All the joy drained out of her face, replaced once more by fear and anxiety. "I've got to go," she said, climbing to her feet. "Stay here. He mustn't see you!"

The fear and urgency in her eyes convinced me to silence my phone and hold still as a frightened rabbit among the bushes while Marion ran to the house, door slamming behind her. Inside, I heard an angry rumble of a man's voice, answered by Marion's frightened, muffled stammers. Then the distinct sound of a slap.

I flinched, but remained hidden, frozen with fear. Then, to my infinite relief, I felt the tug again, of the hole opening.

Bent over, eyes on the house, I hurried over to the hole. I froze at movement in one of the downstairs windows, but it was only Marion. One side of her face was bright red, but she smiled and waved. Come back? she mouthed.

I nodded and waved, then fled back home through the hedge.
***
That night at dinner, Mum noticed how silent I was. "What's the matter, Natalie?" she asked.

80

"Mum," I said after a moment, "what do you do if a friend is being...hurt? If her dad's hitting her?"

"Who?" Mum asked immediately, eyes alive with concern. "Who do you know who's being hurt?" Across the table, Dad came alert too.

I squirmed. There was no way I could tell my parents about Marion. "A friend. And...I'm not sure what's happening."

Mum and Dad exchanged looks, seeming to come to an unspoken decision. "You're old enough to know now, Natalie," Mum said at last. "Your Gran's coming to visit next month. When she was growing up, her father hit her a lot. He hurt her badly."

Just like Marion. "What did she do?"

"She always said a friend told her to call the police," Mum said. "So she did. And she got away from him. Things were hard after that, but better than living with her father."

"So that's what you should do," Dad said firmly. "Tell your friend to get help."

I mulled over my parents' advice, and the next time the hole appeared, I shared it with Marion.

"My dad's not so bad," she said, rubbing the bruises on her throat. The left side of her face was puffy, her eye black. Her broken fingers were still bandaged. "He just hits when he's angry." It was a hot day in 1964, and we skulked at the end of her yard, the windows of the house flashing like accusing eyes.

"My Gran's dad hit too," I said. "Mum always said he nearly killed her. So she called the police and got away from him."

Marion bit her lip and plucked at the hem of her shirt, an oddly familiar gesture. I wondered where I'd seen it before. "I don't know. Would they even believe me?"

"They did for my Gran." I had an idea. "Listen. When Gran comes, I'll show her the hole in the hedge. You can talk to her about it."

Marion's eyes widened and she grabbed my hands. "No! Natalie, what if she tells my dad? Or your parents?"

"How could she tell your dad?" I asked. "She lives in 2024! And she wouldn't tell my parents. Please, Marion. Just try it?"

Marion frowned, then winced as her facial wound throbbed. "I'll think about it." She looked up, and despite her puffy face, her eyes were bright. "Can you tell me more about your Gran in 2024?"

#

Over the next few weeks, I visited Marion many times. We were never caught, by either her father or my parents. Time and again I snuck down to the hole in the hedge and slipped through to 1964, where Marion was waiting for me.

She was never without some injury—bruises, black eyes, her healing fingers—but she never wanted to discuss them. Instead, we played together like any pair of ten-year-old girls, taking Marion's dolls on time-traveling adventures, playing games on my smartphone, or dancing to Marion's record player when her father wasn't home. We didn't dare get too far from the hole in the hedge, in case it opened unexpectedly, but we explored the vast old farmhouse while her father was gone, and I marveled at the view outside the front windows, which showed far more farmland and open spaces than in 2024. I thought Marion would be sad or disappointed when I told her of the changes to the neighborhood in the intervening decades, but she just shrugged. "I won't mind if they do bulldoze the house." Considering that she was only at peace in the farmhouse when she was all alone in it, perhaps that wasn't so surprising.

On my last visit before Gran was due to arrive, it was drizzling on Marion's side of the hedge. I emerged from the hole, blinking at the apparently empty yard. "Marion?"

The only response was a faint sob. Frowning, I went to our usual hiding place behind the bushes. And there I found Marion.

She was curled up, hunched over her knees. When she looked up, I recoiled. Both her eyes were black, her lip split. "Natalie…"

"Marion!" I fell to my knees, taking her into my arms. She wept and shuddered, fragile as a broken bird. "Marion, what happened?"

"Dad…he…" A sob ran through her again. "He…put his hand up my skirt and…I pushed him off. And he…he…" Marion broke down under another wave of tears.

I held my friend in my arms while she wept in the rain, and it felt like the whole world was weeping too. I held her, not knowing what to say, until at last she took a deep, shuddering breath and wiped her tears, carefully around the bruises.

Then I spoke. "Marion. You need to get help."

"Who can help me?" Her hazel eyes were blank with despair behind their bruises.

"My Gran. She got help when she was a kid. She can tell you how. You can talk to her when she comes. I promise it'll be okay!"

After a long moment, Marion nodded. "Yes. I'll talk to her. Through the hedge."

###

The next day, in 2024, I stood back while my grandmother came into our new house, hauling her suitcase and looking around. "My, my," she said. "These new houses are certainly an improvement on when I was a girl!"

Her eyes, crinkled in nests of laugh lines, shone a bright hazel. For a moment, their color tugged at my memory, but there was no time to think about that. I hugged my grandmother tightly. "I'm so glad you're here, Gran!"

"Yes," said Dad breathlessly, coming in after her. "Shall we have tea?"

Tea was an agony of scones and teacups and endless, endless minutes, while the adults talked and I waited for the torture to end so I could get Gran alone. I needed to tell her about Marion. I was sure she'd understand. But it was over an hour before I could accompany Gran up the stairs to the guestroom under the pretext of helping her unpack.

"Gran," I said, "I need to tell you something. I have a friend who lives nearby. On the other side of the hedge."

Gran paused in unpacking. "The hedge, you say?"

"That's right. Her name's Marion and her dad...he's hurting her. Like your dad hurt you," I added with a child's blithe callousness. "She needs to call the police but...she doesn't really know what to do. Could you...talk to her?"

"Through the hedge." Gran sounded like she was speaking to herself rather than me, her hazel gaze turned inward. Then she looked at me and smiled, and again I felt that sudden, surprising similarity, the recognition I couldn't place.

"Yes," she said. "I'll talk to her. Through the hedge."

###

The next day, Gran asked my parents if she and I could have some private time. They agreed amiably enough and drove off after lunch, leaving us alone in the house.

As soon as they were gone, I took Gran's hand and led her down to the bottom of the yard. "I can't always get through," I said. It was a sunny day, but cloud shadows raced over the hills, shadows passing over the lawn. "The hole isn't always—there it is!"

The hole in the hedge stood, a neat archway. I crouched down to crawl through. "Come on!"

With some effort, her old bones creaking and popping, Gran crawled through the tunnel after me. She straightened up on the other side, blinking at the wide yard, the towering stone farmhouse, the clear blue skies beyond. "Oh," she murmured. "Oh…!"

The door opened and Marion appeared, limping slightly, both eyes still black. She fell still at the sight of us, gaze fixed on my grandmother. She stared at Gran, and Gran stared back, and, looking between their faces, I suddenly knew.

"You…you…" Marion gasped, staggering back.

"Nancy Marion, listen to me." Gran spoke with calm urgency. "Listen very carefully. We don't have much time. What your father is doing to you is wrong. He will kill you if this continues, do you understand?" She paused. "Do you understand, Nancy Marion?"

Slowly, Marion nodded, still staring. She seemed speechless.

"Call the police," Gran continued. "Call the police and they will help you." Gran smiled, and in that smile, I saw a ten-year-old girl who had befriended another girl from another time. "I promise they will. They already have, after all. It will be hard, but you will survive and you will be happy. Do it, Nancy Marion!"

I caught one last glimpse of Marion's white, incredulous face before the world swooped, jerked, and fell on its side. A confusing glimpse of blue summer sky, a rustle of leaves—and Gran and I were on the 2024 side of the hedge, the clouds racing above us, the hedge an unbroken wall of green.

"What happened? Where's Marion?" I clawed at the hedge, but found no sign of the hole, only solid leaves and branches.

Gran laid a soft hand on my shoulder. "It's no use, Natalie," she said gently. "The hole won't be coming back."

I whirled on her, to face those so-familiar hazel eyes. She smiled sadly. "My full name is Nancy Marion Heddlestone Mayhew," she said. "I always went by Marion when I was a girl."

"You…you're her?" I gaped.

Gran nodded. "That was the summer after my mother died," she said. "My father was always ready with his fists, but then he started drinking, and he got so much worse. If it wasn't for you, Natalie, for

84

those visits through the hedge, I would have died. He would have killed me. You saved my life that summer."

"But...but..." My head was spinning. "What happened—what happens now? Do I ever...the hole...?"

"It won't be coming back, I fear," said Gran. "I never saw it again after that last time. I think I closed the loop just now when I spoke to my younger self."

I let out a sob, the tears coming, tears at the loss of my friend. Soft, gentle arms enfolded me, and Gran held me while I cried, just as I had held her, so many decades ago.

At last, when my weeping eased, Gran continued, "When the hole closed that final time, I called the police, just as you advised. I got away from my father. It was hard, but I survived. I found happiness. I wouldn't have done that without you, Natalie."

"But...will Marion call...?"

"She will." Marion grinned, the laughing young grin I knew so well transmuted onto my grandmother's face. "After all, she already has!"

I had to laugh at this, a weak, hiccupping laugh. I leaned into her soft, warm side. My grandmother, who had been my friend across time. The friend I had lost, whose life I had saved, long before I had been born.

"And she'll be all right?" I whispered. "You were all right?"

Marion hugged me. "Yes. I was. She will be."

We stood silent together a long moment, before the hedge that bordered the past. Then, Marion's arm still around me, we turned and walked into the future.

###

Rose Strickman is a speculative fiction writer living in Seattle, Washington. Her work has been published over 50 times, appearing in anthologies such as Sword and Sorceress 32, Witch Wizard Warlock and Spring Into SciFi: 2024 Edition, as well as several e-zines. She has also self-published several novellas on Amazon. https://www.amazon.com/author/rosestrickman is her Amazon author's page.

Please contact Rose at rosestrickman@gmail.com. She looks forward to hearing from you!

THE FLORIST

by E.V. Emmons

The clock's ticking echoed louder as its hands reached toward midnight—a reminder that his time was nearly up. He had waited fourteen years for this night to arrive. In truth, it was longer than that by a few months, but no one was going to split hairs. His special meal—slabs of turkey, baby carrots, mashed potatoes, stuffing, and cranberry sauce drowned in gravy—was a memory from both yesterday and a Christmas long ago. It felt strange having this meal in July.

Flakes of pie crust from his dessert still littered the concrete floor, along with a few wisps of hair that had gotten stuck in his collar after they shaved his head.

Death row was a kind of mourning, complete with its stages of grief. The first days after the verdict and judgment were ones of denial. He was innocent. A miracle would happen; it had to. Surely, someone, somewhere, would discover that mistakes were made and prove his innocence. Not only was he not the notorious serial killer dubbed 'The Florist,' he had met none of the victims—except the last. She was his fiancée.

Despite all the news stories about 'The Florist' dominating the national papers for months, he didn't know what the victim's names were until the trial. There were thirteen in all: Rose, Ivy, Pansy, Daisy, Erika, Lily, Petunia, Heather, Iris, Nadine, Inga, Ursa, and Mary. He said their names like a mantra, but only saw one face: Mary's.

At first, they didn't think Mary fit the MO of 'The Florist.' There were no flowers called Mary—until some clever cookie connected that her last name was 'Gold.' Mary Gold was the thirteenth victim. Witnesses placed him at the scene of her death. The police came for him. They established shaky connections to the others, and the rest was history.

Anger came next. No matter what he said, no one believed him. He was certain that the public defender who took his case didn't either. His grief, anger, and frustration boiled over into outbursts that only solidified the jury's belief that he was guilty as hell. A man with that kind of temper had to be guilty, they whispered among themselves. One by one, they crossed their arms, forming a cohesive wall of conviction. The verdict came back in less than twenty minutes.

It didn't help that his parents didn't bother to come to the trial to support him. Their moral upbringing had presumably failed against the persistent genes of the crack-addled teen who had given him up for adoption ten minutes before she died. Their presence would've been an admission that the nice neighborhood, good schools, and church on Sundays meant nothing. Perhaps absence made it easier to dismiss their shame. They were good people, and in return for their goodness, he'd brought them a lifetime of humiliation. No matter what, they would always be 'that serial killer's parents.' He pleaded with God. If only he could prove his innocence—he'd spent the rest of his days making it up to his parents. Depression followed quickly on the heels of his bargaining, and the realization that no one would save him set in.

The clang of the heavy keys against the door returned him fully to his reality. The guard peered into the cell through the narrow wire-laced window and edged the door open. It was time.

He had declined the visit from the priest. He was no stranger to prayer and the good book, but neither ever offered him a good explanation for why this was happening to him. If a miracle was going to happen, surely it would have by now. For a condemned man, there was no point in delaying or denying the inevitable.

The guards came into his cell, and he allowed them to marionette his body as they needed to. He had never shown them any resistance before, and he saw no reason for that to change the moment before his death. They shuffled easily down the long hall, past the other locked doors. They turned the corner sooner than he expected and the guards flanked him as they walked into a large room with a great wooden chair at its center. There was an audience seated off to one side, and a gurney waiting on the other. He scanned the faces of the half-dozen people there to witness the execution, but recognized no one. His gaze settled on one man in a dark trench coat and fedora, who kept his head bowed as if in prayer. Silently, he willed the fedora-wearing man to lift his face, but he did not. The more he watched the man, the more ethereal he seemed to become. Perhaps he was imagining him. It wasn't uncommon for the dying to have delusions in their last moments.

The guards sat him down on the solid wooden chair. It was hard and wide, and the seat was vaguely slippery, like the chairs in grade schools. His thoughts lingered on his first best friend, his favorite teachers, and the girl who would eventually become his fiancée. Tears blurred his vision, and he bit the inside of his right cheek as the guards removed his rubber-soled slip-ons and arranged his feet in a basin with about an inch of water coating the bottom. Another soaked a sponge in the basin and placed it on his head before the other guard arranged and secured the metal skull cap and bolts that would bring the electricity through his body. Rivulets of cool, salty water snaked down to his jaw from the sponge crushed to his scalp.

"Denton William Mosely, a jury of your peers, has sentenced you to die in the electric chair. Do you have any last words?"

"None that would make any difference. I'm sorry."

If dying meant he could bring them all back, he would gladly do it. Panic swelled in his chest as the guards tugged the wide leather straps across his body. Next came the sticky electrodes that would deliver the current into his legs.

His heart pounded in a rhythm so savage that he thought he might die from it, rather than the chair.

Everything went dark after they slipped the black cotton hood over his head. His body shook hard, starting at the knees until the tremor reached his shoulders and the bile remnants of his last meal washed up the back of his throat, burning and biting.

"Oh, please God…" he whispered under his breath.

There was a click and a zapping sound that grew in crescendo, nearing like the spark of a lit fuse. The spark roared. His body wrenched and shook, but he felt nothing except the peculiar sensation of floating for several seconds before being violently pulled out through the ceiling, past the stone blocks of the prison, beyond the rolls of barbed wire lining the roof and fence tops. His ears filled with the rush of what sounded like a mighty waterfall and bright lights twinkled, dimly lighting the dark tunnel churning around him. Somewhere below gasps and sparks and the smell of burned flesh mingled and then that too was gone.

When he woke, he was back home, in his tiny apartment, the air thick with the delicious aroma of Mary's cooking. Rosemary brisket and roast potatoes. And maybe those little carrots in butter sauce that he liked. The remnants of a football game winked on the television set in the corner, and he sat up on the velvety brown floral couch and breathed deeply.

"How could this be?" he asked himself as he stood. His hands skimmed the couch, then the burlap lampshade crowning the lamp on the side table. He stood before the mantel of the fake fireplace, its stone mantel was cool to the touch.

It felt real, all of it. He jumped back, startled, when Mary poked out of the kitchen. "I need your opinion," she said. "Do you think it needs more pepper? Try it." She smiled and extended the wooden spoon to him, her left hand cupping the bowl of the spoon to keep it from spilling.

"You look like you've seen a ghost," she said. "Are you coming down with something? Do you have a fever?"

"I—I don't know. Maybe." He leaned in to sample the broth. "It's perfect."

"Ok, well then, dinner is ready when you are."

He clasped her wrist as she turned toward the kitchen. It was warm and soft, and he could feel the delicate bones in her wrist flex under his touch.

"Is something wrong?"

"Uh—no. I—I just—I'm...I can't believe you're real. If there's a heaven, I must be in it."

Touched, she clicked her tongue against the back of her front teeth, "You say the sweetest things. Come, eat."

He nodded mindlessly and followed her into the kitchen. They ate at the small table in the corner, and he savored the dinner like it was the first meal he'd ever truly tasted. He listened as she prattled on about her parent's new home, her sister's baby, and something about the poodle next door. If there was a heaven, this was it—but how was it that everything felt so real? And yet it felt wrong. The growling spark of the chair was still fresh in his mind. Maybe this was hell, and some horrible torment was yet to show itself.

"You're awfully quiet. Is something wrong?" Mary asked.

"No, I think I just need a couple of aspirin." He disappeared into the bathroom and rummaged through the medicine cabinet to find an empty bottle. "Damnit, looks like we're out. Gonna head over to the store and maybe take a walk. See if I can't clear my head. I'll be back soon."

Mary gave him a singsong reply and, after he grabbed his coat off the hook by the door, he was off.

He turned his collar up against the chilly night air and kept his gaze on the sidewalk. Leaves swirled and crunched under his footsteps and a faint mist dampened his hair. As he approached the corner store, his gaze fell on the red newspaper box beside the door.

He reached into his pocket and found a pair of quarters. Hmph. Strange, the price of papers hadn't gone up after all this time. Then it occurred to him he didn't even know what day it was, or when it was. Panic rose in his gut as he fought the rusty door open and snatched a paper from within. He scanned the front page, and then his gaze landed on the date—Tuesday, November 3rd, 1981. The day before the murder of the Florist's first victim, Rose Campbell.

He felt the blood drain from his face. Dizziness and nausea followed, and he grabbed the store's stair rail to keep from toppling over. His heart raced and his breathing grew shallow. "It couldn't be. This can't be right. The paper must be old, it has to be," he muttered under his breath. It didn't look old, it appeared to be fresh off the presses—no creases, no yellowing. It was perfect.

He sat heavily on the steps and took a long look around the neighborhood. The model year of every car lining the street was mid-to-late seventies except one newer-looking hatchback, a little red Honda, that he was certain was a 1980.

There was only one way to be sure. He charged into the store and squinted as his eyes adjusted to the bright fluorescent lights buzzing above.

"Can I help you, sir?" The clerk called over from behind the counter.

"What day is it?"

"Tuesday."

"Okay, but what date is it?"

"November 3rd."

"1981?"

"Yeah," the young man said incredulously.

Denton rushed toward the stacks of papers piled on the shelves. They all carried the same date, Tuesday, November 3rd, 1981.

"Jesus..."

The clerk craned his neck. "Are you looking for anything in particular, sir?"

He glanced over at the clerk in a daze and stammered, "Uh...yah, yah, I want aspirin. Please. Got a killer headache."

"Sure thing, mister." The clerk reached behind the counter and pulled out a sealed yellow tin box. "That'll be a buck fifty."

Denton slapped the money on the counter, snatched up the box of pills, and charged out of the store, swallowing two of them dry.

"What the hell is this? What does it mean?" he asked himself under his breath as he walked. The last time he had seen a newspaper was the day before his execution—July 11, 1995.

'I know what it means.' He sighed heavily. "I can do something. This is my chance. Save them, save Mary, myself...maybe, just maybe, I can do something," he murmured. His lower lip quaked and tears blurred his eyes.

"It has to be. I gotta think. Need a clear head."

He returned home, and after reassuring Mary he'd be fine, and to go ahead to bed without him, he poured himself a cup of steaming coffee and sat heavily at the kitchen table.

The killer had to be stopped. But how? He looked up Rose Campbell's address in the phone book. It matched the one he remembered mentioned at the trial. He could call her and warn her...but she might think it's a crank call and ignore it. Or she might get scared and think he was the one that meant to kill her. Dammit. He had to save them, but how?

If he tipped the police, there was no guarantee they'd take him seriously, and if they did, they might come for him instead. Rose would still die, and the actual killer would be free to continue his spree. He paced the kitchen, taking a moment to test the creaky tile at the heart of it.

'What are my options?'

He could take Mary and flee. Maybe to an entirely different country. Stay there forever. Get married. Have kids. He didn't know any of the other victims. No one would misidentify him as the killer and Mary would be safe. He didn't owe anyone else anything. They didn't matter.

His shoulders slumped, and he blew out a deep breath. But they did matter. He wouldn't wish the sort of heartache he suffered over Mary's loss on anyone else. There was no reason for a higher power to bring him back in time if it wasn't for him to do something. This was his miracle, and he had to make it work. There was no way he could ride off into the sunset with Mary, knowing full well the others would still die. He had to intervene.

It was up to him to stop the killer, no one else. The clock chimed a dozen notes. Midnight. Today was the day.

He could stake out Rose's place and wait for the killer to show up, but that was the other problem—he did not know who the killer was. In his earnest desire to save the Campbell woman, he might shoot a neighbor, a Jehovah's Witness, or a repairman. He didn't know. And even though this was America, where would a guy like him even get a gun? He'd never even held one.

Getting a gun and learning how to shoot it was not an option. There wasn't enough time.

'Think.'

He had been mistaken for the killer...so the killer had to look like him. That made it a little easier. Various scenarios played out in his mind until nothing made sense. He drew a deep breath, and wrote a detailed letter to Mary, begging her to believe his story, even though it seemed impossible. He explained everything as it had happened—how had he been mistaken for a serial killer, executed, and somehow brought back? This was his miracle. He warned her to get out of town, or even better, the state or country, if anything happened to him. He tucked the letter behind the vase on the open roll-top desk in the corner of the sitting room. If everything went to plan, he would be back before she could read it, and she'd never need to know the horrors waiting for them in the future.

After two in the morning, he fell asleep on the couch and woke at 7 a.m. to the smell of freshly brewed coffee. He crammed a corner of buttered toast in his mouth and washed it down with orange juice. With the excuse that he had errands to run, he took his coffee in a 'to-go' cup, gave Mary a lingering kiss, and dashed out the front door to his car.

He pulled up to the curb across from Rose Campell's home thirty minutes later and watched. The coroner's report from the trial said a concerned neighbor found her bleeding on her kitchen floor around three o'clock in the afternoon, and the estimated time of death was around noon.

His coffee had grown cold by mid-morning. The neighborhood was a middle-American paradise with tree-lined streets shading the road, and each pillbox-sized house had a patch of well-kept green grass. Most of the homes had flower gardens under the large living room window next to the front porch. Some had white picket fences that reminded him of sharpened teeth, while others had children's bikes and toys parked in the driveway, waiting for them to return from school. It was beautiful but boring.

The mail carrier walked up one side of the street and then the other, lingering only at Rose's neighbor's house to pet the lazy golden dog napping on the porch. He passed Rose's home without stopping and continued around the next corner until he was out of sight. The mail carrier was an older African American man in his fifties, so there was no way he could've been the killer.

No, he had to watch for someone like himself—white, with sandy brown hair, and of average build and height.

'How many men in the world looked just like him from afar?'

The pale rose curtains framing Mary's living room window wafted in the breeze. The temperature had gone up since he'd left in the early morning, so much so, he felt compelled to peel off his jacket. No one had come to her front door, nor had she stepped out. He considered the floor plan of the house, and it occurred to him that the kitchen had to be at the rear of the house.

Damnit, did the house have a backdoor? He glanced at his wristwatch—it was almost noon. He swore under his breath—he might have already been too late. If the killer snuck in through the backdoor, she wouldn't be able to answer the front door.

He slipped out of the car and edged the car door shut. With just as much effort to be quiet, he opened the trunk, grabbed the tire iron, and jogged across the street to the rear of Rose Campbell's house.

The fat golden dog next door woke and bayed loud and long. Denton swore under his breath. A dark green chain-link fence framed the yard, and the gate swung open. Inside, he could hear breaking glass and a scream. Without a thought, he charged inside, the tire iron raised high.

He swung at Rose's attacker; the tire iron connecting with his shoulder. The killer whirled about and wrestled Denton to the floor. They rolled and grappled along the black and white tiled floor, trading blows. The tire iron flew from Denton's grip and skittered across the floor.

The killer was strong and landed three powerful punches to Denton's face. His vision grew bleary, and the room spun. Blood roared from his nostrils and sprayed the pristine floor. Rose screamed and fled through the front door. The killer dove for the tire iron and before Denton could roll out of the way, the hooked end connected with his forehead. The ceiling sparkled and spun, and then darkness overtook everything and somehow within that darkness he carried with him the sinking sensation that came with failure, and before the feeling left him, a great boom exploded somewhere above him.

The darkness was comforting and warm, soft even. He could swear a light mist coated his skin and a kindly voice spoke above him, seemingly far away. At other times, the darkness held his hand and crooned to him. The song was familiar, and with it, pinpoints of light and sound broke through the darkness.

"He seems to enjoy having the radio on," Mary said.

"Of course, we'll leave it for him," another woman answered. "When is your baby due, Mary?"

"In about four more months. Somewhere around the 4th of July."

The music became a constant in the darkness and was sometimes punctuated with stories, bible readings, and loving words from Mary, and later his parents joined her.

Soon, smells began to reach him. Sometimes they were pleasant, like flowers and fresh-baked cookies. Other times they were medicinal and sharp, like disinfectant soap.

Another time, the darkness brought the soft cries of a baby— Mary's baby. His baby. The cries were followed by lullabies and soft snuffling sounds.

His mother and father prayed over him when Mary was busy with the baby…and he found himself reaching through the darkness and wondering if it was a boy or a girl.

The scent of strawberries grew strong and exploded against the tip of his tongue and lower lip. Something wet dabbed his face afterward.

"I wonder if he can hear us?" his father asked.

"I think so. He can hear the music and our voices, I'm sure of it," Mary murmured. "I just wish he'd wake."

94

"So do I, but we mustn't rush him. Or the doctors. He needs this time to recover."

And so, it went. Life in the darkness—comforting, warm, but no longer satisfying—he craved more. He wanted to know more.

What happened...Did the woman get away? Rose? That was her name, wasn't it? What happened to the killer?

Mary frowned thoughtfully. "He looks like he's dreaming—but he looks so serious."

"We should let him rest. It's been a long day; you and the baby need to rest too. Let's go home," his mother said.

Were Mary and the baby living with his parents now?

The room fell quiet, but there was a presence with him. He called out, but his voice never left the darkness, and yet an answer came to him.

"No, you're not alone. You never have been. You noticed me on the last day of your life."

"You're the man—the one in the trench coat in the viewing area."

"The very same."

"Did you bring me back?"

"Not exactly—but I was with you the entire time."

"Why?"

"Many no longer believe in miracles, and while rare, they do exist."

"What happened? Did Rose get away? The others too? Where is the killer?"

"She escaped, and Mary found your letter. She called the police and directed them to Rose's home. You gave Rose the time she needed to flee. The police came. The killer was about to strike a final blow against you, and they shot him dead. He will spend eternity in a place I'd rather not speak of."

"So, the girls...they're all safe."

"Yes, they will live the lives they're meant to."

"And what about me? What happens to me now?"

"That is up to you. You have choices to make—you may accompany me and know eternal peace in a loving place, you may remain as you are here and now, or I could return you to the year you left, but on an amended path."

"What does that mean?"

95

"It means you will be awake and able to be with Mary and your child, but time will have passed."

"How much time?"

"Fourteen years."

"No. If I've learned anything, it's the value of time. Please, couldn't I be awakened now?"

The man in the dark trench coat considered Denton's question and nodded. "Yes, but you would know considerable hardship as you continue to recover."

"But I'd be with Mary, the baby, and my parents?"

"Yes, but it would be a struggle."

"Does it have to be? I've missed so much time already. I don't even know if my baby is a boy or a girl."

"Is that your choice? That you wish to wake now?"

"Yes, that's my choice—but before I do, thank you. Thank you for saving me."

"You saved yourself, and those girls."

"But you, or someone you know, made it possible to come back here and do it."

The dark stranger chuckled softly, and as the cheerful sound faded, so did the darkness.

Light streamed in, sunshine bursting in warm rays across the hospital bed. Outside, birds that favored the morning chirped brightly in the trees lining the parking lot.

"Oh my god, you're awake," Mary exclaimed, joyful tears rapidly filling her eyes. She dashed to Denton's side. "I've prayed so hard for this moment."

"How long was I out for?"

"Too long. Over a year and a half, almost two? I have someone here for you to meet."

"I found out the day after you left for your errand. This is your little girl..."

"We have a daughter," Denton murmured. "Can I hold her?"

"Of course you can. But if it's too much, if you have pain, tell me," Mary said, gently nestling the baby girl into her father's arms.

"I feel perfectly fine. What did you name her?"

"Victoria Marion-Rose," after my grandmother, your mother, and our new friend. She told the police you saved her from the intruder."

"You found the letter I left…"

Mary nodded. "Let's not dwell on that anymore. We have the rest of our lives now."

Denton grinned broadly, "That we do."

E.V. Emmons is the author of the novels, ETERNITY AWAITS and, THE SINISTRATI. She is also the author of the writer's advice guide, 'WRITE HERE, WRITE NOW!'

Her short stories include, 'The Flea in the Sake' and 'Beads' in the Unbreakable Ink Anthologies, Volume One and Volume Two, respectively, as well as 'Willow' in the LegionPress anthology which has been deposited on the moon as part of the Lunar Codex Program and successfully delivered by Lunar Lander, Odysseus, in February 2024. The Lunar Codex Program preserves the works of many talented artists and writers on the moon for posterity.

She has also had the pleasure of contributing a short story, 'Eggshells', to the 'Witch, Wizard, and Warlock' anthology, and 'The Florist' to the 'Trouble With Time' anthology, both with West Mesa Press. Her work is available on Amazon.

E.V. Emmons and her family live in Southern Ontario and share their lives with their impish cats, Seth and Syrus, as well as good pups, Vette, and Kyro.

VIVA LA REVOLUTION

Robert Allen Lupton

Doctor Boudreau pushed his horned-rim glasses up on his forehead. "Happy to meet you, Mr. Parson. Welcome to Tulane University. How may I be of service?"

The visitor's chair in the PHD's office was littered with the remains of several clocks and watches. Charles Parson pointed to the chair. "May I sit?"

"Certainly. Toss all those parts in the plastic bin. Don't remember exactly why I'm keeping them, but it will come to me in time."

Parson scraped the chair clean with his hand and then dusted it with a paisley handkerchief. He sat, wiggled for a moment, shifted slightly, reached down, and plucked a small mainspring from the bottom of his trousers. He sighed and dropped it into the plastic bin. "I'll come right to the point. I've got a worldwide business empire to run and I've never been one to waste time. I'm told that you're the world's leading horologist, the man who knows more about time than anyone in the world."

Boudreau smiled. "Yes, I'm a doctor of horology and also of chronology, the two primary disciplines concerning time."

Parson glanced at his wristwatch. "Indeed, sir. I'm paying a thousand dollars an hour for this interview. It will go faster if you don't interrupt me. My researchers have determined that I'm a descendant of Paul Barras, a leader of the French Revolution. He's one of the few to survive. He led the overthrow of Robespierre and his cronies. That plot by Barras was called the Thermidorian Reaction and it brought him to prominence. He masterminded Robespierre's execution by guillotine. The man became terribly rich. When Bonaparte took power, Barras accepted exile to Brussels and then to Rome. He wrote extensive memoirs that were heavily censored after this death."

"I do appreciate the lecture, Mr. Parson, but I did take European history. Actually taught it when I was a graduate student. Is there a point in there anywhere?"

"There is. My ancestor was quite wealthy and he owned land and estates all over Europe. The records of those properties have been lost, destroyed, or deliberately misplaced. My hope is that the

98

records were in his memoirs. I can prove that I'm Paul's descendent and once I have those records, I have the money to lay claim to those estates."

Michael Boudreau PHD laughed and leaned back in his chair. "You and several thousand other people. Paul had dozens of mistresses. Lord knows how many children he had. Conservatively, forty or fifty. Do the math. Starting with forty people and ten or eleven generations, about twenty thousand other people have as good a claim as you do."

"But they haven't the money to prove it. I do."

Boudreau compulsively cleaned his glasses with his tie. "For the sake of argument, let's say that what you say is true. I certainly don't have the missing manuscripts. How can I help?"

"'I should have thought that would be obvious. You're the time guru. I want to go back in time, meet my ancestor, and convince him to hide the important documents somewhere so I can discover them later and claim my inheritance."

Boudreau pointed around his office, a room festooned with all sorts of timekeeping devices. Water clocks and hourglasses sat next to sundials. Pendulum grandfather clocks, cuckoo clocks with weights dangling to the floor, and a variety of electronic clocks filled the walls and shelves. "I know clocks. Does anything in this room look like a time machine?"

"No, but if anyone can build one, it's you. Money is no object."

"I appreciate the offer. While I care about money, time doesn't. Rather science doesn't. You can't pay the universe to work differently. No matter how much cash you offer, the physical laws of the universe won't change. Gravity and the periodic table are funny that way."

"I'm not stupid. I understand, but that doesn't mean that money can't buy a way to accomplish what I want without violating the laws of the universe. How about it, timekeeper?"

"Mr. Parson, there are two major problems with time travel, not the only problems, but two major ones. I looked you up and you made a couple of your fortunes in real estate. The primary rule of real estate is location, location, location."

It's my turn to say that I don't need a lecture."

"But you do. Let's consider going back in time for only one hour and staying in this very room. If we can't do that, we certainly can't

99

cross the Atlantic Ocean and backpedal one hundred and thirty years. Location is critical on many levels. First, in one hour the Earth rotates 15 degrees. At our latitude, and yes, I said latitude, the circumference of the Earth is about 20,000 miles, so fifteen degrees is about 840 miles. So to go back in time one hour, we have to calculate where this room will be after moving 840 miles."

"That's what airplanes do?"

"No, it's not. The airplane and its destination move the same distance relative to each other. Not a problem. The Earth's rotation is only the first location in the real estate quotation. Second, the Earth is moving around the sun at 585 million miles a year or 66,780 miles an hour. So the second location calculation puts us a combined 67,520 miles from my desk. Location three is that the sun is moving through our galaxy. The sun and our solar system are orbiting inside the Milky Way Galaxy at 460,000 miles an hour. So location, location, location, and in one hour we're a half million miles from home and you want to go back in time for 130 years. Think about it.

"Nothing a good computer can't solve."

"But wait, there's more. The Milky Way Galaxy moves through the universe. Think Big Bang. The Milky Way moves at about 1.3 million miles an hour. Simply a time relocation of one hour is a spatial relocation of almost two million miles. Breathtaking isn't it."

Parson crossed his arms. "You said two big problems. What's the other one?"

"Science rears its ugly head again. Remember conservation of mass. All mass, that's you and I, Mr Parson. All mass in existence today has always been in existence. Mass can neither be created nor destroyed. That means that the atoms and molecules that make up you and I today, well, those little beasties were around 130 years ago and they were occupied somewhere else."

"Occupied?

"Yes, occupied. One iron atom in your hemoglobin might have been part of a flintlock, another one was in a sword, and a third was in the blood of a bison in Montana. Every single thing that makes you into you, was making something else what it was in the 1790s. Those little molecules aren't waiting for you to show up and they aren't going to quit doing what they're doing when you do. My guess is that if we went to the past, all of our atoms would be busy elsewhere and we'd simply cease to exist. Probably somewhere in the empty reaches of outer space."

"Thank you for another lecture that I didn't want. If anyone can figure this out, you can and I'll pay you very well to try. No complaints and no refunds. Will you give it a shot?"

"Mr. Parson, the universe doesn't care about money, but I do. You pay me and you fund the research and we've got a deal."

"Done. Martha Dubonnett, my executive assistant will handle things on my end. Communicate directly with her."

"Certainly. I've got a plane to catch. If I did the math right, in two hours, I'll be 1,800, 862 miles from where I am right this second. That's damn good mileage for a private jet. Who knew it was that far from New Orleans to Phoenix, Arizona?"

***

Three years and two billion dollars later, Charles Parson, walked into the laboratory that his money had paid for. Dr. Boudreau and three assistants wore clichéd white lab coats. There were no pencils, no pocket protectors, and no slide rules. Computers and records had replaced them.

The two men shook hands. Parson said, "This place looks more like a hospital operating room than a time machine. Am I here so that you can tell me that you've pissed away the money?"

"No. I could have made it look like something H. G. Wells created, but that would just be window dressing. I've got this figured out. We've made dozens of test runs and I've even used it myself."

"Where is it?"

Boudreau opened a box and removed a hemispherical helmet studded with several electrical connections. The bright overhead lights glinted from the stainless steel surface. Boudreau turned it over. "Each electrode extends inside the Time Helmet, we call it a Time Helmet. Some of them monitor brain activity and some stimulate it. We have to adjust it to ensure that it fits each subject perfectly. I've adjusted perfectly for me and other ones for my staff. This one's ready for you."

Parson picked up the device and inspected it. "Looks like something a man would wear to his own electrocution. How's it work?"

"There are certain limitations. Let me walk you through the theory and the procedure. First, do we agree that distance and the fact that

101

matter can't be in two places at the same time. That would prevent physical time travel. Correct?"

"We do."

"Neither of those prevents the mind, the conscious mind, from traveling through time. First, the time traveler has to be receptive, so a cocktail of relaxing drugs is injected."

Parson crossed his arms. "I didn't invest two billion bucks to take a trip on LSD. I don't like this so far."

"The subject's mind must be willing to accept the computer-enhanced stimulation or it won't work. You'll be aware of everything, I assure you. The computer aligns with the subject's brain and guides the conscious mind into a state of concert with the universe, reality, or whatever. We really don't have a word for it. The Buddhists called it, Dharma.

"Once in harmony with Dharma, the subject can project his mind into the past. Maybe into the future, but we haven't tried that yet. We've found that it's best to have a target time destination as well as a physical one."

"A physical destination?"

"Of course, we can't just go back in time and pop into existence. Our consciousness has to have a physical brain to function properly. We've discovered that we can only occupy the brains of our ancestors. Simply put, if you are really descended from Paul Barras, we can guide your consciousness into his brain, but there are limitations."

"Okay, so this is where the medium at the séance says that it won't work if I'm not a true believer. I expected better from you than drugs and a sideshow act."

"Your beliefs don't matter a rat's ass and neither does your attitude. Here's what we know. In every test we've made so far, we've only been able to occupy the physical brain of a direct ancestor. Search criteria are crucial. We have to know when and where the target is located. You can't just show up at Buckingham Palace on Christmas Eve in 1860 and wander around looking for Queen Victoria. Well, you could, but your consciousness is going to attach itself to the first ancestor it comes across. If there is more than one, it automatically picks the strongest one."

"How can one ancestor be stronger than another?"

"You've studied genealogy. If Paul Barras is twelve generations removed from you and the woman with him is only ten generations removed, your consciousness will choose her as a host. However, Paul could be your ancestor multiple times through different children. He was a busy boy. If he is your grandfather twelve times removed twice and his paramour de jour is your grandmother ten times removed once, you share more DNA with Paul than with his lady, and your mind will choose him."

"We're back where we started, Doctor. Thank you for the lecture, but why do I care?"

"To be sure that your consciousness chooses Barras, we have to pick a date and a location where we can place him with a great deal of certainty. History only gives us a few dates and times to choose from. There are a few other issues."

"Of course there are. If I don't say mother, may I, will I be trapped in the past?"

"Nothing like that. Barras is French. He speaks French and he thinks in French. If you don't speak French you won't understand his thoughts. "

"That makes perfect sense. As it happens, I do, but I'll brush up on my *Français*."

"The traveler can't control the host. The traveler understands his thoughts and can access his memory, but can't direct his actions. The traveler hears, sees, tastes, and smells everything the host smells, but can't control what the host does or says. You'll be a spectator."

"The last issue is the duration of the visit. We've limited our visits to an hour. That's arbitrary, but it lets us evaluate how well your body handled the transition period. We want to be sure that your conciseness returns to where it belongs. We use an automatic protocol that withdraws the chemical stimulus and changes the computer guidance to bring you back."

Parson put the helmet on and then took it off again. "Sounds like that old television cartoon about that turtle. *Drizzle drazzle drozzel drone, time for this on to come home*, or something like that."

"If it helps you to think of it that way, sure. We'd like to calibrate the helmet and the programming to you. Once we do that, we want to test it. We'll send your consciousness back to your fraternal grandfather for a couple of minutes. You okay with that?"

"Let's do it. When do I get to visit the French Revolution?"

"Whenever you say that you're ready to *parle français.*"

"Oui, oui. Three weeks should be enough time. Shall we say July 29th? That would be the anniversary of the 10th day of Thermidor according to the calendar that the French Revolutionists created, the day that Robespierre was beheaded. Barras will be at there at 6 PM local time He didn't want to miss the execution and neither do I."

Boudreau took the helmet from Parson. "A fitting date. Let's calibrate your helmet. We'll need about an hour and we'll need to give you the injection to ensure your receptivity."

"I'm fine with that, but if the ghost of Timothy O'Leary pops up singing "White Rabbit," we're going to have a problem."

###

Boudreau's assistants strapped Parson in what looked like an old-fashioned dentist's chair. They adjusted each electrode for contact pressure and location. The wiring was switched around on four electrodes to ensure that their purposes matched the desired locations in Parson's brain. Boudreau made a quick wipe with an alcohol swab, tightened a tourniquet on Parson's arm, and said, "You're going to feel a pinch and then you'll begin to relax."

The time traveler was sound asleep before Boudreau finished the injection. He removed the hypodermic needle and looked questioningly at one of his assistants, who responded, "He's under. Vital signs are fine."

"Excellent. Begin the stimulation and mental projection program. Let's send Mr. Parson to meet his grandfather. Confirming December 18, 1941, the day that Darrell Parson arrived at Fort Polk, Louisiana to begin basic training. He was in processing from ten that morning until noon."

"Yes, sir."

"Duration set for three minutes and on my mark, Mark!"

Charles was aware of the entire process. He never felt relaxed or like he lost consciousness for a single second. A voice murmured softly in his ears. He watched the scientists working and realized that he wasn't watching them from the dentist's chair, but that his vantage point was above them, near the water-stained ceiling. His body, six feet below him, jerked with the fear-of-falling relaxation response that sometimes precedes going to sleep. Charles tried to grab something to brace himself, but he didn't have any hands. He looked at himself, look being an arbitrary term since his self-inspection made it clear that he didn't have eyes, or even a body for that matter.

He felt pressured to leave the room. He tried to stay near his body as his area of consciousness expanded. He was in the room and beyond the room simultaneously. The scope of his vision continued to grow. He was above the building, and then above the town. He watched clouds moving across the face of the Earth and next, he sensed the sun growing dimmer in distance as his consciousness expanded. Stars grew bright as his mind raced past them and soon faded into darkness as other stars grew larger.

Galaxies were next and he became dizzy as the star clusters swirled, spun, and danced with seemingly aimless abandon. They shrank in apparent size and Charles' universe became a disorientating nothingness with only occasional flickers of light in the distance. He needed an anchor. Something to hold onto before he was lost. On the verge of panic, he felt a soft tug, a rope, or he hoped a lifeline. He couldn't tell, but in desperation, he grasped the ephemeral thread and followed it.

The galaxies reappeared and he followed the tread into a spinning pinwheel. Stars grew larger and they came and went. One called to him and he focused on it. Before Charles reached the star, a blue planet caught his attention. It grew larger and his scope of consciousness grew smaller. He chose a continent and then an area near a swamp. He entered a building. Dozens of men dressed only in their underwear stood in a long line waiting for their turns to have haircuts.

Charles's awareness was sucked into one man with the irresistible pull of a whirlpool. Charles's point of view changed and he looked at the room from Darrell Parson's eyes. He could hear through his grandfather's ears. It was like using one of those ocular devices with audio enhancement except for two things. He could feel what his grandfather felt and he could hear the man's thoughts. His initial effort to investigate the memories was interrupted.

A barber shouted, "Next. You, Okie, I said next. Get your ass in this chair."

"Yes, sir."

"I ain't no sir. Hold still." The man shook a large electric razor in Darrell's face. "Nice hair, cowboy. You want to keep them sideburns."

"Yes, I would."

The man snickered and ran the razor across the top of Darrell's head. "No problem, cowboy. Hold out your hands and catch 'em. Here they come."

In less than a minute, Charles and Darrell felt their bald head tingle under the breeze of the ceiling fan. They ran one hand over their smooth scalp and it came away with a touch of blood. Darrell glared at the barber. "You cut my ear!"

"Boo hoo! Move on, cowboy. No purple hearts today. Next!"

Charles felt a sudden tug and moved to the ceiling and then into the sky. His passage through the cosmos was much quicker than before and he coughed himself awake in Boudreau's laboratory. The assistants removed the helmet and unstrapped him. The first thing he did was run his hand through his hair. He wasn't bald.

Boudreau monitored the readouts. "Your vital signs are fine. That's good. Do you know where you are? What's your name? What day is it? Who's the president?"

"Why ask me those things?"

"Remember this is new to us. We want to be sure that the Charles Parson that went back in time is the one that came back. Don't imagine that Darrell took your place, but we don't know what we don't know."

"I was there during his intake processing. I got a haircut in about fifteen seconds. The barber cut our ear. Darrell didn't get a purple heart for that, but he got one on D-Day, along with a Bronze Star."

"Okay. We have some concern that under extreme stress, both the occupied mind and the occupying mind might try to leave the body and if that were the case, we have no idea what would happen. We don't know which mind would arrive in the time traveler's body. Maybe both."

"Been nice to know that before I went to see my grandpa."

Boudreau labeled Parson's helmet and stored it safely. He pointed at one of his assistants. "This is Pandora Parcells. That theory is hers. We don't give it much credence, because she's a doom-saying worrywart, but nonetheless, we do a brief verification when each traveler returns."

Parson straightened his clothing. "That's just stupid. If I can sense my ancestor's thoughts, it's only reasonable to assume that he can sense mine and would know the answer to whatever you'd ask him.

See you on the twenty-ninth. Barras didn't speak English. If I show up without this Midwestern twang in my voice, just shoot me. Is there anything else about this rinky-dink outfit that you haven't told me?"

"You know everything we know, but again, we don't know what we don't know. This is new technology. Miss Parcells' concern is speculative at best, but you asked, so we told you. You might as well have asked if using the machine too many times will give you a skin rash. We have no reason to think so, but no one has made over three trips, so could be. Will you grow an extra set of arms? Science says that you won't, but there is no empirical evidence either way."

Fine, I understand. You don't have to be a smart ass about it. I'll be here on the 29th.

Parson walked immediately to the laboratory chair and sat down. "Let's do this. The French Revolution is waiting."

Pandora unboxed Parson's helmet and fit it carefully in place. Boudreau said, "You haven't had any alcohol or mind-altering drugs today have you?"

"Another thing you didn't mention as a potential problem, but as it happens, I haven't"

"Don't know if it's a problem or not. Relax. The program is set for six o'clock local time on the evening of July 29, 1794, and the location is set for Concord Square, then called the *Place de la Révolution.* You'll have an hour. Ready when you are."

Parson closed his eyes and shifted to make himself comfortable. "Ready."

His mental journey of expansion and contraction through the universe was quicker than before. Parson was impatient and he rushed the process as much as possible. His consciousness hesitated briefly at the sight of a guillotine standing prominently on the bloodstained cobblestones. Hundreds of the worst-dressed people he'd ever seen crowded the area. Some of the filthy revolutionaries glowed slightly and the glowing ones tugged gently at him.

He realized that he was descended from more than one person present, but surely he could find Barras. He wouldn't be in the crowd with the unwashed peasants. Parson mentally inspected the area. A strong tug came from a raised dais near the guillotine, a spot not

107

unlike the good seats at the theatre. A bright glow shone from an immaculately dressed man. It had to be Barras. Parson moved his mind closer and felt a strong pull toward the man. It was him. Parson didn't resist it.

A horse cart carrying a dozen chained men entered the square and stopped near the guillotine. One man had his arms chained behind him and his face was tightly wrapped with bandages. Robespierre thought Parson. Robespierre had tried to kill himself the day before and had shot himself in the face. He'd botched the job.

Parson directed his consciousness toward Barras, but he couldn't force himself closer. He focused harder, but to his shock, he was pulled toward the horse cart. Robespierre was as bright as sunrise. Parson fought the pull, but like a moth drawn to the flame, he flew toward the light and his mind merged with the chained man.

It wasn't like joining with his grandfather. Robespierre's mind was a jumble of fear, confusion, anger, and pain, mostly pain. His lower face was on fire, his jawbone shattered from the bullet, and his skin was charred and freckled with black powder marks. His left wrist throbbed like a drummer's backbeat. The jailors had broken it deliberately when they'd handcuffed him.

Parson tried to control his reaction to the overwhelming pain but it came in waves. He searched for the underlying consciousness hoping to learn something useful, but Robespierre's mind was a shadow in the wind, now here, now gone, briefly focused, and then lost in agony and fear.

Parson withdrew his consciousness into a small corner and battled to build a wall against the throbbing torture, the unrelenting torment He couldn't make it stop completely, but he reduced it to a manageable standstill. He held it at bay and, once more he reached for Robespierre's mind. He found it, or rather Robespierre found him.

The disgraced Revolutionary was aware of Parson and his hastily erected sanctuary and his consciousness seized on Parson as a drowning man seizes a floating branch. His mind shoved Parson's and Parson shoved back. The two men fought for the safe place like children playing king of the hill, but there was only room for one.

Parson gained the upper hand for a few seconds, but was distracted by movement. The executioners dragged Robespierre up the steps to the guillotine. They shoved him to his knees. Parson lost focus with every jerk and shove. He couldn't speak and he couldn't control the body.

Robespierre's panicked consciousness was like a troop of army ants, relentless, probing, and grasping for the slightest opening, for any entrance into the safe area.

Parson was stronger. He shoved Robespierre from the mental refuge. He visualized his fist around the nobleman's throat. The body was rudely shaken and it collapsed on the guillotine.

Both minds were shocked when the guillotine's guard hit the back of Robespierre's neck. It didn't fit properly and the executioner smashed it down three more times. He lifted it up and cursed. The large bandage around the injured jaw kept it from fitting properly. The man said, "*Merde. Fils de Pute. Maudit Bandage* is in the way. He ripped away the bandage and a part of the injured face tore away with it.

The body screamed and Parson screamed in concert with it. He lost focus and Robespierre shoved from the safe place before Parson could react and resist. He clenched his fists. He realized he'd clenched his fists, but he shouldn't be able to do that. He shouldn't be able to control the body. He shifted his feet. He was in control. Somehow Robespierre had switched places with him. His mind turned to fight the Frenchman, but Robespierre's consciousness was gone. He was alone with the pain.

And then the pain was gone. He opened his eyes and saw the guillotine above him. The blade was in the down position and covered with blood. He tried to turn his head. He couldn't. The crowd noise grew quiet and the light faded to black.

***

Martha said, "Mr. Boudreau, he's waking up."

Parson shivered violently, shook his head rapidly, and jerked awake. The panic in his eyes was immediately apparent. Martha wiped his face with a damp towel. "Relax, Mr. Parson, relax. Let Pandora and I check your vital signs and we'll get you out of this chair."

She released one of his hands and Parson touched his undamaged face and smiled with relief. "English," he mumbled. "*Mon Dieu*, they speak English in heaven. Who knew? This is heaven, is it not?"

"No, Mr. Parson. This is New Orleans. Remember?"

Boudreau spoke too fast for Martha to follow the Creole patois common in Louisiana. Parson replied. "Your French is deplorable. It's worse than my English. Speak English. Am I in heaven?"

"No, and you aren't in hell. As my assistant said, "Mr. Parson, you're back where you started, New Orleans."

"My name is Maximilien François Marie Isidore de Robespierre. I know of Orleans, but nothing of a New Orleans."

Boudreau nodded and refilled the hypodermic. He injected it quickly into Parson's arm.

Once Parson, or at least, Parson's body, went back to sleep, Boudreau said, "This is a nightmare. I've got to think. It seems that Parson merged with the wrong Jacobin. Evidently, Robespierre was a stronger genetic match than Barras was, and somehow, he managed to overcome Parson's consciousness."

Pandora looked terrified. "Mr. Boudreau, are you saying that this is the same Robespierre who was a leader of the French Revolution. What are we going to do?"

"We mustn't lose our heads. The man is an incendiary orator, a rabble-rouser, and a notorious philanderer. We can't just turn him loose in our world. We need to send him somewhere else, I mean sometime else. Any thoughts, Martha."

"How about World War One. We'll send his mind into the trenches. Aim for the German side, just before they lose the war. No recall protocol. Leave him there. Maybe he'll be killed"

Robespierre looked out of the eyes of a frightened German courier. The mind in the body he now occupied cowered in one small corner of consciousness. Robespierre crushed it. He wore some type of uniform, a wet dirty uniform. He heard gunfire and explosions faintly over the pouring rain.

Another uniformed man handed him a sealed packet and spoke in German. "Adolf, deliver this to Haupleute Schmidt. Quickly."

Robespierre smiled. "Jawohl." He saluted, placed the oilcloth package inside his greatcoat, and hurried outside where the rain-sodden landscape was intermittently illuminated by lightning and mortar fire.

110

Robert Allen Lupton is a retired commercial hot air balloon pilot. Robert runs and writes every day, but not necessarily in that order. Over 200 of his short stories have been published in various anthologies. Over 2500 drabbles based on the worlds of Edgar Rice Burroughs and several articles and interviews are available online at www.erbzine.com/lupton. He has four novels, seven short story collections and three anthologies available from the finest purveyors of reading material.

TO BEGIN AT THE BEGINNING

By Rie Sheridan Rose

I didn't intend to ruin time. Let's get that straight from the start. Initially, I had an idea to explore its byways through the aid of a conceptual masterpiece of scientific engineering which would set the world on its ear. In other words—a time machine.

Of course, every scientist, or even dilettante, who contemplates the intricacies of time and history designs a time machine. Society considers it *de rigueur.* Not to do so says one isn't serious about the matter. After all, one doesn't just lie down on one's bed, close one's eyes, and travel backward or forward to another time and place. That isn't how it works. Believe me. I tried.

Not that anyone has presented actual *proof* they have succeeded in the matter either. A few of my more promising colleagues have disappeared, never to be seen again, and the scientific community assumes they fulfilled their goal and are now living comfortable lives in another era. But no demonstrative proof of that exists.

My apparatus was intended for travel without boundaries. Nothing would tie it to the conventional methods of disapparation and recombination that most such machines used to voyage the sea of time. No, it would cast the user back or forth as desired in an incorporeal state. The traveler's body would remain safe and sound in the apparatus while their mind traveled to their desired destination unincumbered by material trappings, or the need to attempt to match the clothing or customs of the period visited. It would be like traveling as a ghost.

Of course, of necessity, this would mean no interaction with the denizens of the chosen time would be possible. No opportunity would present itself for any of the shenanigans befalling characters in the novels of the day—my day, that is—where the traveler from the past or future winds up falling in love with a citizen of a bygone or future era and settling down. The community had decided this to be the case for at least two of the missing. That's why I thought my intended solution would be perfect. Strict scientific study with none of the mess.

Unfortunately, the best-laid plans and all that. It turns out that noncorporeal travel has its own pitfalls. No matter how I set the parameters, I could not manage more than a day or two to the past or the future. And I could only observe my chosen timeframe for two or three days before my physical body had needs I had to address.

I could venture to last Monday, say, and observe the staff going about their business until Wednesday—the day I set forth—but I couldn't see what they did Thursday, because my body needed sustenance...and other practical considerations. Also, once I arrived at the point where I had departed, things would get hazy, as if I were watching events through a thick layer of gauze. I came to hypothesize that this might be because the cosmos did not intend for me to see my immediate future lest I disturb it somehow. Moving to the extreme end of my tether forward gave me a glimpse of household affairs—Mary, the maid, dropping a China cup; the butler polishing the silver; the housekeeper scolding the footman for sneaking a bottle from the wine cellar...—but allowed me to see nothing of interest or venture outside the walls of my own home.

I finally bowed to the inevitable and decided I must build the traditional type of machine to traverse the currents of time in a tactile, physical way. Revisiting my colleague Herbert's *Time Machine*—a veiled treatise on his experiments. I also perused his lesser known—and more private—*A Treatise on Time Machines*. I know of only four copies of the latter in existence. It took all my persuasion and a bottle of very fine claret to get my hands on one of them.

Herbert's machine was straightforward, but I hesitated to follow his instructions to the letter, considering the lack of control evidenced in his purported adventures. I intended my machine to follow my dictates and take me to precise locations and moments in time.

My colleague Bertram Haversmith and I collaborated on the building of the device. After all, even in our enlightened times, prohibitions existed about certain people in certain places, so Bertie had to collect all the materials required.

Our conjecture hypothesized the trouble with Herbert's machine lay within the materials. He had relied on brass for all of his structural fittings. I felt, and Bertie said he agreed with me, that steel would be a more compatible component for the basic machine itself, with copper forming the electrical conduits and fittings. We were all charting unknown territory, so our guess had as much validity as anyone else's.

Bertie and I constructed the steel armature of the machine in no time, using the empty carriage house out behind the manor as a staging area. When it came to covering the structure, we dickered to obtain several yards of naval-quality sailcloth from the sail makers, which adapted to the new function quite well. Then the intricacies of the mechanisms came into play. I consulted often with Herbert, as well as William Morris, who had also dabbled in the mists of time. The entire project had firm roots in speculation. A sea of ivory, copper, and brass bits flowed into the workshop, to be contorted into the inner workings of the machine. Neither Bertie nor I had the slightest idea of what we were doing, but the bliss of working together to conquer the vagaries of that most elusive dimension felt invigorating.

With the aid of our more experienced colleagues, we finished our machine just before Christmas in 1896. As a gift to ourselves, we intended to set our first course on Christmas Day. No question had arisen regarding who would pilot our maiden voyage. We would go together—as we had every step of the way leading up to this moment.

Bertie handed me up into the pilot seat of the machine and then joined me in his own seat. "Fingers crossed," he whispered, flipping the switch on his console that powered up the machine. Holding my breath, I eased forward the lever that would send the both of us— and the machine—back to our chosen destination of the original Christmas Day. It had seemed as good a choice as any and held deep significance for us both.

"We will see the birthplace of Christ," I said, my fingers trembling with excitement.

We had set the coordinates for Bethlehem in late April. Despite the general attribution of the birth to December, many historians put forth April or even May. We had determined to put an end to the speculation by going to see for ourselves.

The machine started whining and then shimmered around us. Within instants, it had dissolved around us, taking us with it.

Then passed a moment of utter blackness, where I struggled to breathe. It felt as if I had become lost in a void. I panicked, reaching over to clutch at Bertie. His arms came around me—the only modicum of comfort in the featureless dark.

It only lasted a matter of an instant, but it felt like an eternity before the darkness lightened and the world started reintegrating around us. We waited with bated breath to see the mud-built houses and the blazing sun of Bethlehem.

That was not to be. As the world came into focus, we found ourselves in a pastoral countryside with green rolling hills, tree-covered meadows, and swaths of waving grain.

"I suppose Herbert was right about the travel aspect too," Bertie sighed. "You can travel in space, or you can travel in time...but you can't do both at once."

I felt my lip curl into a pout. We had so hoped to prove his theory wrong. "Ah, well," I replied, trying to keep our spirits up, "we may not see the Christ child born, but there are doubtless things of interest to be explored in Ancient Britain."

"Indeed. It appears this period predates the Roman invasion by several decades. It would be fascinating to see what circumstances existed in actuality from a first-person perspective."

My Bertie was always foremost a historian. I was the more scientific of the pair, with a fondness for the natural world.

"Let us test our hypothesis. It seems to be a consensus that the Romans founded Londinium in the mid-40s AD. Therefore, whatever civilization currently occupies this area is pre-Roman. If Herbert's theory is accurate, we are currently sitting in the exact spot that will become our workshop in the future. I must confess," I confided, "I really hoped we would prove him wrong about that." I rose to my feet, smoothing the rough linen of my clothing. "Let us see if we can verify our position."

I wasn't sure how we would do so, to be honest, but it would provide an intriguing distraction. If we could verify we had traveled backward in time to pre-Roman Britain, it would at least give credence to the fact that time travel itself was possible, shoring up Herbert's claims as fact, not fiction. That alone should be enough to provide us all with cachet in the scientific community—and likely dinner invitations for the next decade to come.

The two of us covered our machine with loose branches to hide it from any potential prying eyes. Not that we expected anyone to stumble across it. We could see no sign of human habitation from where we stood. The machine itself stood in the middle of a clearing surrounded by open fields and trees as far as the eye could see. We equipped the supplies we had brought with us—planned for trade and commerce in the markets of Bethlehem, not wilderness exploration—and started off to see if we could find any denizens of the area.

The day proved pleasant, if a trifle muggy, and we enjoyed the chance to see what the countryside around where London now stood had looked like almost two thousand years ago. The verdant freshness of the air proved the most interesting feature. Gone was the constant pall of smoke and soot hanging over the city. The air seemed almost too fresh to breathe.

After a bit of walking, we came upon the edge of a river surrounded by marshland. Its water sparkled and danced under the midday sun. With wonder, we realized from its proximity to our arrival that it must be the Thames. Bending to cup a handful of the water, I had never tasted such purity in a liquid. There appeared no sign of the sullen waterway it would one day become, walled-in and muddy.

We found a place shallow enough to cross to the other side and picked our way through the marsh on the far bank. We had still found no signs of habitation.

"Surely we should have seen some vestiges of civilization by now," I commented to Bertie. "Even if the Romans won't invade for several decades, there should be small villages dotting the countryside, shouldn't there? Where are the people?"

"A very fine question indeed." Bertie pulled a map of Britain from his knapsack. "If I am correct in my calculations, the city will eventually lie behind us, and we are now moving south toward the coast—though I wouldn't advise we travel that far since no landmarks have appeared to return us to our machine. We already risk losing it if we don't turn back."

I sighed. As always, Bertie had the right of it. Unless we wanted to remain here and watch the Romans eventually conquer Britain, we needed to keep track of our machine. To state the obvious, it would prove impossible to recreate it in these primitive surroundings.

"You're right, Bertie. We should return to the machine. It is obvious we will learn no more here. Perhaps we'll have better luck on our next venture."

We started to retrace our steps, discussing where to try next, since we had determined that we could only travel in time.

"I would quite like to see Queen Elizabeth," Bertie offered. "Look at all she did for the Empire, and all on her own."

"I am amenable to that. But only if I can witness a play at the Globe. The queen's life overlapped with Shakespeare's. Two birds, one stone."

We passed the remainder of the walk back in a convivial debate over which was the greater masterpiece—*Hamlet* or *Macbeth*.

I walked a pace or two behind Bertie, examining a specimen of unusual flora I had found. I had seen nothing like it in my botanical studies. When he stopped dead in his tracks, I almost ran into him, as he let out an uncharacteristic oath.

"Bloody hell."

I peeked around him and saw what he meant in an instant. Where we had left the machine covered by its protective camouflage of branches, there now lay a flattened sea of broken plant matter. Something had destroyed the machine.

"Perhaps it's not as dire as it looks," I murmured. "Perhaps someone has stolen it, and we can deal with them to retrieve it."

Bertie strode forward and began throwing the broken branches right and left. He soon uncovered the flattened remains, removing all doubt. Chest heaving, he turned to me. "We cannot go home."

The stunning statement hit me like a knife to the belly. "W-What?"

"They—whoever they are—have destroyed the machine beyond repair. Even if we could somehow manufacture replacement parts, we have no way to generate the electricity to charge the components and set course for home. We will have to carve out a new existence here as best we can."

I sank down upon the ground as all the strength left my lower limbs. Marooned…in a past where we didn't belong. With no way to alleviate the situation.

Seeing my distress, Bertie hurried to kneel at my side. "Be of stout heart. I am sure we will find others if we keep exploring. We'll just go in a different direction next time. Don't fret."

117

Mustering my resources, I gave him a tremulous smile. "Of course, we will prevail. Do we not have two of the brightest minds in the Empire? For now, we should see about raising some sort of shelter for the night."

I sighed and rose to my feet, brushing off the clothing I would now have to wear for the foreseeable future. Walking over to the destruction, I surveyed the remains of the machine with despair. Bertie was right. The two of us would never repair it with the materials and circumstances to hand.

We gathered the branches into a pile and spread upon it the fabrics we had brought as trade goods for the Bethlehem market. The components of the machine we thought might one day be useful, we set to one side. Any parts deemed unusable, we tossed into a separate pile.

By full dark, we had everything sorted and a small campfire started by Bertie's flint and steel. The rising wood smoke held the aroma of home.

April had a wintery bite with no buildings to radiate the day's warmth. We huddled together, sharing the meager rations we had brought on what we thought would be a brief trip to a market town.

"We'll need to forage tomorrow," I whispered, unwilling to break the silence of the night more than necessary. "I am so glad I have brushed up on botany this spring. I believe I should be able to recognize most of the local flora."

"That will prove useful," Bertie said, smiling down at me. "Just think…we can build a farmstead here. Experiment to cultivate the hardiest plants. There have to be animals here somewhere. I can fashion a spear or a bow and hunt for meat."

I couldn't help but laugh. "So, we will become hunter/gatherers?"

"Why not? If we must exist in this…this forsaken environ—and I fear, we must—we might as well be useful in some way. Perhaps we will invent the practical techniques used by the farmers of our day. Passed down from generation to generation through time."

"I suppose we will have to keep an eye out for potential partners to facilitate those generations," I said with a wicked grin. "Best part of the wilderness—no competition."

This time, Bertie's laugh rang out in the night. "Bless you for your wit. It will make the days to come less devastating."

I felt my cheeks heat. Desiring to change the subject, I blurted out, "What will we call it, this new farmstead of ours?"

"Eden, of course."

I feigned shock. "Have you gone mad, Mr. Haversmith? Look around you—do you see anything that even vaguely resembles a garden?"

"Not at the moment, but that is the entire *raison d'être* of a farm, isn't it? To grow crops—form a garden of sorts?"

"Eden, it is," I conceded, with a nod of my head.

Smothering the fire, we curled up on the pile of branches to attempt some semblance of sleep. To conserve body heat, we slept as children do, curled into a dog pile of entwined limbs. We had a single length of wool to cover us both, so such proximity was necessary.

When I next came to my senses, the sun was rising. *That must be to the east*, I reminded myself. We should mark the compass points somehow, so that we could keep vague track of our location.

I turned to mention this to Bertie, but he had left the camp. *Off to hunt*, I supposed.

Rising from the pile of prickly sticks, I started to give the place where the machine had been a cursory search to make sure we had overlooked nothing of value. Tracing my bare foot through the dirt— we had removed our shoes to sleep, and I had not yet re-donned mine—I saw the glitter of glass. As there had been few components of that material on the machine, I squatted down for a closer look. Brushing away the remaining detritus with careful fingers, I uncovered the window that had protected the delicate ivory dials. The entire mechanism had been ground into the earth. I gazed in amazement to see that the dials remained in their places, undamaged by the disaster. I squinted harder as something I had never noticed before caught my eye.

Above the dials, Bertie had carved increments—1s, 10s, 100s, 1000s...millions. In our excitement to be off the day before, I must have hurried as I entered the number for our destination, -1928. This meant that only the first four dials should have shown a number. The fifth dial should never have a number. I felt sure Bertie had added it as a joke. But instead of exhibiting the unnumbered space it should have, I could clearly see a zed. We had not traveled back

2000 years, give or take, but, instead, found ourselves nearer to 2,000,000 years from home.

As I say, I did not mean to ruin time...

Rie Sheridan Rose's prose appears in numerous anthologies, including Killing It Softly Vol. 1 & 2, Hides the Dark Tower, Dark Divinations, and Startling Stories. In addition, she has authored twelve novels in multiple genres, six poetry chapbooks, and dozens of song lyrics. She is a native of Texas and lives there with her husband and several spoiled cats. When not writing or editing, she is usually walking—being a Virtual Race addict. Member of the HWA and SFWA, she X's irregularly as @RieSheridanRose.

Her website is www.riewriter.com, or find her on Facebook at https://www.facebook.com/RieSheridanRoseAuthorPage/.

THE TIME SLIDER

By David Lawrence Morris

Robert Henderson was a physicist. He was a retired physics professor and had been retired for some time, but still worked for hours every day in his personal lab. He'd created it over several years in the cellar of his mountain cabin. The cellar was an unusual feature in a cabin, but when he'd had it built he knew he'd always need a lab. Investigating the world around him and the way it worked was the one thing that could occupy his time for hours, sometimes days at a time.

The cabin was now his principal residence. He'd rented out the house he'd raised his kids in when his wife passed away a few years earlier. After her funeral, he'd packed up and moved to the cabin, planning on spending the rest of his days there. It took a while, but living alone eventually grew on him.

Being able to work for hours on end in the old cabin was rewarding, a way to forget that she was gone. It wasn't uncommon for him to see the sunrise and only then realize he'd been working all night.

At the university, he was best known for developing different theories about time. After much thought and research, he was about to publish what he planned to be his last paper. He'd studied the concept of time for years and he'd already published two papers detailing his theories. This third paper unfortunately would make the first two irrelevant.

His prior theories both led to the same conclusion that was much simpler than scientists had "proven" in the past. While math supporting prior theories, made them sound plausible, this time he'd approached it from a different angle, leading to different conclusions altogether. His new mathematical equations relating time with the physical world were much simpler by comparison and made more sense.

Using his new concepts, he was able to propose ways to slow, speed up, and even move through time. While his mathematics seemed valid, the technology to test the new theory was not yet available, and developing it would be too expensive for anyone to test it.

Being retired and something of a loner, he didn't feel like he had to defend his new theory, but felt obligated to publish it. His faith was unwavering and with what vanity he had left, he wanted the credit to be his, even if it might be years before it was proven to be true.

He was over seventy, and while he was in good health, this paper seemed like a great way to go out, to be remembered for all time. *Maybe someday someone will be able to test it.* He thought. *It would be easier to build a skyscraper.*

Once the new concept occurred to him, he worked for months on his supporting equations. He'd traveled to CERN in Switzerland only to find that even their technology wasn't adequate to prove or even hint in support of his new ideas.

Just after he left his computer to finish the printout of what would be his final publication the phone rang.

Robert still had a house phone, finding it easier to use at his desk, and more reliable than the cell service in the mountains. He answered the phone with an attitude. He hated interruptions, finding he'd have to go back and sometimes start over. Breaking his concentration was something he detested and he'd hoped living in the cabin would keep it at a minimum.

The voice on the phone was familiar, belonging to a good friend. "Robert, this is Aaron, I'm so glad you picked up. I need your help. I found something I think you should see."

Robert had known Aaron from the archeology department at the university where he taught physics. He'd known him for almost twenty years. Oddly their friendship began during a discussion about how archeology and time were related. Back then, Robert had misgivings about the very existence of time. It was only a personal suspicion, something he'd now overcome. As excited as he was about binding the printout of his paper, Aaron came first. Friendship had its privileges.

As a professor of archeology, Aaron always chose to take summers off, taking that time to practice what he preached. He'd explore the ruins left by the area's first occupants thousands of years ago, traveling the Americas and investigating ancient civilizations.

###

It wasn't long before Robert heard someone pounding at the door, he was expecting Aaron, but this was very unlike his normal knock. Peering through the peephole he confirmed that it was indeed Aaron, and opening the door he saw him standing there like a child with a new toy. Robert motioned him inside and they both sat at the table by the cabin's small kitchen. "Okay, what's so important?"

Aaron carried an object with him and sat it carefully on the table. "Let me tell you about this thing," He said. He sat back and with the pride of an archeologist discovering a new mystery he started to tell his tale.

"I was hiking in the mountains, not far from here looking for signs that might hint to any ancient occupation. I was about to give up when I turned a corner around a rock outcropping and came across an old decaying one room cabin. Part of the old roof had already caved in. There was no telling when the whole thing might fall. It was easily over a hundred years old, likely unoccupied most of that time, but I was way too curious to be stopped. The door had disappeared somewhere along the line, so entry to the cabin was easy.

"I walked around the old ruin of a building looking through the windows, just to make sure it looked safe. When my eyes grew used to the darkness, I saw what looked like an old iron figurine, the thing you see before you. As you can see, it isn't cast iron. Later when went inside, I picked it up and took it outside. I held it in the light and could see that it was some kind of device. Something told me not to mess with it. Its very existence there made no sense.

"For instance, it's shiny clean, but everything else in that old cabin is covered in years of accumulated dust, bird droppings, bits of rotting wood, all kinds of filth." Aaron carefully picked up the object. It reminded Robert of an old toy train engine.

"I thought at first it might be some kind of ancient machine, but its condition would indicate it was recently left there and the material it's made from is a mystery to me. Never seen anything quite like it. It looks to be in perfect shape. There's no corrosion or scratches, and like I said it isn't even dusty! Have you ever seen that old broken down cabin up in the backwoods?"

"I saw it once, even looked inside, but there wasn't anything there except that old rotting table. The door had come off, but it was lying on the ground back then. The rest of it already looked like it was ready to cave in. I decided it best to just leave it alone.

Aaron was anxious to finish his story. "I thought the same thing. At first, I just thought it odd that there was something on the table and I continued up the hill. A few minutes later it started to rain. I'd just seen the old cabin, so I turned around, ran back, and waited inside for the rain to stop. The roof is crap, but luckily parts of it were good enough to keep me dry."

Aaron leaned over the table holding up the device. "This thing was sitting on that old rotten table."

"Someone had obviously been inside and recently. I could still see footprints in the dust. So tell me, why would someone just walk in, set something like that down, and leave?"

"They're probably coming back for it. There could be someone out there, probably freaking out because they forgot this thing, or maybe he meant to leave it there. For all we know this could be some kind of bomb left to demolish that old cabin. I doubt it though. It's too unusual."

Again Aaron turned the gadget over, examining each side. Robert watched him turning what looked like an old iron children's toy. A series of little buttons and dials lined one side. The buttons were what looked like small bumps arranged in two rows. Each one was labeled with an engraving, but the marks were foreign. Egyptian like little squiggles, or animal images.

Each side had textured indents where fingers could wrap around it. The shape appeared to have been designed so whoever held it could easily keep a tight grip on it.

"I haven't touched anything. I wasn't going to mess with it until running it by you. I hoped, being a physicist, you might have some idea of what it is."

"Well, it's designed to be carried. It's some kind of mechanism, so there's got to be a power source inside somewhere, but I don't see a place to open it. I'm stumped."

Without any warning, Aaron reached down and pushed a large button on the gadget. He found himself standing outside looking at the eye looking through the peephole. The door opened, and Robert greeted him. Aaron entered and went through the same routine of explaining the origin of the gadget he held. This time he knew what he was carrying. "I traveled through time using this thing! I was just here! We talked about this thing for at least five minutes. I pushed that button," pointing to the bump in the array of buttons, "then I was outside! Again!"

Robert paid careful attention to the claims of his friend Aaron. It had to be some kind of joke. He now believed that time travel might be theoretically possible, but Aaron surely didn't expect him to believe he'd accomplished it with that little gadget. It didn't make sense. Rather than comment, Robert reached out, quickly grabbed the strange contraption, and pushed the same button Aaron said he'd pushed a few minutes earlier, only to watch Aaron disappear.

There was a knock at the door and this time he didn't bother with the peephole. Opening the door, he saw Aaron excitedly holding up the time travel gadget he'd held the first time he'd arrived, except this time he was completely unaware of his first trip. *This really is his first trip*, Robert thought. *but this time I had initiated it.*

Before Aaron could repeat the rant that Robert had heard the time before, Robert raised his arm, showing off the gadget he still held. Aaron was studying Robert's expression. He seemed deep in thought, finally, almost angrily, staring at the gadget in his own hand. "You have one too. So, what are they?" "

All the laws of physics told him that having two changed masses was not possible, but there were two anyway.

Taking the original gadget gently from Aaron, Robert held it up for him to see. *He doesn't know what this is yet*, he thought. "Earlier, you came to me with this. You pushed this large button." He said pointing. You ended up outside, arriving for the first time…again. In the future you'd traveled back from, I'd already seen you and you had already been inside, but that time I didn't know what it was. You explained it to me because you remembered being here. I didn't really believe you, so I took it from you and tested it, pushing the same button you'd showed me. I left you in our future, a future that will not happen for us now, I moved back to your arrival, but since I was holding this thing, it's still here and I still remember our earlier…I mean later discussions. That's why there are two of these now. So, we need to change something.

The odd thing is getting rid of it is going to leave you in the dark about this thing once again. Aaron sat on the couch. "MORE", he said.

"This is a time travel gadget," he started. "You just told me all about it." It's my turn to tell you." In the next few minutes, he continued to detail the events of the last fifteen minutes.

"I've been working on theories about the very existence of time my entire career. For years, I believed it was a construct to make sense of memory, that in reality there was only the present and it changed. I was wrong. You just proved it. I proved it again. The scary thing to me is the source of this thing. There's no way I can be working on new concepts that agree on the existence of time with the mathematics to back it up while someone already developed a time machine this small, besides who would leave a treasure like this in an old cabin?"

Aaron stared at Robert like he'd lost his mind.

Robert walked toward the bookcase, found an empty slot, and sent them both down where they wouldn't be bumped. "Why don't we put these somewhere safe? They could be really dangerous. We've already changed things that took place right here just a few minutes ago and we don't know what the rest of those buttons do. The big one is well… .miraculous. Thank God, it only moved us a couple of minutes."

"First things first," Aaron said walking toward the bookcase. Reaching up to one of the gadgets he pushed the button, making contact but not picking it up. This time he held it down for a few seconds.

In the blink of an eye, he was standing in the old cabin, looking across the room at the table. The slider was not in his hand, but was sitting just as it had been when he first saw it. Following his steps as best as he could recall he picked up the slider and started for Robert's house. When he arrived, he knocked on the door again, only this time it would be the first time for Robert and there would only be one slider. The second one was lost in the future which would never happen quite the same way.

This time the explanation took a lot longer than before, but with all of the new details Robert seemed more inclined to believe him, at least for now. Aaron sat the slider on the same bookshelf. "Whoever left that thing in the cabin must never use it again. It's not a game…that thing is way too dangerous to be allowed to exist, but I don't know how to destroy it."

Robert asked Aaron to stay overnight. They didn't sleep, but instead spent hours discussing how the Time Slider, as they'd come to call it, could somehow be destroyed. Robert still had his reservations, but there it was. He'd never seen anything like it. Nothing about it looked like anything he'd seen before. The story Aaron told him seemed too detailed and most of all, he knew from his own mathematics that time travel was very likely possible.

The next day, they decided to photograph it from every angle, and then Robert set it on the shelf again where it would be safe. Studying the image, enlarging it, and looking at the markings for each button wasn't much help. "Those buttons must adjust the time travel settings. Can you imagine what could happen if you just started pushing buttons on that thing?"

Aaron pulled up one of the images they'd taken of the little box. "The reason this thing is in such good condition makes perfect sense to me now. This hasn't been in that cabin very long. There were footprints all over the place in there. I assumed they were from other hikers. Someone, whoever left those prints, went to that cabin, sat that gadget on the table, and left. Who knows? They may have come here from another time."

Robert gestured toward the door. "If they did, they're out there somewhere, probably freaking out about this thing missing."

"We could leave a note, but really…can you imagine a time traveler coming to this time and ending up in that old dilapidated cabin. Why there?"

"Someone came here and sat that thing down, knowing the cabin was abandoned and unfit to live in. Assuming it would be safe, they left it there. I'll bet they were only a minute or two away when you found it."

A few miles away, Paul was returning to the old cabin. He knew he had to do this, but he had no real plan. He'd been hiking through the area looking for Robert's cabin. According to his records, it wasn't far, but he was working from ancient records that were already historical documents when they were compiled. The records described a woodsy area with a few cabins. *Well,* he thought, *that's where Professor Henderson lived. The first thing I have to do is see if he really lives there.*

Following a makeshift map he'd created from data buried inside the old records, he soon found the nearby cabin he was looking for. Comparing it to ancient photos, he was able to confirm that he'd found the right place.

Once inside he set the Time Slider on an old table and began hiking to find the cabin the professor should be in. A short while later, he saw a small cabin. Seeking out the address numbers he confirmed that he'd found the right cabin. Through the window, he could see that a man was working inside. *I've found it*, he thought.

He returned to the old cabin, to retrieve the Time Slider. He was temporarily blinded while his eyes adjusted to the darkness. As his eyes adjusted, it was soon obvious that the Time Slider was gone. Searching the cabin, he saw new footprints in the dust. There was a design in the print that wasn't the same as the one his shoes left. Pushing his shoe onto the soft floor confirmed it. Something had gone terribly wrong.

"Someone's been here," he said to no one in particular. He didn't know if the prints were already there when he arrived, or if the abandoned cabin had been visited while he was gone. He hadn't paid attention. Then, seeing the strange print over one of his answered the question. Someone had been inside. They had apparently taken the device.

Losing the time travel machine was a disaster. Besides not being able to return without it, anyone messing with it could inadvertently change everything in the future he knew, he could easily just disappear, having never existed. The ripples from a minor change would grow. The changes to his time could be enormous. He couldn't even guarantee the Time Slider would cease to exist. The professor's theories already existed. He had to retrieve the slider, destroy the records before they could be published, and kill the professor. He had to move and he had to move fast.

Following the newly discovered footprints he crept along the path until they disappeared, being replaced by tire tracks.

Someone from this time had discovered the cabin, gone inside, and walked around, leaving the prints on the old dusty floor, then taken the Time Slider. If he was playing with it, he was likely already in some other time wreaking havoc and not even knowing it. If it was still here, it had to be recovered or Paul would never see his home again.

After scouring the cabin, he stepped outside looking down at his footprints. Moving the sand around with his foot, he wondered what he was going to do. The wheel tracks had to be from the car of the person who took the Slider. So, slowly, carefully, he followed the tire tracks, assuming that whoever took it, had driven away without trying to fiddle with it. When he'd walked slowly a few hundred feet away, the tire tracks grew fainter and started to disappear. Reaching into his pocket, he retrieved a small device and pointed a violet beam of light across the area where the tracks had disappeared. A faint image of the continuing tracks appeared, revealed by the unusual light.

For the next few minutes, he slowly followed the faint tracks

After a few minutes, the tracks turned, traveling up a small dirt road winding into the pines.

The tracks were visible now so he put away the light. After a short hike, he came across the same cabin he'd found earlier. Whoever took the slider was inside. Was it the professor? Looking through the window he saw the two men, then one of them disappeared and was standing on the porch knocking at the door. They definitely had it.

Walking up the driveway, he inched toward the door. He pushed a few buttons on the translator of the little pad he carried with him, and waited to see what they did next. After a minute, he knocked on the door.

The man who opened it looked surprised. It was Robert. At a time like this, the last thing he needed was another person in the vicinity. Robert shook off his surprise. "Can I help you?"

As Robert studied the stranger standing at his door, the man began to speak. The words sounded like a bastardized blend of English, French, Spanish, and German. Seconds after he stopped speaking a perfect English translation came from the device on the man's wrist. "My name is Paul. I am looking for Professor Robert Henderson."

"I'm Robert, why are you looking for me?" He was suspicious and glad he wasn't alone at that moment. *Why would someone come to a cabin in the forest, and what the hell is that translator.* Knowing there was no such thing as this quality of instant translator and knowing he'd never heard a language like this gave the man's motives away. This had to be the time traveler. Paul was looking over Robert's shoulder at the interior of the house. Then he saw the Slider sitting on a shelf lined with old books.

Again, looking at the two men, Paul began to speak followed by the translation from the mechanism. It spoke in English with the inflexions and tempo of 2024 America. "You have the...machine from the old cabin?"

Aaron stepped out from behind. "I found it. I came across that old cabin today while I was investigating the area. I saw the table inside and that was on it. You called it a Time Slider? Who are you and what is your connection to it?" More importantly, how did you know it was here? This place isn't far from the old cabin, but it's only one of several in the area and it's not that easy to find."

As the man was ushered into the house Aaron stepped back while he and Robert listened to the translations as Paul explained his presence there.

Slowly, awaiting each translation they carried on their conversation. Robert motioned for everyone to sit on the couches facing the fireplace. Sitting comfortably, Paul set the translator on the coffee table and began to explain in detail why he was there.

"Professor Henderson, I already know who you are. In my time...well that's three hundred years from now, your theories about time sat buried in the archives. It was stored there for literally hundreds of years before we started the preservation project. The paper was starting to fall apart and rather than lose it all, everything was translated and stored electronically. Without it, I never could have developed the Slider. I was helping manage the project, so I had unlimited access.

"One day I was running a search of the papers we'd preserved that day when I came across your thesis. I only got through a few pages, but I was so intrigued that I saved it and deleted it on the system. I could always either return it to the electronic archives or destroy it if it had no merit, but something in your introduction just sounded plausible. The future is very different. Most work is done by intelligent machines. In my lab, I have several. I modified them so they would have no ability to communicate with other machines which makes them unique. Once they absorbed the details from your thesis, they gave me lists of items they would need to test it. Most of them were older parts and easy to locate. Over the next few years, they, with my supervision, were able to build the first Time Slider." It was the size of my desk. I tested the device, moved an hour holding the device, and moved back. Once I knew it worked I left the "boys," as I call them, to miniaturize it.

My excitement kept me awake at night. No matter how anxious I got, it was another year before the boys had designed and manufactured the parts for the "Mini-Slider."

Looking back to Paul, he explained that they'd already both moved through time. They talked about the concept and the dangers. Robert explained that they thought it was too dangerous to be used by anyone. "We plan to lock it up, for now."

"So," Aaron interrupted. "Why are you here? How did you know where I'd be?"

Aaron had an idea. "What if you take that thing, and travel back to your time? Then, your time will hopefully be unharmed and we won't have to worry about how to destroy it, and you'll be home. Why are you here in this time anyway? Why here and now? Did anyone see you?"

"No one saw me. I made sure of that. I came here to this place at this time because I'm on a very specific mission. As you know, that thing has the capability to change the present over and over again. This...this thing is the worst, the most dangerous thing ever devised, and I made it! Before I revealed it to anyone, I tried it, as I mentioned before."

Aaron seemed puzzled. "Not to change the subject, but isn't it just a little more than odd for you to travel within walking distance from the man whose theory eventually led to the development of that thing," he said waving his hand toward Robert.

Paul was quiet for a minute. His original idea was to murder Robert so he could not develop the theory, but it'd already been written, something not detailed in the history. "According to the records, you published that paper. The historical record about you said you kept your published works here in this cabin. The error in his logic had evaded him, but it was perfectly clear now. For the time being he kept it to himself.

Robert walked toward the fireplace and pulled out a large manually bound manuscript from the bookcase. It was at least two hundred pages long. In a few seconds, he'd crossed the room and tossed it into the fireplace. Soon a roaring fire lit up the cabin, sending a radiant heat through the room. There were no tools to retrieve the manuscript and nobody wanted it to survive, knowing what it might lead to. The three men just stood watching the pages burst into flame, the rising heat lifting one page and then another.

Robert's face filled with disappointment. "It was my greatest work."

Paul was looking around the room and patting his shirt. "I'm still here!"

Robert and Aaron were looking at each other studying the reaction of the other. At the same moment, their faces seemed to light up as both men understood the problem.

The last of the pages were burning. Robert walked to Paul and put his hand on his shoulder. "Relax...There are backups." I'm the kind of guy that never destroys them. I'm like a theory hoarder. The time has come for me to put all of that away. I need to give this research up and in the years I have left, live my life normally. This lab will make a nice man cave." By the way, none of the backups are online. I don't hook anything up to the "Cloud." The computer I work on isn't hooked to the internet. I have another computer for that. All of the backups are here, right here in this cabin.

Robert walked to his desk, sat down, opened the drawer, and began to remove hard drives and stack them on his desk. He'd always backed his files up and often. Once the drawers were empty, he excused himself a minute, and went upstairs and into the garage. A minute later he returned with a bucket full of water. One by one he dropped the backup drives into the bucket. "Now, I'll erase the hard drive on this computer, and that should be it."

In a few seconds, the computer started to delete all of its storage. Minutes later, the screen went black.

Spinning around in his chair he saw Aaron and Paul still standing there. "You shouldn't be here!" He said. The backups are gone, but time is still fluid.

"If I have another backup somewhere and destroy it, theoretically Paul should disappear in this time. Because the publication won't exist in his time. He will never discover what it contains. He'd never make the Time Slider."

"Good name," said Paul

Breaking his explanation a second, Robert explained that they'd been calling it that and then continued. "He'll never travel here to

132

stop me from publishing because he will never make that thing. Because he'll never show up with the Slider he'll never try to stop me, so I'll publish anyway. All of the copies and backups will still exist eventually to be retrieved by Paul in three hundred years. Then he'll still invent the Time Slider and come here to stop me. Sound familiar? If I throw this into the fire, Paul returns to the moment he started to travel here. In seconds he'll be back.

Paul understood completely. "I'm the key. If I stay here, I disappear forever in my time which will affect the future from the moment I disappear. I'm not supposed to be here, which will have effects. I am supposed to exist in three hundred years, but will disappear and that will have an effect. But...if I travel back to the time I take your publication, I'll still remember all of this. I'll never make the Time Slider. So, you have to publish the paper anyway, just as you would have if I'd never come. You have to. When I take it from the archives, I can make it disappear forever. I'll never be able to warn you so a few things will change here, but the three of us have not interacted with anyone.

Paul picked up the slider, made a few adjustments, pushed a button, and disappeared. At the same instant, he found himself on the road by the old cabin. Stepping inside he picked the Slider off the table, made a few more adjustments, and disappeared.

In the year 2324, Paul removed the publication from the archives. This time he burned it.

The future from that moment forward would likely be different, but to Paul, it hadn't happened yet.

Aaron and Robert, who'd just watched Paul disappear didn't move for a few seconds. The Slider had disappeared along with Paul.

Walking into the closet the printer was in, Robert picked up the copy he'd started the day before. "Here it is! Ready to publish." He sat the printout on his desk and turned to Aaron.

"So, why exactly did you come over?" said Robert, not realizing he'd been there overnight.

"I was hiking. I guess...I don't really know. You were nearby...well, I better get home. What day is it anyway?

David Morris is one of the three cousins in Three Cousins Publishing. He grew up in Phoenix, and retired to Palm Springs where he started to write short novels. He says that getting together with his cousins, Robert and Carol to publish these anthologies has been a highlight in his retirement. This collection is about Time Travel, his favorite genre. One of his novels, 'The Time Ship,' taught him that writing about time is filled with pitfalls & traps. See if you can find any in this anthology.

PERFECTING THE MUNDANE

By Tim Pulo

Henry yearned for something simpler.

The thrill of altering timelines had faded, replaced by a desire to perfect the ordinary, to use his abilities to simply treat himself.

He focused on a humble goal: making the perfect waffle.

7:00 AM, the ideal time for breakfast, Henry would tweak his recipe. On the first attempt, he added too much baking powder, and the waffles puffed up like balloons only to deflate into sad, soggy discs. He sighed, did his thing, and went back at 6:59 AM the next morning.

Armed with the knowledge of his failure, Henry reduced the baking powder and added more flour. This time, the waffles turned out dense and chewy, sticking stubbornly to the iron. "If I could almost save JFK, I can sure as hell do this," he said, doing his thing and returning to 6:59 the same day for another attempt.

He whisked the batter more vigorously, hoping for a fluffier texture. The result? Tough, rubbery waffles. "Shit." Frustrated but determined, he did his thing once more.

Adjusting the temperature, he lowered the heat on the waffle iron. The waffles emerged pale and undercooked, the batter still gooey inside. "Fuck it," he groaned, contemplating a more drastic use of his abilities.

Resisting the urge, he tried again, increasing the cooking time by a minute. The edges burned while the center remained raw. Back he went.

Henry experimented with different ingredients—almond milk instead of regular, a hint of nutmeg instead of cinnamon. One batch was too sweet, the next too bland. Each failure brought him closer to giving up but ultimately sent him back for another try.

His kitchen became a temple of trial and error. It was a cozy, sunlit space filled with the aroma of fresh ingredients and quickly became his laboratory. Gleaming copper pots and pans hung from a wooden rack above the stove, and the countertops were cluttered with an array of measuring cups, spoons, and bowls. The waffle iron, an old but reliable cast-iron model, sat prominently in the center, its

135

surface seasoned from countless attempts. He learned the alchemy of batter, the subtle art of heat, and the delicate balance of flavors. He experimented with every variable—temperature, ingredients, resting times—refining his process with the meticulousness of a watchmaker.

Through his waffle failures, his mind wandered – he was capable of big things and had proven as such on many occasions throughout the course of his wonderful lifetime… but he also failed just as many times.

As Henry poured more batter into the waffle iron, his mind drifted back to one of his more ambitious time travel escapades: the attempt to rescue Archduke Franz Ferdinand and stop World War I from happening. He remembered the tension and chaos of Sarajevo in 1914, the weight of history pressing down on him as he maneuvered through the crowded streets with a clear goal in mind. He had rehearsed his plan countless times, calculating every move to prevent the assassination that would ignite chaos across the globe. Despite his meticulous preparation, he found himself thwarted at every turn by the sheer complexity of altering a profoundly fixed point in history. The bullet still found its mark every single time, and the war began every single time, unchanged by his intervention.

The failure haunted him, a stark reminder of the limits of his powers. As he watched the waffle iron hiss and sizzle, he reflected on how his grand gestures often felt futile against the tides of time. It was his reflections that had brought him to this kitchen, seeking solace in the simplicity of perfecting a single, humble task. In the quiet of his kitchen, surrounded by the familiar scents of vanilla and cinnamon, he found a peace that eluded him in the grand theatres of history. Perfecting the mundane, he realized, offered a different kind of satisfaction—one that did not rely on altering the course of nations but on mastering the small, everyday moments.

After countless attempts, Henry poured more batter into the iron, the sizzle promising something extraordinary. As the waffle cooked, he could feel it in his bones: *this was it*. Though long in the tooth, he *was still* capable of extraordinary things.

Henry smiled as he patiently waited, remembering a more successful use of his time-travel abilities. It was the late 1970s when he had traveled back with insider knowledge of future market trends. He carefully chose a modest sum to invest in a fledgling tech company called Apple. He recalled the modest office and the young, ambitious Steve Jobs, who barely glanced at him as he signed the investment papers. Over the years, his modest investment blossomed into a fortune, securing Henry's financial future and allowing him the freedom to pursue his less grandiose ambitions without worry.

The memory of that triumph was a comforting contrast to the chaos of his failed historical interventions. It was a reminder that while he couldn't always change the course of human events, he could still wield his unique gift for personal gain.

After seconds that felt like days in a lifetime of repetition, the iron opened to reveal a perfectly golden waffle, its aroma filling the room with the promise of perfection.

"I fucking did it," he exclaimed, fetching a plate from the bench.

As he poured syrup over the perfectly cooked waffle, he reflected on the balance he had found between grand adventures and personal successes. He savored the small victories that brought him genuine contentment, a balance of the extraordinary and the everyday.

He took a bite, and for a moment, time itself seemed to pause. The waffle was everything he'd hoped for—crisp on the outside, fluffy on the inside, with a taste that was both rich and subtle.

Henry smiled, savoring each bite. He'd conquered time itself, yet it was this small victory that brought him true satisfaction. The waffle was a symbol; a new kind of mastery, one that didn't require majestic gestures but the simple joy of getting something exactly right.

Timothy Pulo is an aspiring author from Sydney, Australia. He enjoys writing in his spare time and is passionate about playing guitar, judo, and spending time with his family. With several of his short stories published, he hopes more people will one day read his creations.

TIME ENOUGH

RJ Meldrum

For my Arabian princess

In the depths of his rage and grief, he'd isolated himself from the world and from his family. Grief, he realized, was both a cliché and intensely individual. He'd never really thought about it before; why should he? He'd lost grandparents and other relatives, but it had always been natural and expected. They had lived their lives in full measure. It was just part of life. To lose her, only in her early fifties and in such a short time was devastating. The diagnosis had come from nowhere; she'd gone to the doctor complaining of pain and headaches. The doctor, unusually astute, had sent her for further tests. The diagnosis, and prognosis, didn't take long. The tumor itself was untreatable and, worse, the cancer had uncontrollably spread throughout her body. The doctors informed them she only had weeks left.

After a few days in hospital, she'd been sent home. She was placed on palliative care; primarily oxygen and morphine. They knew she wouldn't live long enough to get addicted.

He became her home nurse, a willing role. She had no appetite, but he cooked anything she fancied. She slurped a cold beer or two; something that was on her wish list. He smiled through tears, trying to stay positive for her, trying to hope for a miracle. But there was no miracle and she slipped away in the early hours of a cool September morning. He was suddenly, inexplicably alone.

The machinery of death took over. Nurses, doctors, undertakers. Lawyers, the bank. Coroners. Family hovered on the periphery, but were unable to help. Perhaps he had been unwilling to let them.

He had been her support; her family, her best friend and she had reciprocated. Living in a foreign land with no family and few friends, they had stuck together, not by need, but by choice. Now, he had to deal with the dual torments of loss and loneliness. Unable to deal with the platitudes of condolence, he'd locked himself away. It was instinct, like a wounded animal crawling away to hide itself. But it nearly broke him. The tempting darkness and peace had been so tantalizingly close, but he had fought back and had not gone easily into the night. Slowly, the darkness receded. He began to drink less and eat more. He regained the weight he'd lost. He began to see people again.

But he did not recover from the damage caused by the trauma of her loss. He slowly realized the damage was permanent. He'd changed, darkness and sadness was now always going to be part of him. He smiled and tried to appear normal, managing some limited socialization and, after a short break, working again at the university. Work did make him feel more normal, but outside work, when he was home, the pain continued.

During the long days and nights at home, stuck alone, thoughts crowded into his mind, fighting for prominence. The good times were forgotten, only the bad times remained. He would wander around their house for hours on end, raving to himself, trying to make sense of the chaos. Slowly it got better, but the memories and the guilt never fully left him. The darkness never left.

When he decided it was time, he started to clear her belongings, but he was constantly triggered. He realized he could barely look at her photographs. He knew he had to find a way to fully recover, otherwise the darkness would catch up with him and consume him.

He made a decision, one he was aware probably reflected an unhinged mind. He had to find a way to reach out to her, to see her again. To talk to her about the loss he felt, about the guilt and regret. He had to say sorry and tell her he loved her. No sane person would decide such a thing, but he was sure he was no longer entirely sane.

Frenetically, he set about his task. Part of him knew it was just his mind, finding a diversion. An activity to help heal his mental wounds, but he knew he had to do something, even if it was a fool's errand. His mind craved an activity, something that could help him heal. The task was to find a way to reach out to her. Various options suggested themselves immediately, even if he didn't believe in most. The process of whittling down the options took weeks, and, because he was a scientist, he recorded everything. He scribbled his progress in a hand-written journal.

Religion is no good...nothing but platitudes and nonsense about resurrection or heaven. I've talked to so many, but it's all about acceptance and/or meeting after the 'veil of tears'. Not good enough. I can't wait.

There is no supernatural, I am not far gone enough to believe in ghosts or the afterlife, comforting as the thought is. Psychics and mediums are all fake. I won't see her again unless I do something myself.

Science is the only answer. I cannot resurrect her; she is nothing more than ashes in a box, nor would I want to perform this act even if her body had been buried. I want her alive, not undead.

It is clear…I must warn her, and let her know what is just around the corner for her. For both of us. I must warn us both.

If she is warned, say, six months before, will it be enough? Perhaps a year.

I must find a way to travel back to her. Science is the only answer.

I must do the unthinkable and create a machine that can allow me to travel back, perhaps not physically, but in some way where I can communicate

I must try…

He realized he had something more than just a Band-Aid; perhaps he had accidentally identified a possible way to contact her. Perhaps it was the grief, the imbalance in his mind, but his instinct told him this new idea just might be worth pursuing. What harm could it do? At the very least, it would give him a distraction.

He wasn't acting completely irrationally. His profession was theoretical physics. He thought about the coincidence; the luck he had in terms of his expertise and profession, which gave him access not only to the understanding of the theories of time travel, but also to the machinery and equipment that could make it possible.

Everyone with even the slightest knowledge of the topic knew no person could travel back. It wasn't as simple as the books and movies depicted. Biological material could not be physically sent in either temporal direction, back or forward, at an accelerated rate. At the cellular level, time was unidirectional and fixed, but quantum time travel had been identified by multiple researchers as theoretically possible. His investigation of the problem was therefore focused on quantum flow, where infinitesimally small particles existed without the influence of time or physical factors such as gravity.

If he could send one of these particles back in time, if he could trace its progress, even direct it, then it was possible he could use the particle to both view the past and interact with it. The theory was sound, the practical aspect less so, and the notion of viewing and interacting with the past via a quantum particle was almost impossible to imagine, yet he decided to focus on the possibility.

He'd never imagined he would now be using this theory to try to reach out into the darkness of the past in order to save a life. Two lives, his mind reminded him, for he needed saving almost as much as she did.

He contacted the oncologist who had dealt with her case and pressed her about the disease progression. She was unhappy about making such a diagnosis but ventured if the diagnosis had been six months earlier, the tumor was probably small enough to be surgically removed. After that point, it had become too big to remove, as well as having metastasized and spread to other parts of his wife's body. That clinched it; if he could just talk to her before that point, there still could be time to cure her.

If he could simply travel back, then she could be warned.

He took a sabbatical from the university, promising to work on his research. Technically he wasn't lying, it was just his research was taking a different approach. He would be free from teaching and service, and able to concentrate on this new, pressing project.

The computers in the laboratory were powerful enough to run simulations of his idea. Most of their work in the lab was theoretical and the computers, all jerry-rigged from standard models, were powerful enough to simulate even the most outlandish ideas. The key was finding a method and a particle he could control. He was well aware he could not send a particle back in time, that was impossible, but it was absolutely conceivable he could force a particle to exist in the present and in the past simultaneously, and also control when in the past. The computer churned away for hours, running different models and theories. He was content to let the machine do the work for him and he thanked whatever scientist had developed the lab's super computing technology.

After approximately twenty hours, the computer burped out an answer. Hybrid laser-microwave schemes with oscillating magnetic field gradients should provide enough control over a quantum particle to be able to make it oscillate, and therefore exist, in both the present and past. Viewing and controlling it was theoretically possible, albeit it had never been tried, let alone successfully. This was where his particular brand of drive, despair, and genius came into play. He entered the various requirements into the computer then sat back and waited. After another fifteen hours of computer run-time, it burped out a number of theoretical mechanisms for controlling and viewing the particle. He read the notes and decided to rely on the computer's 'dumb' intelligence to have figured out the basic science. It was now up to him to introduce the human element, and translate the computer's concepts into a practical reality.

It took four weeks for him to develop the plan suggested by the computer into a reality. Luckily, no one challenged him about his lab time or equipment usage. It was summer and the place was inhabited mainly by postgraduate students or research assistants. The occasional visit he had from faculty colleagues created no concerns. Each faculty member worked on their own research programs, and these were rarely discussed with other faculty since the field was highly competitive. His pivot to new and sometimes borrowed equipment probably did raise some eyebrows, but only in the sense he was following a new, novel research area unknown to his colleagues. Their probing, unsubtle questions were easily rebuffed. Tenure did have some benefits.

He found by manipulating the fields around the particle he could control its oscillation and fluctuation. The activity of the particle, naturally chaotic, could be determined and predicted. It was hugely complicated, a bigger challenge than he had ever considered even trying. The knowledge and the certainty he could use this infinitesimally small particle to talk to his wife drove him onwards. The madness of grief was replaced with the madness of needing to find a way. Hours spent at home were replaced with hours spent in the laboratory. He was generating huge electricity bills as the computer and other equipment raced to find the perfect balance in the conflicting fields. Eyebrows raised by the university were quickly quelled when he used research funds to cover the cost. In the background, the university authorities were pleased, something big was clearly in the pipeline. A breakthrough. Breakthroughs meant publicity, and publicity meant more students interested in the program, more awards, and more prestige.

Eventually, his mind on overdrive and reaching new heights of intellectual power never imagined, he developed a way to manipulate the particle to be able to both exist in a defined time period and also have physical presence, allowing him to control its actions. His scribbled notes were written in his version of shorthand. His mind was moving so fast his left hand barely could keep up as it moved like lightning to record the methodology that would no doubt change humanity, if it was found to be a viable technique. But he had no thought of this, no vision or care for what the benefits and problems quantum time travel could bring to the world. He was entirely focused on her.

He set his first attempt for a Sunday morning. He reckoned the lab would be empty at that time and he was right. He consulted his notes and configured the machinery to generate the required fields. The 'viewer' was a computer monitor, but this was no high-definition picture. It was fuzzy and out of focus, as befitted an image from the quantum world. He fine-tuned the equipment, altering the subtle oscillation of the chosen particle. It was under his control, no longer free to move chaotically in the quantum world. He had reined it in and it followed his clumsy direction. His method was far more technical and scientific, but it amounted to 'telling' the particle to exist at a time a year before she died. He knew 'exist' was not the right word, much in the same way he was not 'telling' the particle, but at the quantum level, even human language broke down. There were simply no words he could use to describe the technique he was using to manipulate the particle into doing his bidding. It was related to the interaction between microwaves and magnetic fields, and the computer was doing much of the required computational heavy lifting, translating his clumsy commands into a subtle, beautiful quantum dance.

The picture on the monitor showed a grey world until he ordered the much-needed temporal resolution. To his unbelieving amazement, on the screen he could make out their study at home, the room she used as an office. The vision was fuzzy and black-and-white but it was there. The computer had adjusted the particle's oscillation to where it not only existed both then and now, but also its location could be viewed. Now for the true acid test. Could he make the quantum world interact with the physical world? The computer had told him it was possible. Quantum particles were physical, albeit infinitely tiny, but the huge potential energy they held inside themselves could be used, if the controlling fields were manipulated correctly. These tiny particles, after all, were the powerhouses of the universe. He typed in the requisite commands.

143

The computer whirred and clicked, controlling the opaque box sitting on the bench, surrounded by the paraphernalia of physics. The view on the monitor moved, settling in front of the computer keyboard she always used. He typed another command.

He watched awestruck as the keyboard keys started to depress without any human or mechanical intervention.

From future. U R ill. Go doctor

The picture faded then went to black. He was amazed he'd managed to focus the particle for the seconds it had taken to write even that short message. He prayed she would read the message, understand, and respond in a way that just might save her life. Perhaps he would, since he still existed in the past.

There was a sudden pop as the magnetic field generator gave up. Smoke started to rise from the machinery. The computer had commanded these bits of steel, glass, and plastic to drive themselves beyond every conceivable operational limit. The particle was free again to behave as nature intended, no longer constrained by a lifeform inconceivably larger than itself. It had done the job and he silently thanked it.

He stared down at the still smoking equipment. Overcome by stress and exhaustion, he slipped gently from the stool onto the floor. Darkness overtook him.

He woke, confused and unsure. It was dark outside and it took him a few moments to work out where he was. Then he remembered. The experiment had been successful, at least in transmitting the message to her.

He stood, groggily shaking the exhaustion he still felt out of his body. His watch told him it was a little after 8 p.m. He'd been out for the count for nearly five hours.

He flicked on the lab lights, amazed and also somehow disgusted he'd been left to lie on the cold floor for all that time, without a single security guard or student finding him. He made a mental note to discuss the matter with the laboratory safety officer, then smiled to himself at the incongruity of the thought.

He glanced at the bench and the ruined equipment. His notebook was full of scribbles, detailing the method, but there was only one question in his mind. Had it worked?

He was aware of time travel paradoxes; you couldn't go back and alter time because it was metaphysically impossible, but he hadn't traveled back. It had been his little friend who had done the work, and because the particle could exist in both worlds, there was no paradox.

There was only one way to prove if it had worked.

He headed to his car and unlocked it. It was Sunday evening so she would be at home if she had heeded the message; if it had been early enough for treatment. Was she there, curled up on the sofa, about to remonstrate with him about the lateness of the hour. Too many questions flooded his mind. There was only one way to find out.

He pulled into their driveway, seeing warm yellow lights shining from the lounge window. He couldn't remember if he'd left the lights on when he left that morning.

He made one last silent prayer before he exited the car and climbed the steps to the front door. Let her be there, he prayed to an unseen god. Let her be well.

R. J. Meldrum has had stories published by Midnight Street Press, Culture Cult Press, Horrified Press, Infernal Clock, Trembling with Fear, Black Hare Press, Darkhouse Books, Smoking Pen Press, Breaking Rules Press, Kevin J Kennedy, West Mesa Press and James Ward Kirk Fiction. He also has had stories in The Sirens Call e-zine, the Horror Zine and Drabblez Magazine. His novellas "The Plague " and "Placid Point " were published by Demain Press in 2019 and 2021. He is a contributor to the Pen of the Damned and an Affiliate Member of the Horror Writers Association.

THE NULL

By Gilbert M. Stack

By the time I regained consciousness, the ambulance was getting ready to leave without me. The EMTs and police continued to ignore me. It was one of a traveler's worst nightmares. My stabilizer had malfunctioned. If I didn't do something quickly, all of these well-meaning people would go about their business and leave me to bleed to death, or I'd get run over by the first car to be allowed to drive back down this road.

There was not even time to self-assess my injuries. I pushed myself to my knees, making no effort at all to stifle my urge to scream. My left arm was a blood-drenched mess of white-hot agony and my chest felt as if some jack-boot had tap-danced on top of it. It literally hurt to breathe, and my screams ignited a whole new kind of pain throughout my body.

The EMTs lifted the empty stretcher into the back of the ambulance. Clearly, at least one person had noticed me for a few moments since the emergency personnel arrived. The poor guy had probably tripped over me and terrified himself with the sudden appearance of my body.

Obviously, the experience hadn't been enough to keep me in his conscious mind. He had probably turned to the EMTs and screamed: "Get a stretcher over here. We've got an injured man by the wrecked car."

The EMT grabbed the stretcher, but looking away had been enough to push my presence out of the first man's mind. Without the stabilizer, I was null in this time - just far enough out of sync with reality that these twenty-first-century Americans couldn't remain aware of my existence.

With an effort of will born of abject terror, I clambered to my feet. Tears streamed freely down my face and my vision briefly blackened. I stumbled forward, keeping my balance by pushing off a policeman. He actually saw me for an instant, but then reality intervened, and I was gone from his mind again.

It was only at the ambulance doors that someone truly recognized my presence. The doors were already closing when I lunged between them and they caught me in the pinch. My scream was harsh enough to wake the dead. That, and my physical obstruction of the doors, was finally enough to bridge the gap between my physical existence and these peoples' reality.

It couldn't have hurt that one of the EMTs accidentally put his hand on me as well.

"Oh my God," said the man who'd touched me, letting go of the door and stepping back in surprise.

I reached out with my good right hand and took hold of him again. If I didn't, I was afraid that the lack of contact might let this time frame re-erase me from his senses.

"Larry," he croaked, "where did this guy come from?"

That comment was enough to spread our bubble of shared reality to the other EMTs. His eyes widened with shock. I'm certain it would have all been very comical if I just hadn't hurt so much.

"Please, help me," I begged.

The EMTs took hold of me and began to help me to the ground.

I couldn't let them do that. If they forgot me again, I'd be right back where I started, helpless victim to the first car to pass this way.

"Stretcher," I pleaded, fighting to remain standing on the street between them. Despite the unbearable pain in my chest, I just wasn't ready to lie down and die.

The first EMT took firmer hold of me and I collapsed against his body. "Larry, get the stretcher!" he commanded.

Larry hesitated. He may have been blinking with confusion. I could not see him through my pain so I don't know. What I do know is that the stretcher banged down onto the asphalt behind me and the first man helped me onto it.

Even through the pain, I felt relief. I hadn't gotten into the hospital yet, but it was highly unlikely now that I would be left behind on the pavement. The stretcher was a strong artifact of the EMTs reality. I didn't think that they would drive away and leave it behind.

The first man began to examine me, his professional routine aiding me in more ways than the obvious one. His actions were guided by habit and only informed by thought. His conscious mind had far less to do with his preliminary examination than it did with other critical activities such as finding my injured body in the first place.

I screamed heartily, almost happily, as he poked and prodded me, despite what this did to the pain in my chest. The more senses I could engage in this man, the less likely he was to suddenly forget my existence and drive away.

"My name is Carlos Sanchez, by the way. I'm a graduate student at Fordham University in the new Applied Social Sciences Department. And as you might have guessed, I don't belong back here in the early twenty-first century.

"I was born one hundred twenty-eight years from now and twenty-five years after that I chose to write a PhD dissertation on "The Evolution of Social Protest to the War in Iraq in Northern New Jersey, 2002-2007." It's a topic of limited interest in my time, but so are most dissertations. To jazz it up for the job market, I decided to include a couple of chapters analyzing oral histories with a nice fat appendix of transcripts at the back of my thesis. But, as you might have guessed, there aren't any people from the first decade of the twenty-first century remaining around one hundred fifty-three years later—so I had to travel to them.

"Naturally, it wasn't actually that easy. First, I had to get my advisor's approval, then she had to get the approval of the department chair. After that, we had to get Institutional Research's backing as the project involved historical living subjects.

Then I had to take a four-week seminar exploring ethical issues involved in interactive time travel, followed by another four-week course in the mechanics of the process. That last course was a waste of time. Everyone knows that the first time machine was only expected to open a window into the past. When Southerland got too close and fell through, it changed everything, even though no one in late nineteenth century Philadelphia noticed her sprawling on the ground beside them. Eventually, scientists figured out that a traveler from our time could force a person from the past to recognize his existence, but no matter what he did he could not form a lingering impression in any of the subjects' memories.

The physicists eventually decided that the problem was one of temporal resonance. People were tied to the time stream at the time they were born in and the consciousness of people and the majority of animals from earlier time streams could not process the higher resonance of later time periods. Translation: we could see them, but they could not see us.

If you stop to think about it, this problem can be awfully convenient in a lot of situations. We have 3D recordings now of just about every conversation connected to the Constitutional Convention in 1789. Even the strictest originalists were shocked to learn what some of our Founding Fathers really wanted.

It has also proved very useful for art collectors and other criminally minded individuals as the growing number of scandals in this area continue to demonstrate.

But the one thing time travel did not permit was meaningful interaction. No one could hold a true conversation, conduct an interview, make a friend, or anything else of this nature, until the development of the temporal stabilizer.

The EMT finished recording my vital signs while his partner bound the gash in my arm and immobilized it with a splint. Both of these activities made me happy. The first actually recorded my destabilized existence in this time frame—an exceedingly rare event worthy of a paper or two in itself. The second significantly lessened my ability to further hurt or damage myself. Things were really looking up before they slid me into the back of the ambulance and didn't follow me inside.

I don't really know what happened. At the time, I didn't know what was supposed to happen. I certainly thought that one of the EMTs would ride in the back to the hospital with me, but they didn't. Something distracted my rescuers as they slid me into the back of their vehicle and that was all it took for reality to reassert itself and wipe me out of their memories.

The men casually waved to their friends and then seated themselves in the front cab. They were in no hurry at all as they made their way back to the hospital waiting for their next call.

Panic nearly overwhelmed me. I was strapped securely to a stretcher with a tremendous pain in my chest and a clearly broken arm. There was no way that I could free myself. I was going to die here in the back of an ambulance because a chance accident had broken my stabilizer.

I shouted and screamed to no avail. I tried to shake my stretcher but had to stop due to the pain in my chest. My breath came in increasingly shallow and ragged gasps. My vision blurred.

Suddenly, the ambulance turned on its lights and siren and swung into a steep U-turn. Its speed increased dramatically as it hurried toward a new emergency.

149

I struggled to maintain a hold on my panicked senses, picturing the EMTs callously tossing me off the stretcher to make room for their new patient. I knew that was unfair. None of this was their fault. But I wasn't feeling particularly generous toward the men who had forgotten my existence.

The ambulance screeched to a halt on a suburban street in Lodi and I could hear the EMTs open and close their doors to the vehicle. A few moments later the rear of the ambulance opened and the stretcher and I were sliding back into daylight.

My eyes actually met the driver's.

"Jesus Christ!" he said.

As it had the first time, it took the other EMT a moment to re-recognize my existence. Then he snatched up the clipboard with my vital signs and started cursing under his breath.

"I can't believe we forgot him!" the first man said. "How on earth did we forget about him?"

"We didn't even radio it in," his partner whispered.

I found a new fear to add to my others. They had made a potentially career-ending error. This was an intensely litigious era. The temptation to cover up their apparent incompetence must be overwhelming, but I was being unfair to them. I don't know what thoughts ultimately passed through their heads, but they did not dump me off my stretcher and pretend I didn't exist.

Instead, they pushed me back into the vehicle and began to call for a second ambulance.

The second EMT looked nauseous as he rode with me to the hospital. Every time he glanced out the back window, his body would relax, but then the ambulance would bounce across a pothole and he'd look down again and his eyes would widen like he was seeing a spirit from beyond the grave.

Still, his presence was enough to get me into the hospital. The driver had forgotten me again by the time we arrived, but when he opened the rear doors for his friend a kaleidoscope of memories came flashing back to him.

They lifted my stretcher to the ground and rolled me into the Emergency Room. The staff there was ready for me—having no problem at all until I was physically in their presence. Then the different temporal continuities tended to push their senses away.

Until then I was just some notes on a clipboard and a bizarre story about two EMTs who forgot about their patient. Now I was a null swirling against their senses actively interfering with their ability to think about and interact with me.

The floor nurse in the emergency room hurried over to us when she saw the EMTs. She had a smile on her face that seemed inappropriate to me considering my circumstances. "We've been waiting for you guys," she announced. "Where's the patient? Don't tell me you've lost him again."

Neither EMT found her joke funny. The first pointed down at my face and the nurse's eyes dropped, following his finger until she suddenly met my gaze.

She jumped backward in shock and surprise. "Oh my God, I didn't see him."

"I know,' the EMT said. "Spooky, isn't it? There's something really strange about this guy..."

His voice trailed off without completing the thought. I actually understood his problem, but I was getting mighty impatient with my circumstances nonetheless.

"Pain, please," I reminded them.

The nurse jumped again at the sound of my voice, but this time she was moving into action. She grabbed the stretcher and began rolling me deeper into the ER. "I'll take him from here," she told the EMTs, then shifted her attention back to me. "What's your name?"

"Carlos," I croaked, relieved that she had not lost me again during that brief instant of distraction. I didn't know how I was going to actually get help here when no one could remember my presence from one moment to the next.

"Well, Carlos," the nurse promised, "I'm going to take care of you now."

She slid me into berth twenty-two. I thought thirteen would have been more appropriate.

Things got worse and more complicated.

The nurse started my chart, checked my vital signs, and hooked an IV to my right arm. She told me they would make an appointment for an x-ray and that a doctor would stop by to check on me.

She walked away holding my chart, but never made the promised call. Another patient demanded her attention and my chart got laid

151

awkwardly on a desktop—as if she couldn't quite remember where it was supposed to go.

I watched the clipboard sit on that desk for twenty minutes, uncertain what, if anything, I could do about it. The pain in my arm had dulled to an endurable throb, but the agony in my chest increased with each shallow breath. The thought of pulling myself out of this bed and over to the nurse's desk was nearly unbearable.

The nurse appeared to jot a few notes on another patient, noticed the clipboard, and picked it up to glance at what she had written. Her eyes widened as she realized what she had done. I assumed she could remember the story about how the EMTs had lost me, but I was not certain of it. To my knowledge, no studies had been done on my precise situation, so it was difficult to predict what these twenty-first-century people would do and how they would react.

The nurse sat back down and called x-ray, scheduled my appointment, then slid my chart into its proper place next to a lot of other patients' records.

Relieved that progress was being made, I laid my head back on the pillow and tried to make my breathing even shallower than it already was.

I looked up again an hour later. I don't think I'd fallen asleep, but I wasn't totally conscious either. The floor nurse was arguing with someone on the phone. "What do you mean you can't find him? I'm looking at the patient's chart. He's in berth twenty-two. It's right behind me."

She turned in her seat to face me and almost dropped the phone.

"Alright then, I'll send someone back over to get him," a voice carried through the speaker.

The nurse wasn't listening. She hurriedly dropped the phone into its cradle and rushed over to my berth. Her eyes took in the stretcher and the IV, but she really had to focus her concentration before she could see the rest of me.

Her right hand tentatively touched my knee and then jerked back as if the contact shocked and burned her.

She shook her head emphatically back and forth as if trying to jiggle her brain inside her skull. "What's wrong with you?" she asked. "For a moment there I could swear I could see right through you. And before that…"

Her voice trailed off, but she kept looking at me. A patient a few berths down from me began calling out, "Nurse!"

She ignored him, still staring at me like I would disappear if she looked away.

Her suspicion was correct. If she looked away, I likely would be gone.

The transporter arrived from x-ray looking both put upon and defensive, totally ready for an argument. The nurse had left me long before he arrived so I suspected he would return again to x-ray empty handed.

My fears were well founded. He took one look at berth twenty-two and turned around complaining loudly. "I thought you said the patient would be here this time! Well, where is he?"

Of course, no one paid any immediate attention to him. Emergency rooms are busy places. I don't know where the floor nurse had gotten to; she had thirty patients under her care. Then there were the doctors. To the best of my knowledge, none of them had looked at me yet, which was puzzling considering that someone had approved my x-rays.

The transporter groaned and complained some more before sorting through the racks to find the clipboard with my number on it. A bright orange post-it note was stuck to the front and he read it carefully before beginning to complain again. "Is this some type of joke?"

He looked around, but no one was laughing at him. He read the note again before tentatively making his way over to my bed. He was clearly nervous, not with fear but with the certainty that someone was pranking him. He leaned down over the bed as if searching for something.

"Hello," I greeted him.

The transporter leapt backward into the curtain which separated my berth from the next one.

Despite the pain, I lifted my head off the pillow and tried to keep eye contact with him.

"Of all the freaking things," he muttered.

"Are you here to take me to x-ray?" I asked him.

"I—"

The transporter stopped talking and crossed himself. "Yes," he agreed.

"You're going to have to stay with me while they take the picture," I told him. "Otherwise, I may never get back here. For some reason, the hospital keeps losing me."

"I, uh, yeah," the transporter mumbled, "right."

He tossed the clipboard on the bed. For the first time I could read the Post-it note: Look carefully at bed to find patient.

By the time the transporter finished pushing me to x-ray, his face had grown pale with unease. He'd spent the short journey experimenting with looking at me, half turning his face away and then looking back down at me again. He never said what he saw, but it clearly unnerved him. His eyes couldn't quite keep me in focus. His brain didn't want to grapple with my reality. But for all of that, he didn't abandon me when we reached our destination. Instead, he stayed by my side and actually helped to draw attention to me.

"Hey, Molly," he called to the x-ray technician. His eyes barely flickered from my face as he spoke. "Did you hear the story about the two EMTs who forgot they put a patient in the back of their ambulance?"

"Crazy story," Molly agreed, walking over next to him without appearing to notice me. "Did they really drive to a second site to pick up another patient?"

"Yeah," my transporter confirmed, his eyes never leaving my face. "They couldn't explain it. Said they didn't understand what happened."

"It's weird," Molly said. "I hope it doesn't cost them their jobs."

"It really shouldn't," my transporter said.

"I don't know, forgetting about a patient..."

"But there's something really strange about this guy," the transporter said as if I wasn't lying right in front of him. "If you don't keep your eyes right on him, he just sort of fades away."

"Who? The patient?" Molly asked, clearly not understanding what her friend was trying to say. "Have you met him?"

"He's lying on the stretcher right beside you," the transporter told her.

Molly jerked as if struck by an electric shock as she noticed my existence for the first time. "Oh, I, I am so sorry," she apologized. "I don't know how I didn't notice you there."

"It's okay," I said, "it's happening a lot today."

"It's like he's a freaking ghost," the transporter mumbled with what, even in my weakened condition, seemed an unnecessary loss of professionalism.

Molly's eyes snapped up disapprovingly, but no words escaped her mouth as she suddenly struggled to remember what they were talking about.

The transporter lost me then also, eyes coming around as he prepared to defend himself against Molly's coming criticism.

Instead, the two people stood staring at each other in confusion.

I had to act quickly or risk losing them forever. My right hand grabbed at Molly's arm, not quite getting hold of her but pushing at her sleeve.

Molly's eyes darted back toward me and widened again. Evidently, her strange reaction was enough to remind the transporter of the peculiar phenomenon he had been considering for the past ten minutes. I think he actually succeeded in pulling me into his mind before his eyes settled back upon me.

"That is unbelievable," Molly whispered. Cautiously, she extended her right hand and touched my shoulder. "You're really here."

"Please help me," I begged. The transporter's ability to overcome our difference in resonance was giving me new hope. If I could just force enough people to recognize my existence... If I could just find enough ways to document myself within this time stream...

It was a slim hope, but I held tight to it as my single most likely chance of survival. "Please, I need an x-ray to show them what's wrong with my chest."

Molly seemed to gather up the tattered shreds of her professionalism. "Help me get him into the chamber," she told the transporter, "Then you stay with him so we don't lose him while I take the picture."

As they pushed me into the x-ray room, the transporter snatched a pad off a desk and began scribbling.

"What's it show?" I asked.

155

Molly was working very hard at remembering I was present. Like the transporter, she was writing notes to herself, and while I couldn't actually read any of them, I was assuming that they said things like: Remember, the patient is lying on that stretcher.

In the short term, I was undoubtedly doing myself an important service. In the long term, well I had signed lots of papers promising to in no way compromise the secret that visitors from the future were here in the present.

There are all kinds of rules. For example, we aren't allowed to make bank accounts and then collect the accrued interest one hundred years later. We also aren't allowed to gamble on lotteries or sports events. And we certainly aren't allowed to tell anyone or try to prove to anyone that we aren't supposed to be in the time we are visiting. Big fines and long prison terms awaited rule breakers, but honestly, right then, sitting healthy in a future prison cell seemed like a pretty good deal.

"Please," I repeated, "it's genuinely possible that the hospital will lose me again when you send me back to the Emergency Room. I just want to know why I'm hurting so badly."

"We're not going to lose you again," the transporter said confidently. His discomfort at my condition appeared to have vanished, replaced by excitement at the peculiar challenge I represented.

"Please," I said for the third time.

Molly conceded. "I see two separate problems," she told me. "The first is very straightforward. You've got two cracked ribs. As for the second thing—I don't know what it is—but it looks like you've got some sort of device in your chest pressed up beneath your rib cage. I've never seen anything like it."

A cold breath of fear penetrated my pain. She was describing my stabilizer. It was surgically implanted in my chest to make certain I couldn't lose it. It was mostly composed of synthetics and was supposed to be invisible to X-rays and metal detectors. I hadn't even considered the possibility that it could be broken so badly that these machines could show it was there.

"I'll bet that has to come out," Molly said. "It looks to me like it's pricking your heart. That could be really dangerous."

She transferred her attention from the X-ray to me with only a little difficulty. It appeared that practice increased her ability to see

156

through the disturbance of the resonance. It probably didn't hurt that she'd been reading my x-ray and speaking to me before she tried to look at me again.

"Do you have any idea what this thing could be?" she asked me.

I lied. "I have no idea. I mean, I've never even had surgery since my appendix was taken out as a kid."

She shook her head. "We'll just have to see what the doctors say—if we can get them to look at you."

As great as my pain continued to be, as frightened as I was of dying, I was no longer certain that a doctor successfully examining me was such a good idea. Molly was talking about removing my stabilizer. Even broken they were going to be able to study it. I might have just violated the biggest rule in the book. I might have just substantially altered history.

Unfortunately, matters had gotten well beyond me.

"I think I have the doctors covered," the transporter said.

Unfortunately, he did.

The idea was remarkably simple and from his perspective, it worked beautifully. The transporter simply stopped every hospital staff member he came across and asked: "Do you want to see something really cool?"

Often the staff members were walking in pairs. This greatly enhanced their chances of remembering the encounter. They watched each other's reactions and followed the shock and puzzlement back to the source—me.

A couple of staff members even followed us back to the ER where the transporter began loudly calling all of the doctors over. Somehow, he seemed to break the laws of temporal physics. I went from being a complete non-entity, a temporal null out of resonance with the present, to a super-nova medical sensation.

As word of the strange effect that surrounded me circulated, more and more doctors, nurses, technicians, and staff found an excuse to drop by the ER and experience the phenomenon for themselves. They read over my growing file, consulted my x-rays, and discussed just how and if they should go inside me to take the strange object out.

Naturally, the growing interest terrified me. It only remained now for a news team with cameras rolling to invade the ER and start

157

filming the medical (temporal) oddity. If I ever succeeded in getting back to my own time, I was sunk. It was prison for sure.

It wasn't all a hundred percent bad, however. All of this attention did get me the help I so desperately needed. I got a morphine drip for my arm that didn't really take my pain away but dulled it quite a lot. My broken arm was properly set and re-splinted. And finally, I was comfortable enough and secure enough that I was able to drift off to sleep.

A hand on my good shoulder quietly wakened me. "Carlos," a voice said. "Can you hear me?"

I was groggy from sleep and didn't immediately remember where I was or what had happened.

"You've had quite an adventure," the voice said. "Can you tell me what happened?"

My thoughts and vision cleared and I suddenly recognized the man behind the voice. He was the protocol officer for the portal home.

I tried to sit up but he gently held me in place. It wasn't hard. I was weak as a kitten with my injuries and the painkillers inside me.

"Easy," he said. "You're not in trouble. We're here to get you home to some proper care."

I laid back against my pillow.

"Now can you tell me what happened?"

"I got hit by a car," I mumbled.

He grinned. "We kind of figured that out for ourselves. I mean here. What happened here? How in the world did you get all of these people to help you with your stabilizer broken? Do you realize they're now talking about you in every hospital in northern New Jersey and who knows where else? It's how we found you."

"It was the transporter who did it," I began to explain.

The officer reconsidered his request. "I guess we better hear about it later when you can make sense. With stabilizers off, we're going to carry you out of this building, but expect a full debriefing when you're recovering at home."

Gilbert M. Stack has been creating stories almost since he began speaking and publishing fiction and non-fiction since 2006. A professional historian, Gilbert delights in bringing the past to life in his fiction, depicting characters who are both true to their time and empathetic with modern sensibilities. His work has appeared in more than a dozen issues of Alfred Hitchcock's Mystery Magazine and is available online. His most popular series include Legionnaire, Musket Men, Winterhaven, and Preternatural, all available on Amazon. He lives in New Jersey with his wife, Michelle, and their son, Michael. You can find out more about Gilbert at www.gilbertstack.com.

WHAT COULD HAVE BEEN

By Caroline Ashley

There was a patch of air where the light refracted and danced like fireflies. The movement drew Joe McMillan forward like a moth, unable to look away. He pulled out his phone to record a video, but his camera couldn't capture the true essence of the flickering movement.

Joe's stomach lurched like he was peering over a cliff edge. He stood in the Meadows, a large park just south of Edinburgh's city centre. This was always his route home, a familiar comfort after a long day, and somehow it felt tainted. He feared the beauty of the light disguised a poison underneath.

To his right, uniformed men in black approached the flickering anomaly, chests covered in armoured vests and weapons holstered at their hips, their authority as certain as the rising of the sun.

They herded him away and constructed a transparent box around the space, carefully ensuring not to step too close. Their makeshift prison concealed the subtle distortion, though the surface flickered with reflected movement. Next came a metal shipping container, the walls rising to enclose the space entirely. Once their task was complete, the men stood sentry around the building's walls, humans forming the final layer of defense. Joe's discovery was encased like an industrial nesting doll.

A few others had gathered nearby, watching the construction with their phones raised.

"Hey, what's going on here?" one man asked.

A woman pointed her camera at a guard's face. "We have a right to know what you're hiding in there."

"Do you work for O'Neil?" came another voice.

Everyone knew Arthur O'Neil. He sat in news interviews wearing his satin three-piece suits, hair slicked back and glistening like slug trails in the sun. When he spoke, he would spray spittle at the camera lens as he paced the room, arms attempting to encapsulate the breadth of his ire at the state of the world. Arthur O'Neil acted like he was certain that he knew best. He treated his audience as if they were misbehaving toddlers who he had to force into line.

No one knew where he came from. One day he appeared, a self-made millionaire, and predicted all the details of Chernobyl and the Challenger explosion right before they happened. It was too late to prevent them, but Joe was certain that had been his intention. He wanted to prove himself, to ensure people believed the importance of his words. He wanted to be the pied piper, leading willing rats out of the village and lauded him for his achievements.

The government tried to lock him away, and interrogate him, but he had surrounded himself with an army of lawyers. Now he was one of the most powerful people in the world.

Joe's watch vibrated, reminding him of a dinner date with his wife, Ashley. She always had plenty to say about O'Neil.

He could still picture the sparkle of light drifting through the air, shining like a gas cloud deep in the vacuum of space. Shaking his head, he cast the image from his mind and pushed past the crowd that was forming around him.

The morning sun stretched its fingers across Joe's wooden floor. Photographs of Ashley and his adventures across Europe lined Joe's path to the kitchen.

He had never planned to travel – his father had an inherited career in the police all lined up for him. But he and Ashley turned eighteen just as the government introduced the universal wage and they thought, Why not?

Two decades ago, he had stood on a balcony at Neuschwanstein Castle in Bavaria, surrounded by whispering trees and snow-peaked mountains, and realized that his father's footsteps were impressions in powdered snow, easily swept away.

As Joe opened the fridge to search for eggs, he hummed a tune. Ashley stopped in the doorway, tying the cord of her dressing gown. "What is that?"

"What's what?" Joe asked.

"That song."

He paused to think, thumb tapping on the fridge door. "Must have heard it on the radio."

"I heard someone at work sing it too, but they didn't know the name either."

Echoes, some people called them. Fragments of songs and snippets of conversations, haunting the ether and drifting into people's consciousness. Some believed they were voices from a different timeline, one without O'Neil. Some said it was just déjà vu, and the experience had been twisted into more than it was by the social media echo chamber.

Ashley said she had never felt one. In Vienna, she had perched on the edge of a bar stool and declared herself free of the shackles of fate. "I don't need any signs from the universe that I'm following some predetermined path."

She chugged back the dregs of her beer and pulled him up to dance. Her cheeks were rose pink and she moved like a bird launching into flight, ready to follow the call of the wind.

I miss those days.

"Judith Alexander is doing a talk tonight at the University," Ashley said. "Do you want to come with me?"

"Judy Alexander? Is it not she who sings the song?"

Years ago, he watched the X Factor with Ashley and had been sure afterward that a woman from Edinburgh was the winner, even though no one from Edinburgh competed. A lot of people online had thought the same. Was Judy Alexander her name?

"No, she's a physicist. The one I told you about with all the theories about O'Neil."

Joe held back a sigh. He focused his attention on frying eggs. "Why does it matter so much?"

She raised her hands in the air, tension rising through her limbs. "How he got here... how he knows what he does... it changes our understanding of the universe."

Joe shrugged. In this age of prosperity, a contented life was as easy to achieve as opening the fridge for a beer.

Instead of the police, he worked in social care, a role he had never considered until he broke free of his father's shadow. Ashley, on the other hand, had flitted from one job to the next, an anxious hummingbird trying to source enough nectar to sustain herself.

He had wanted to build a family with her but she had never felt ready and had treated the creation of a child like consigning a convict to death row.

A picture above her head in their kitchen showed her gleaming ivory teeth, eyes shining like fireflies, as she held a shot of milky ouzo to the camera. She didn't care about the universe back then; was content with the experiences life offered her. If only he could catch that feeling and hold it captive for Ashley so that she wouldn't have to keep searching for it.

He turned back to the eggs, gaze fixed on the bubbling egg whites. "Yeah, we can go if you want."

###

Joe and Ashley crossed the Meadows to reach the University. Barriers had been erected around the new structure, spotlights marking the boundary. A crowd of people surveyed the building, and they were largely ignored by the stoic guardsmen.

Joe pulled out his phone to check the local news as he walked – the articles he found called it a research station, conducting scans of the soil.

Social media was certain this was a lie.

Some people had seen the anomaly and believed O'Neil had paid the government to hide a time portal, restricting access to the means by which he had created this world.

"Did you see he's releasing his memoir in a couple of weeks?" Ashley asked.

"Who?"

"O'Neil." She rolled her eyes at his question – there was no one else whose memoir would interest her.

Ashley had increasingly struggled with O'Neil's existence. When she allowed herself a moment of contemplation, she often said that it felt as if the ground vanished beneath her, leaving her falling, swimming, reaching outward for a life vest that never came. Her mind was an unanchored ship and every second of lapsed attention sent her drifting further out into the midnight depths.

X O'Neil's most recent major prediction had been uploaded to all of his social media accounts four years ago. He sat, alone, hands clenched together to obscure the trembling of his limbs. Time had drawn lines across his face, and bent his body forward under its weight. His brown eyes stared straight into the camera, a circle of white LEDs reflected across his irises.

He predicted a pandemic and he shared the tools needed to develop a vaccine.

Ashley had watched the man's address to the nation with a scowl of distaste. O'Neil sought to shape the world in the image that he had chosen, a puppet master directing his creations. Ashley railed against his control and refused to inject herself with any vaccine

163

inspired by his words – not that it mattered when the majority of the population followed him like loyal rats.

The latest publications suggested that the nCov-19 virus wasn't nearly as deadly as O'Neil said it would be. Ashley had seen that as vindication of her actions; Joe was just grateful there was nothing to worry about.

Joe reached for her hand, entwining his fingers with hers. "You going to read it?"

Ashley lifted a shoulder in feigned indifference. "Maybe."

Joe lowered his head against hers, eyes drifting to the metal cage once more, his stomach twisting with unease.

Judith Alexander stood at a wooden lectern, her colleague Ben Anderson at her side. The woman was a vision of sharp edges, golden hair brushed tightly against her scalp as if she had wanted to tear it from her skull. Her companion was a hunched shadow, eyes locked on his tablet as she spoke.

Joe could swear he knew both of them as he watched from the rear of the lecture theatre.

Judith seemed as broken as Ashley sometimes did. A vase fractured and pieced together but never quite the same again. She presented her theories with the anger of a scorned lover.

Fifteen minutes proclaiming that the rules of physics as humans knew them were proof against any earth-based time travel. Einstein-Rosen bridges would tear the earth apart with the strength of their gravitational pull. Quantum tunneling predicted the possibility of a particle moving in time, but the world would be waiting until the end of the universe for probability to allow for the movement of a human being.

And then, the juxtaposition of the scientific facts with her own certainty that time travel was the only explanation for Arthur O'Neil's existence. She drew a picture of a line, had the line double back to halfway along, and then sent it off on a sideways angle. But what if Arthur wasn't the only traveler? She doubled back on the branch and sent another line on its own path through space. Then again, then again. Her hand shook as she pressed the lid back on her pen and turned to face the audience.

"The echoes are proof. You find yourself in the same time, the same place, as another version of yourself and you hear someone speak who isn't there. You find yourself thinking something that doesn't make sense. You hear a song that no one knows."

Ashley flinched at the woman's words. The older she got, the more it seemed to bother her. Joe had never understood why it was important – the echoes were just an irritation, like interference on a radio. What difference did it make?

They were slow to leave, one of the last in the queue from the lecture theatre. Judith was leaving the building at the same time they were. Her eyes were fixed on the ground, shoulders hunched forward.

Ashley waved to get her attention. "Dr Alexander? Dr Alexander?"

She reached out to tap Judith's arm when it looked like the woman wasn't planning to stop. Judith jumped back as if she had been bitten by a snake. "Can I help you?"

Ashley lifted her hand in apology. "I'm sorry. I just wanted to thank you for the presentation."

Judith looked between Joe and Ashley. "That's okay. Do you struggle with the echoes too?"

"I've never heard any echoes," Ashley said.

"Oh. I..."

"Joe thought you were a singer," Ashley added.

Judith nodded, a sad smile lifting her lips. "Maybe I am, somewhere on another branch."

"Do you really think there might be other time travelers like O'Neil?"

"His appearance and the information he's shared wouldn't suggest an astronaut," Judith said. "More likely a UK-based theoretician. So, if he had access to some means of time travel, more than likely others did... or will... too."

Joe considered the distortion hidden from view in the Meadows. "What would it look like if it wasn't a machine?"

Judith turned to look in the direction of the newly constructed building. "I don't know. The physics we know would say a natural phenomenon on Earth is impossible. But we used to think the earth was flat once too."

Ashley plucked at a stray thread on the sleeve of her jumper. "Just the existence of time travelers is... terrifying. What does it mean for our lives if it's all so easily changed?"

"It means life as we know it is fragile… but we knew that before O'Neil came along."

Joe pulled at Ashley's waist. "Come on, let's leave her to get home."

"None of what I say really matters, you know," Judith said. "You can love it or hate it, but we live in O'Neil's timeline regardless."

Ashley nodded, though her features tightened and she clenched her jaw. Joe shook his head, wishing Ashley could just move on and live her life. He reached for her hand but she thrust hers deep into her pockets and walked away.

For years, on certain streets, Joe would walk much slower than his usual pace. He would slip into a steady gait, his gaze shifting to watch his surroundings. He would find himself reaching to his shoulder for a radio that didn't exist, or turning his head to speak to a person who wasn't there. Sometimes, he could half-hear a distant voice calling, "Sierra four five, Sierra four five, this is control, over."

He didn't talk to Ashley about those moments – they would only inflame her paranoia about the world O'Neil took from them.

Maybe somewhere nCov-19 killed people. Maybe somewhere he was a police officer and Judy Alexander was a pop star. Here and now was the only time Joe cared about.

In the Meadows, the crowd now encircled the barriers. An air of agitation surrounded them, like a tiger pacing a cage, waiting for an opportunity to breach the boundary. Some people carried placards, condemning government secrets, and asserting their right to public information. A smaller crowd wore yellow Amnesty International t-shirts and decried the government's laws against refugees.

O'Neil had called it a collateral cost of the West's prosperity. He said you had to put the resources into the developing world, not just let the developing world move in next door. He didn't write the policies, but he always had a say.

The small building had become an altar for people like Ashley to worship at. I wonder what she'll write on her placard when she joins them?

Joe continued his walk to work, leaving them to their ire.

His office was in the city centre, not far from the train station. In the distance, Edinburgh Castle perched atop a grass-coated cliff, the unchanging sentinel of Joe's city.

When he was younger, the streets he walked would have been choked with cars and buses, the faint smell of exhaust and oil drifting through the air. The daily 9-5 was a relic of the pre-tech age, with many people like Ashley working from the convenience of their home devices.

Commuting traffic hadn't stopped, but the vehicles formed a trickle rather than a wave and were silent as a whisper, all powered by electric fuel cells. The scent of pollen tickled his nose and the rustle of nearby trees was the rhythmic pulse of Princes Street Gardens.

He climbed the stairs to his office, where his colleague, Martha, sat scrolling through her emails. Martha was two decades older than him, of the generation who were old enough to remember a world before O'Neil. He poured them both a coffee and propped himself against the desk, voicing his frustration about the previous night's lecture.

"Ben Anderson?" Martha asked. "Was he not the one whose family all won the lottery?"

"Did they?"

Martha rubbed at her temple and her features creased in concentration. "I don't know. Maybe I'm muddling him with someone else."

"Do you think it's happening more often? People misremembering things?"

"Clients I work with talk a lot about regret. Missed opportunities. Events they couldn't control." Her lips formed a wistful smile as she raised her coffee. "But they always did."

"He says he's going to explain everything in the memoir that's coming out soon."

Martha shook her head. "He should have told us before. The government lets him get away with murder and no one even knows where he came from."

"Does it matter?" Joe asked. "He's made our lives better."

"Better than my Mam had it, yeah, better than we could have it? Who knows."

Martha had always been vocal in her distaste for the universal wage. Joe was certain it had changed his life, but Martha believed that people needed to earn what they were given. She pointed out youngsters in their twenties, out partying or joining bands or posting on social media, safe in the knowledge that the government would pay them no matter how little they contributed. She resented that her earnings were filtered down through tax to strangers instead of to her family. On her most vitriolic of days, she told Joe, that he couldn't understand, since he had no children of his own.

Joe offered to take their cups and clean them. He stood in the kitchenette, looking out over the city street. Is police officer McMillan happy with his life? Am I?

The crowd was spreading across the Meadows, hundreds of people, all uniting together in protest. The story of a research base persisted, but the crowd remained adamant that they would not be deceived. They pushed at the barriers, a river pressing against a dam, forcing the guards to increase their presence.

The European Union had been built on a platform of transparency. People weren't used to their leaders keeping information from the public sphere. They railed against it, the notion of a patriarchal government, hiding truths from its children, a bitter tonic that they sought to expel.

"He just wants to keep his time portal from us," one woman said. "He made his billions, took over the government, and now he wants to stop us doing the same."

"You don't know it's a time portal," Joe countered.

"Aye? What else would it be that they need to hide it?"

In the back of his mind, he heard a voice, clear as a bell despite the clamouring crowd. "Your job is to let the researchers do their job, Sergeant. Professor O'Neil will give you a list of university employees with clearance to enter."

The protesters near the front were growing agitated, rattling the barriers and piercing the sky with their placards. The disgruntled complaints were growing more urgent. Like a wave sweeping up over a rock, it was only a matter of time before the building was engulfed.

"We have just as much right to it as he does!"

"Who does the wanker think he is, stopping us from getting to it?"

Did he see Judith and Ben walking into the makeshift building, their backs turned, lifting ID cards to a police officer? Joe rubbed at his forehead, feeling pressure building at his temples. There were no police here and the guards weren't letting anyone venture through the door.

His stomach twisted like it had when he first saw the distortion. He pushed against the flow of the crowd, a salmon rising through a ladder, fighting the force of gravity itself. He headed for the security of home.

When he walked into his flat, Ashley was on the sofa, hunched forward over her phone, the voice of the crowd he had just left snaking towards him through her speaker. Her shoulders strained with tension and she tapped a discordant rhythm against the back of her phone.

"Are you okay?" he asked.

"O'Neil's just posted a video."

She swept a thumb upward to sync her screen to the television. Joe sat beside her, elbows on his knees, lips tight with concern.

Arthur O'Neil was at a desk, a shrinking figure embraced in the leather arms of his computer chair. He clasped his hands together, shaking his head, and turned to the camera. His jaw lifted upward, defiantly pointing at his dissenters. "I have been asked to make a statement about the situation in Edinburgh. My statement is... go home."

His eyes flashed with the same arrogant spark that propelled his body during interviews in his youth. He denied the existence of a time portal but cited national security as he avoided revealing what was hidden inside. He lifted a hand to point at the screen. "Trust me. I know what's best. Leave us to sort this and enjoy your lives."

Ashley un-synced her phone but her eyes remained fixed on the blank television screen. Her thoughts were as opaque as ink, leaving Joe walled off from her world. Talk to me. But she was like a castle, raising the drawbridge against him.

"I think they're right, you know," Joe said. He turned to look out the window, the sparkling lights dancing across his vision. "I think it is a time portal."

Ashley inhaled a breath, then leaned back, arms folded. "He's just an arrogant old man. Who is he to decide what we should or shouldn't know?"

169

"I'm surprised you're not out on the Meadows with the protesters." He spoke as if he was teasing her, but frustration leaked out, hardening the edges of his words.

"I don't want to know the truth," Ashley admitted her voice a fledgling, struggling to find its wings. "I just want him to not exist."

Their phones buzzed and they both lifted their screens. The crowd had breached the barrier and was fighting the guards. Joe felt a sense of dread coiling like a snake in the darkness. He reached for Ashley's hand but she lifted hers to her hair, his approach unnoticed.

The crowd overwhelmed the guards, an avalanche of human will. Joe and Ashley watched as the first fists struck at the metal door.

Joe could see the flickering lights dancing across the air, in his mind's eye. Will o' wisps luring the unwary to their downfall. All they needed was to be set free.

His eyes welled with tears and he fought to swallow the lump of emotion building in his throat. He forced words through the obstruction. "Let's not watch. We can find out tomorrow."

Ashley stared at her screen, petrified, hypnotized. Joe reached out and pulled the phone from her hand, forcing her to reply.

She nodded. "You're right. Let's focus on each other."

They turned off their phones and spent a night in a blackout surrounded by photographs of their youth. Ashley's attention kept drifting, her thoughts lost among the stars, and Joe didn't know how to pull her back to Earth. She fell asleep with her cheek pressed against his chest, her breath warming his skin. He held her close, melding his body with hers, as if physical contact could bind them together. Is the other me as scared to lose you?

In the morning, Ashley was gone. Their home was an empty body, last breath exhaled, life dispersed in the aether. Joe walked into the kitchen, his wife's photographs haunting his path. She had packed a bag while he slept and slipped off into the night.

The message on his phone said she planned to fly somewhere far away, where O'Neil's influence was more of a brushstroke than a painting.

Her phone lay on the kitchen counter, a severed limb, torn free to escape the clutches of her cage. He closed his eyes to hold back the grief welling beneath the surface. Should I follow her?

Ashley had been a part of his entire adult life. Her voice echoed in his mind far more than any ghost from another timeline. She might have broken free, but she had left him alone on the ground. He didn't know how to fly after her – didn't even know where he would start.

Why wasn't being here with me enough?

He escaped the house and walked to the Meadows. The parkland was filled with a roiling mass of life. The air sparked with fury, a tinderbox about to burst into flame.

A row of army vehicles lined the street – reinforcements may have held the tide at bay overnight but Joe could feel the pressure building all around him. Have they broken through yet?

He tried to push to the front of the crowd, to see what was happening. A part of him hoped to catch a glimpse of his wife, facing the fears that haunted her instead of bending to their will.

The scent of body odour and perfumes filled his nose. Placards swooped in front of his face and he grew flushed with the swell of body heat. Ahead, excited voices rose above the background hum, declaring themselves victors against an uncaring authority.

Unable to reach the building, Joe pulled out his phone and turned to the news. The crowd had breached the door and we're sharing footage of the glass enclosure.

Flashlights flared against the reflective surface, faces and limbs and screens forming a sinuous movement as they approached the anomaly's prison. Joe held his breath as he waited for the glass to shatter.

Caroline Ashley is a clinical psychologist who works for the NHS in Scotland. She primarily writes fantasy with the occasional foray into sci-fi and horror. She also posts a monthly blog about the psychology within storytelling on her website. If she had any free time around work, writing and raising her two young children, she would spend it playing board games.

Visit her website for her work: www.carolineashley.co.uk

DOUBLE-SLIT TRAVELING

By Ginger Strivelli

Dr. Edgar Fisher was an excitable man. He could get excited about anything, his favorite cereal being on sale, finding a parking space close to his lab entrance, or inventing teleportation.

He didn't invent it by himself, of course. His partner Dr. Lancelot Lorrin and six junior scientists assisting them had helped quite a bit. Lorrin was not an excitable man but inventing a new instantaneous way to travel makes even stoic men celebrate. Fisher and Lorrin had been celebrating and being celebrated for weeks since they had taken the old Double-Slit experiment and turned it into a teleportation machine.

The assistant scientists working with them were trying to make the invention work internationally. Then they were aiming for interplanetary travel. The word interstellar had been whispered.

The first trials were on ants. Lorrin and Fisher had teleported three old fashioned ant farm colonies of ants from one side of the lab to another, one at a time. There had been only ten percent casualties. The scientists fine-tuned the procedure. Dr. Mary Baker had figured out a mathematical tweak of the particle acceleration equation that stabilized the wormholes which led to fewer and fewer ants disappearing. They moved to mice.

The mice fared much better. The scientists spent a month teleporting mice all over the lab. There were three hundred trials and only four mice didn't reappear. They counted that as acceptable losses.

Then they graduated to monkeys. Amazingly they only misplaced one monkey out of fifty that they teleported. They even started teleporting monkeys to one another's homes, not just around the lab. On the last day of the monkey trials, they all gathered around a big round table to meet and discuss what was next.

"It is time to try Double-Slit Traveling on a human subject." Fisher proudly announced to the group.

"I have an idea for a volunteer. Dr. Baker's mother is dying of stage four cancer. She only has days left. If we lost her...it wouldn't be so tragic." Lorrin emotionlessly reasoned.

Fisher was used to Lorrin being more of a brain than a heart so he didn't flinch much at the

unethical comment. Luckily, Dr. Mary Baker was almost as smart and not much more sentimental than Lorrin. So, Fisher wasn't too shocked when Baker said her mother might go for it and agreed to ask her about it that night.

The next day, Dr. Baker came to work with her Mother in tow in a wheelchair. The elder Baker woman was eager to be the first human trial, though Lorrin explained thrice that they had lost ants, mice, and a monkey. He told her that they were just gone. She could just be gone. The old lady shrugged and said she was about to be gone anyway and this way she'd be helping her daughter's work. She gushed over what an amazing discovery they had made and how proud of her daughter's contributions to science she was.

"Mom is ready today. She wants to make history as the first human Double-Slit Traveler. Let's do it!" Dr. Baker said high-fiving the other female Doctor on the team, Dr. McMahon. "Where are we sending her?"

"Whoa now, that is your mom, Mary. You sure?" Fisher said in amazement.

"We discussed it all night. She wants to go first. She wants to make history. It is her chance to do something great with what is left of her life." Dr. Baker reached to pat her mom on the back.

"We could lose her like we did all the ants, the four mice, and the monkey," Lorin said bluntly, even though Mrs. Baker was right there in front of them.

"We know." Dr. Mary Baker said. "But we won't lose her. She's going down in history. We all are."

"Let me do this...I'm ready to make history." Mrs. Baker said calmly.

Dr. Mary Baker's mother, Florence Baker did indeed go down in history as the first human to teleport using the new Double-Slit Traveling technique. She only teleported from one side of the lab to the other but she teleported nonetheless. She died four days later but it was from her cancer not from any malfunction of the Double-Slit Travel machine.

They proceeded with the human trials for weeks. All the doctors shot each other around the lab umpteen times a day. They never lost anyone.

The two lead doctors started teleporting across town to a second site where they set up a Double-Slit Traveling station in Lorrin's garage.

It was only three months into those human trials when one morning Dr. Fisher suddenly popped a bottle of champagne in the lab drawing everyone's attention.

"Ladies and gentlemen, we've been green lit to build Double-Slit Traveling stations at JFK, LAX, and ATL, since our human trials have gone so well. "Dr. Fisher was almost glowing with his new record level of excitement.

The technology was all ironed out by then, with all the bugs found and fixed. They could build a station in a day. They had those first US Double-Slit Travel stations at the airports up within a week.

Dr Fisher was the first human to teleport across the country from JFK to LAX in less than a second. He arrived safe and sound and very excited, naturally. It was all going so well, the government funding stuffed shirts and the military oversight board moved up the timetable. They had international Double-Slit Travel stations up and running by the end of the year.

Nothing was going wrong, which should have been a clue that something was about to go very wrong. No one picked up on that clue, however, so things kept going right for a few precious more days. Dr. Fisher came in late one morning looking more excited than usual. He was jumpy as a lab rabbit. He motioned for the six assistants and Dr. Lorrin to gather around. He announced that the government had approved their request to set up Double-Slit Travel stations on the Moon and Mars!

Dr. Fisher and Lorrin let Dr. Baker be the first person to transport off world. In honor of her mother, the Double-Slit Travel station at the newly set up Moon Colony was named; Florence Station. Dr. Baker teleported from the lab on Earth to Florence station on the Moon without incident. The world celebrated. Traveling was now quicker, easier, and just as safe as flying, they thought.

After that travel just took off...ironically as fewer and fewer airplanes were taking off. By March they had added Lorrin Fisher Station on Mars and people were being shot across space between the Earth, The Moon, and Mars like laser beams. It was amazing, the future was here.

Alas, the whole system was about to crash. Not because of any malfunction but because of an

unknown dangerous function they had not intended to invent.

Dr. Lorrin had just Double-Slit Traveled to Mars the morning of April Fool's Day. He'd teleported so many times he'd lost count now. He was working on the station and telling Dr. Baker how she had been selected to set up the new station on Eupora when Dr. Fisher came rushing into the station all excited, yet again.

"What is it now Fisher? Did they give us another Nobel prize?" Lorrin laughed.

Fisher didn't answer the question. Instead, he pulled Dr. Lorrin aside and thrust a printout into his hands.

"What am I looking at Fisher?"

"Our lost monkey has turned up." He whispered and motioned for Lorrin to look at the copy of a newspaper article.

"Damn. That is him, ole Number P-64." Lorrin was holding the paper close to examine the photo with the article. Then he pulled it back to arm's length to read the headline. "Monkey appears out of thin air at the Opera in front of an audience." He read.

"Note the date, Lorrin." Fisher pointed to the upper corner of the page. "November, thirteenth, eighteen ninety-three! We haven't just invented teleportation. We've invented damn time travel."

Lorrin stared down at the date. He shook his head. "We have become Death, destroyers of worlds." he paraphrased.

"We gotta fix this! End this! Sabotage it. Hide the research and never tell anyone about the damn monkey." Fisher whispered.

Lorrin nodded. "I'll get the others. We will write some virus code...blow up all the stations."

That is just what they did. The eight scientists were the only ones who knew that the Double-Slit Traveling stations didn't all malfunction and destroy themselves that very night. The

eight of them took the secret to their graves. No one else ever knew about the monkey. They had lost their amazing invention but they had saved all of history and all of the future.

Ginger has written for Marion Zimmer Bradley's Fantasy Magazine, Autism Parenting Magazine, Flash Fiction Magazine,

Third Flatiron, Silver Blade, Greenprints, Solarpunk Magazine, several other magazines, and several anthology books.

PAST AND PRESENT COMPANY EXCEPTED

By Lawrence Dagstine

In the darkness, Gabe Smith got up from his bed and dressed with no particular destination in mind. He walked into the air beyond the white terracotta house which had belonged to three generations of Smiths. The time? He had forgotten his smartphone on the nightstand by the bed.

Fifty. The turning point. Fifty. Earlier, the cake with two edible candles, a five and a zero, for the time of numbering the years with separate supermarket-bought candles had passed, and now these two shaped cookie cutter numerals served to stand for the single ones as well. Fifty. A brittle breaking. A mortal wound never recovered from. Entrance into a deep dark cavern. A handful of 'Hey, granddads' from here out.

Would she miss the warmth of his body? Not likely, for Matilda slept as though drugged, exhausted by her own day, as he had been by his until restlessness left him turning with pointless thoughts of time as the day passed into tomorrow. That was all last night, now.

The air was filled with ocean mist, a refreshing feeling coming from an unusually high tide. The clean moisture entered his lungs from the boardwalk, bringing youth again. The world blurred into a dim reality of shifting lights. A silent car came, its headlights flaring out and then lost. No sign of the passage of the car, only the white, moving mist and the distant sounds without identity.

He walked, putting his hand in his pocket, feeling the change there between the thumb and forefinger: twenty-five cent pieces, nickels, perhaps a dime or two. The Old World currency, which had usually been reserved for the Laundromat down the street from his house. They had done away with pennies some time ago. Nevertheless, still redeemable.

At first, his fingers couldn't distinguish the small coins, and there was an impulse to bring them out and hold them close to his face for identification, for a kind of certainty. He looked down at the swirling mist made alive by his movement. What kind of magic is this? He walked on, turning from street to street. The bulge of the coins in his pocket. The coins only. He'd forgotten his billfold, lying with the smartphone on his nightstand.

Lights came from the darkness, smeared away in the ocean mist, and were absorbed. Lights falling into white darkness like his breath. Far away sounds, bright as though near.

Now and then, passing him, the cars; he, now and then, passing the lights of some late-night establishment. The bulge of the coins in his pocket.

A café or perhaps a tavern ahead, after the timeless walk. A Woolworths here, a Caldors there. Obviously shuttered with vandalized gates. They all seemed so archaic now, out of place. They seemed like establishments from some long-forgotten era.

One place in particular seemed very nostalgic to him. "This shouldn't be here," he muttered. He came abreast, paused, and peered inside through the moist glass into the warm, bright interior, his face haloed with orange neon. "Well, I'll be damned. Is that a jukebox I see?"

A beer bar, he decided, drawn by its warmth. The kind of watering hole renowned for its dollar Budweiser and two-dollar Coors Lights. Inside were kids, a dozen or more of them, most gathered at a long central table, sitting quietly in the lateness of the hour. It was very cozy. There was a small pool table, but nobody seemed to be in a billiards kind of mood this misty night. There was an acoustic guitar on a wooden chair. A girl with long blonde hair, and large clear eyes; was seated beside a youth in an Angels baseball cap. The team emblem was from when Reggie Jackson might have played for the franchise. Designated hitter. Slow sipping of beer and talk. The taste of beer came to his mouth, bitter with hops, bringing thirst.

The young man in the Angel's cap looked toward the window. He smiled recognition and gestured, inviting the Gabe inside.

Gabe turned to continue his solitary walk, feeling the coins in his pocket, but after a few steps, he hesitated and came back. After an indecisive moment, he entered the tavern, the ominous mist swirling around him like a cloak. The young man in the Angels cap smiled again, more distantly, as though identification, once certain, now hung on the rim of a memory unabsorbed.

Gabe nodded without any sense of commitment. The tavern was small yet vaguely familiar, and he crept silently inside and squeezed himself behind a corner table. Even the booths looked like something out of a history book about dives and small-town pubs.

He was only a few feet from the central table, but far distant in time, now, cut off forever from its youthful occupants.

Besides the savory smell of hops and a particular moistness of young bodies, there was the sleepy, late-night softness of conversations, reluctant to end. On the jukebox, You Spin Me Right Round by Dead or Alive was fading out, and no one decided to pop in another quarter. The young man in the Angels cap turned to look at him, as did his blonde companion.

Gabe looked away and waited for someone to come and take his order. Behind the bar, the bartender, resting on an elbow before the waitress with her tray. They were both looking up at a small Zenith television drilled into a hanging wall pedestal. Thirteen inches at best. The mirror presented the curly-haired waitress's full face, and he saw himself too, at the table, peering back from the reversed world, a world borne of nostalgia, captured in the hard, bright surface.

A few minutes, he thought, thinking of the coins in his pocket. Then back into the night and the swirling mist, home at last to rejoin his wife with his body pleasantly tired from the unaccustomed late-night exercise.

The young waitress came, smiling. She put a smooth hand lightly on his table.

"A glass of beer," he said and removed a bunch of quarters and nickels from his pocket.

"That's a pretty big purse you have there," she said. "For that much, I'll get you a pitcher. Besides, we have a special tonight. Refills included."

The conversation at the central table was of unfamiliar worlds, illuminated with the crystalline brightness of youthful fantasy. He studied the people, most of whom seemed like seniors in college. One wore patched corduroy pants, like he hadn't seen for years, and sat far back in his chair, eyes partly closed.

Another man wore a faded MTV t-shirt with a tapered denim coat, while he held his gum-chewing girlfriend close to him. She wore a flight jacket and Doc Marten boots—the shoe style was unmistakable, even from a distance—with fishnet stockings and a slightly frayed Depeche Mode shirt beneath. Another tall man in a Benetton sweater lifted the guitar and strummed idly, the strings capturing his restless fingers but not his tongue. Another heftier-

179

looking fellow poured from a pitcher to the brim of his glass, spilling none, and forming a head hardly thicker than the mist outside, so slowly was the last careful tilt.

The waitress returned. "That'll be a dollar, hun," she said.

A dollar. It had been many years since he had bought a pitcher of beer for a dollar. The spare change in his hand suddenly extended time. He brought out the rest of the Old World currency to inspect it in the light, so as not to make a fool of himself.

Everything was monetarily correct.

He gave her a handful of quarters. "Keep the change," he said.

She smiled. "Thank you, sweetie," she said. "Enjoy."

He settled back with the beer, cool and dark. The glass made circles on the tabletop, and the condensed moisture on the surface was cold to his touch. The taste was bright and flowery, more characteristic of European lager than American beer. He drank a long swallow and the liquid moved in his throat as though across an internal desert. He could not remember a time, since early childhood, when from his father's glass, beer had held that excitement for him.

"Won't you join us?" the young man in the Angels cap asked.

He put down the glass.

"Please do," said his blonde companion. Her voice was soft, bringing memories of some former time. As she turned, he noted the flared jeans she wore were faded. A masculine white shirt, open at the neck, did not fully conceal the contours of her upper body, and part of her high, smooth collar bone was visible as a rise in the flesh. The broad belt above feminine hips embraced a waist scarcely thicker than he could encircle with his hands. She couldn't be over twenty-five, twenty-six at best, he thought, noting there was no glass before her place.

He was made welcome at the empty seat beside the woman half his age. "Please go on with your conversation," he said. "Don't let me interfere. I'll just sit here and listen."

"We were saying," the young man in the Angels cap said, "when we saw you out there at the window that we'd seen you somewhere before."

"Oh? Where could that be?" asked the woman, puzzled.

Gabe smiled. "Perhaps you've confused me with someone else?"

Sitting with them at the long table, he felt a sense of belonging, as though in some way he was a contemporary of theirs, inexplicably grown older. They were talking about a Michael J. Fox movie he couldn't remember having seen but seemed vaguely to remember. There were some old stars in it.

He felt his body slowly relax and he drank again from the dollar pitcher before him. Then, once more, the glass was empty, the foam a little white circle near the top, and breaking invisibly on his upper lip. Suddenly, he wished to remain in the soft quiet of this warmth and brightness, while the clock above the bar progressed to an uncertain hour.

"This all feels so…so very surreal," he said to the young gentleman in the baseball cap, "as if I have the early signs of schizophrenia. Sorry, I must seem like an old fool to you."

"Nothing of the sort," said the youthful Angel's fan. "I'm actually in my final semester and taking psychology. I hope to work in the mental health field one day. Schizophrenia starts off very similar to depression. You feel tired, unmotivated, and sometimes numb. "You don't strike me as tired and unmotivated. Then you'll eventually begin to get confused and things won't seem like they used to seem, but you won't know why. Further down the line, you'll begin hearing voices and possibly other types of hallucinations. You knew to accept my invitation, order that beer, and quench your thirst. That's a good sign."

"Is this a hallucination?" Gabe asked, smiling. "Old-fashioned bars with neon signs and beers for a buck? It almost seems like one."

"No. This is so very real," the blonde woman said, extending her arm. "Here, pinch me."

The flesh on her hand was as real as Matilda's, pale and fair and leathery to the touch.

"I wish I could remember where I've seen you," said the woman now.

"I've lived in town my entire life, down by the beach, except the years I was stationed on a military base with my family. Before that, my parents and grandparents had the property. I even went to grade school three counties away. Maybe you've seen me in a restaurant, or at the bowling alley, something like that, somewhere around."

"I'm not even sure it was here exactly," said the girl. She wrinkled her brow and caught her lower lip with her front teeth, thinking long and hard.

The waitress came with a new pitcher, and he reached into his pocket again for a pile of quarters, dimes, and nickels. The twenty-five cent pieces were old, with milled edges worn to parent metal rather than inner construction of new technology and recent mintage. George Washington's face and the Capitol Building were emblazoned on them.

"One dollar, hun," she said.

He passed a pile of coins to her. "Keep the change." He returned any remaining coins to his pocket. "Pass it around."

The young man in the Angel's cap complied, and poured most of the contents of the pitcher into three other glasses, bright, cold, and foamy.

"Funny," said the blonde, her thoughts still on the identity problem. He was conscious of a perfume he did not recognize and needed the time to place it. It was too faint and subtle to activate pathways to other thoughts.

In the moment, it seemed to him that, in former days, the confused sense of identity might have arisen had someone from one of his own groups returned, say a fellow member of his bowling league—one evening, his name lost to both age and amnesia. So again, the feeling came that he was their contemporary, but had returned from a long exhausting journey. Perhaps a journey to other worlds, even other dimensions, while they had remained ageless and outside of time, suspended.

Meanwhile, coexistent with his thoughts, their conversation flowed as did time itself, and the lateness grew. He listened momentarily. "I saw him down the street on a motorcycle," said the man in the corduroy slacks. The dark-skinned guitar man strummed, "That was last Friday."

An unfathomable subject, he partly closed his eyes, hoping eventually to catch the background of the conversation, but feeling no compelling need to do so.

"That reminds me," the man with the guitar said, hitting the strings heavily for emphasis. "Same thing happened to a friend of mine about a year ago, although I think in his case it was an accident

182

more than anything else." He stopped strumming the strings and poured from the pitcher.

Gabe was content to sit among them, accepted as a member of the group, as if some temporary initiate to a fraternity, seeking to recreate a memory that he could not, for time had aged all his youthful companions and many were lost in memory and more were lost in the world. The people around him tonight might, in their way, saw themselves in him.

And there was the mist, swirling off the coast.

Outside of his thoughts, the conversations went on, talk of persons and places veiled with familiarity from an outsider. He drank again, and the pitcher he had bought was soon empty.

"Yo! Earlier, we were talking about the beach," the man in the corduroys said. "We can sit in the cars there. Who wants to come?"

He looked at the faces around him, all eager and full of youth. His body had absorbed the warmth of the room, and for the first time, he was conscious of the chill outside. He pictured the beach and the dark waves beneath the overcast skies, and the mists swirling around automobiles like smoke from some ice fire. The picture he drew in his mind was beautiful, but filled with a strange heartbreak.

A sense of panic came to him. He desperately wanted them not to leave him here in the tavern but, rather, to stay until the inevitability of the clock and the reversed world took them from him. In some respects, he was desperate to keep the soft murmuring conversation around him as a cloak against the night.

"Here," he said, counting the rest of his coins. "I still have some change left. Let me get another pitcher of beer."

"They'll be closing soon," the man with the guitar said, strumming idly, looking at the remaining beer in his glass.

He signaled the waitress for a refill and she came with it.

"If we're going to the beach, we'd better go," said the man in the MTV shirt. "It's getting late."

"Might as well finish this new pitcher," Gabe said. "Here. Let me fill your glasses."

Then feeling foolish, he sank back into his chair, waiting. The blonde girl bent over him and refilled his glass. "Anyone else?"

The man with the guitar, glancing upwards at the clock, said, "Maybe a last one."

The pitcher was passed around.

Gabe sat back, grateful.

The blonde turned to him and moved her hair with a hand. "You'll come with us to the beach? You will, won't you? I've got my car. We can take it, let them go on."

"Thanks for the invitation," he said. "I don't think I can. But it's been very nice sitting here with you."

"They're about to close," she said. "We'll be leaving in a few minutes."

He could feel the alcohol moving in his thoughts, mellowing them. "I don't drink too much," he stammered, "or too often. I'll be leaving myself in a minute. Just finish this." Still, there was a sharp disappointment, and his eyes went to the bar mirror. Perhaps the regained hour of time was nearly passed, and closing time was inevitably upon the tavern.

"Oh, please come," the girl said. "I'm not with anybody."

"What about your California fanboy over yonder?" he asked.

"He's just a friend."

He shook his head, but still found himself sitting when she stood, last to leave the table. There was nothing really to keep him any longer. She called to the parting troupe: "See you on the sand!"

Gabe waved goodbye to the bartender and waitress. At the door, the mist greeted him again, and when everybody moved outside, he and the girl were lost together in the swirling whiteness. He was pleased to be isolated with her.

"See me to the car, at least," she said.

He took her arm to guide her through the enveloping mist, hearing the sounds of car doors closing and laughter, then soft talk and motors revving.

"I'm right over here," she said. "Back here." She stumbled, and he held her for an instant by the waist, the consciousness of her body exploded in him, leaving him short of breath and, in a way, frightened.

The car appeared from the white shroud, a model long out of date.

"It'll be bad driving tonight," she said. "High tide too. Perhaps I won't go to the beach after all. Want to sit and talk a moment?" The voice was raspy, and her perfume came to him out of the mist. Her features blurred. She opened the door, and he saw it swinging as an invitation. "Slip through," she said, "sit under the wheel."

He was surrounded by the darkness of the car and the clean leather smell of the upholstery. Outside was endless isolation, and dense fog. She was beside him, small and comfortable.

Again, the fragrance, and he was conscious of her youthful warmth. Again, of the moist smell, perhaps coming from her hair where the mists of the ocean mingled with her scent.

She started the motor and let it idle, the car heater slowly bringing up the inside temperature with a warm and distant purr.

"You're very beautiful," he said, feeling no particular strangeness sitting here with her. Instead, feeling as he had felt in the parking lot when he momentarily supported her with an arm around her slender waist, above the softness of the hips. She, too, seemed conscious of the emotion and she leaned back with a catch in her breath. He studied her face in the dim light from the dashboard and marveled at the whiteness of her skin and its smooth and pliable youth, noting for the first time the absence of lipstick and any apparent makeup.

"I like this," she said, closing her eyes. "Here in this dark silence, us in the warmth here. The mist out there, cutting us off from the world. Just the two of us have a secret world in here. Kind of like a pocket universe." She smiled towards him. "I'm glad you came tonight. I'd hoped you would, when I saw your face out there, in the window. It was as if I was waiting for you."

He wondered what memory of a lost love he represented for her, what particular formulation of experience had unlocked what swelling need for the quiet intimacy here. And there was a sudden all-encompassing sense of nostalgia. He sat back, waiting, knowing what his next move should be, and yet unable to make it. She sat waiting too. For a long time, there was silence, except for the sound of the heater and the sound of their breathing.

At last, she said, "Whatever you're looking for—and you're looking for something—I can't ever give it to you, can I?"

"No," he said.

"I thought I could. This is some kind of a dream that's real for both of us...isn't it?"

He shrugged. "I don't know."

"And what I'm looking for, I'll never find," she said. "...There's going to be a war on Earth, right here, and we're going to get involved. I'm going to lose my friends and lose my future in it." She waved her hand toward the mist swirling outside the car. "This world...It's already vanishing. No thanks to the robots."

"Robots?"

"AI, silly. Artificial Intelligence. It's us versus them. We're fucked." She wiped a tear from her eye. "We're going to vanish because of them, you see. The war talk is in the air. Man versus machine, that sort of thing. Everybody knows what's coming. It might take thirty years, it might take forty. We're all just waiting. And nothing will ever be what we expect it to be. Nothing will ever be the way we find it in the secret dreams we have. After all, machines don't have dreams. They don't have emotions like we do."

He didn't reply.

"You're sad," she said.

"Everybody is sad, girl. Everybody, everywhere. But sometimes it takes a long time to admit it to yourself. Well, thank you for letting me sit in here for a little while. I guess you better go join your friends. I'd like to go with you, but I can't. It's late for me, and my wife will be worried."

She reached out to touch him, tears in her eyes, but already he was opening the door. He stood outside the car, looking in, seeing the small figure illuminated by the dash light.

"Didn't you say back at the tavern you lived on a military base?" she asked.

"I did. I was a colonel."

"What kind of colonel were you?"

"I was a colonel in a war. A war unlike any other. In a future scenario exactly like the one you depicted."

"Really?" For a moment, a bright outlook. "Who wins?"

He closed the door to the car without reply and, without looking back, turned and walked away in the ocean mist. He wondered what time it was.

He walked several blocks before he regained his orientation and located a familiar street. He turned toward home. There was an aching tiredness in the muscles of his legs. In his memory lingered the flowery taste of beer such as he could not remember since childhood.

He knew that the future is uncertain, and that time is the one problem that everybody faces that has no solution. Someday man might build machines, then conquer those machines, and then spread itself across all the stars, but the future is a conundrum unto itself. It is an order of magnitude more complex than the three-dimensional world. The future is always in the beginning and will be in the end. We make the future before it happens, so we are forced to live it, fixed, immutable, and eternal. Men and women are forever helpless before it. All we have to show from it is nostalgia.

As he walked, his hand went now and again into his pants pocket to feel for the coins. There was only one quarter left. Over and over again, he tried to will for there to be a bulge of change in his pocket.

But one coin alone was all there was.

Lawrence Dagstine is a native New Yorker and speculative fiction writer of close to 30 years. He has placed around 500 short stories in online and print periodicals during that period of time. He has been published by houses such as Damnation Books, Steampunk Tales, Wicked Shadow Press, Black Beacon Books, Farthest Star Publishing, Calliope Interactive, and Dark Owl Publishing (of which he has a new book out called The Nightmare Cycle). Visit his website, for publication history past and present, at: www.lawrencedagstine.com "

WHAT GOES AROUND

By Gargi Mehra

On the way home from the prenatal check-up, Chris Bransford leaned in and kissed his wife as they snuggled together in the back seat. He rested one hand gently on Jen's stomach, and draped the other around her, drawing her close. Her pregnancy had not yet acquired the bulge and swell appropriate for a mother of twins.

She curled her brown fingers around his white ones. "I've been thinking. Remember when this whole VYYS thing started?"

Chris sighed. "Jen, I'm not good with technology. You know that."

"The time-traveling campaign, Chris!"

"Oh, that one – Visit Your Younger Self. Yeah, it's exciting, isn't it?"

"All our friends have done it. Only we haven't. Yet. "

He rubbed his thumb along her ring finger. "We made a pact, remember?"

"I know, but I think you should visit now."

"My younger self?"

She shook her head. "No. Mine."

He withdrew his arm and looked at her quizzically. "What are you saying?"

She gazed up at him. The specks of green in his blue eyes muddied her thoughts, even after all these years. "Just think about it. The doctor said we have to take precautions now. We can't have sex for some time, and, I don't think I'll even want to. And soon I'll lose my figure and you won't be interested in me anymore."

"That's ridiculous, Jen!"

Perhaps it was her hormone-addled brain, but his protests rang hollow. She could even detect a tinge of hope in his voice. "Hear me out. I would rather you did it with a younger, hotter version of myself rather than one of your 'actress friends'."

Chris turned to face the window. The marketplace of Kensington drifted past. "Let me think about it."

Jen smiled. She pecked him on the lips, and on the line of freckles that ran up the side of his neck. "We'll call Mitch and get him to arrange it."

###

They stood at the edge of an abandoned power station at the cusp of sunset. Streaks of purple and orange were cutting across the sky. A little thrill bubbled up in Jen's heart.

Chris' PA, Mitch, stood beside the couple as they held hands. "It's not as long a journey as you might think. Only all the way to the other end of the galaxy!"

Mitch roared with laughter at his own joke. Chris grinned, but Jen only forced a smile.

Chris lifted her palm to his lips. "Don't worry, I'll be fine."

Jen said, "Five years in the past, to a planet at the edge of the Milky Way. It's the journey that worries me."

Mitch said, "You don't have to worry, Jen. It's barely even time travel, more like good old spatial travel."

In the distance, a closed carriage floated through the sky towards them. It had no wheels, and no driver pulling the horses by reins.

Chris said, "Mitch, how come the timelines haven't been affected? Isn't there a time paradox because all these people have been visiting their younger selves and telling them what they should or should not do?"

"Good question. The jury's still out on that. In fact, they can't even say for certain what will happen if the Whizzer kills himself in the earlier timeline. And Chris, don't forget this."

Mitch drew out a device that resembled a television remote. Chris took it from him and examined it.

"Your forgetonator. Just point it at the target, and they lose the memory of their meeting their future selves. The second time onwards, you point it at the target straight away, and the memories of their earlier meetings with you will be revived. This way you don't have to introduce yourself each time."

Mitch turned to Jen. "VYYS has been declared safe for pregnant women as well, up to and including the eighth month."

Jen laughed. "No way, Mitch. I am not going to travel. Only Chris will."

"Do you plan to stay alone when he's off time-traveling?"

Jen snorted. "What's the big deal? I've stayed alone before. I'm not scared."

Chris said, "Don't worry. She keeps a dagger under the mattress where she can reach it."

"Great, I wouldn't want to mess with that."

The driverless carriage came floating down to them.

To Chris' disappointment, the insides of the coach didn't hold a mirror. He smoothed an errant curl of hair from his forehead. If he'd stolen one last glance at his reflection before stepping out of the house, he might've felt surer of dazzling his young wife.

Five years ago, Chris and Jen had lived separate lives, unaware of each other's existence – he, a rising megastar in the British film industry, and she a financial journalist, whom he met entirely by happenstance.

Before he met Jen, he'd dated a string of smart actresses without feeling a tug at the heartstrings. But Jen combined beauty, wit, and brains in one enchanting mix. He fell in love at first sight, something he never imagined would happen.

A sound like the wind blowing at hurricane speeds rose above the noise of the coach. Where was the engine of the coach anyway? Chris glanced around, wondering if he'd find anything more than the velveteen sofas and plum curtains that worked as a window to outer space. Nothing inside the coach revealed its inner machinations.

In the darkness of night, they rattled through space and finally skidded to a halt. The double doors of the coach slid open. A footman, as Chris privately thought of him, stood outside, floating on his anti-gravity mat. A staircase rolled out from the bottom of the coach.

The footman gripped Chris' elbow to help him gain a steady hold on the steps. Chris climbed down onto the balcony of his young wife's apartment in Canary Wharf.

"Why the balcony? Can't you set me down at the front door?"

"No sir, that's against the policy."

And without another word, the steps rolled up and disappeared, the double doors swooped in and hid the interiors of the coach from view, and the footman-cum-driver drove off.

Chris shook his head. At first flight, time travel didn't feel so worth it.

The door slid open, and young Jen came through holding a fat book. Chris knew what it was – a financial guide that she cracked open every few years to brush up on the basics.

He stared at her. His wife flaunted curves in all the right places, but young Jen looked almost skinny. The strap of her spaghetti top clung to her jutting-out collarbone. Her hair lay in permed curls over her perky breasts. Her features were sharper, but her cheeks were still slightly chubby.

"Jen?"

She glanced up from her book, startled.

A mixture of fear and excitement glinted in her eyes. "Yes?"

"Jen, I come from the future, in which I'm your husband and we've been married for seven months. We've known each other for three years. I can show you the evidence."

He rattled off the official words as he'd been instructed. The speech had sounded absurd in his head, but now it just rolled off his tongue. How else would he explain his presence on the balcony?

She blinked. He sensed her disbelief. Maybe he had spoken too much. Maybe she would refuse to let him in.

But then she said, "Show me your proof."

He whisked out a seven-inch tablet from the inside pocket of his topcoat and loaded the photographs. She swiped through the list. He had arranged them in reverse order, starting with their wedding photos – she in pristine white, he looking dapper in his tuxedo with a carnation pinned to his lapel. From the recent ones she moved to the old photos, their first shoot together when they had posed for a magazine.

She turned the full force of her deep brown eyes on him. He gazed into them, hypnotized, just like when he first met her.

A light blush crept into her cheeks. "Why don't you come in for a beer?"

Young Jen probed into every detail of their lives together.

"Can't I go meet you in my world now?" she asked, her eyes shining.

"That wouldn't be advisable. It could cause variations in the timeline – problems between your world and mine."

For more than an hour he satiated her curiosity, and then he led her to the bedroom.

"I'm not sure about this. I mean, after all, you are –"

"Your future husband. That's the only thing that should matter. You know we are not allowed to meet strangers. If I wasn't who I said I was, I wouldn't have been able to come and meet you. How would I know where you lived?"

"It's not that. I trust you. But…do you really want to…?"

They locked eyes for interminable seconds. He gathered her hands in his, raised the tips of her fingers to his lips, and kissed each finger in turn. He felt her sharp intake of breath as he unleashed a wet kiss on the back of her hand.

He placed her hands around his neck, put his arms around her small waist, and drew her to him. He bent low and kissed her full on the lips, pushing her mouth wider open with his tongue. She responded in kind.

She broke off and placed a firm hand on his chest. He held on to her palm, but instead of pulling free, she led him to the bed.

###

"How was it?"

"Weird, at first."

Jen laughed. "Weird? Why? Didn't you enjoy it?"

"Of course I did, but in the beginning, it felt a little odd. Like I was shooting a love scene with someone I hadn't met before."

"And then…?"

"Then she got comfortable, and so did I. I didn't want her to feel like her consent didn't matter."

"What happened…when you left?"

"Pointing the forgetonator at her felt even weirder – like she was a TV and I was holding the remote. I did it when she was sleeping."

Jen fell silent for a minute. Then she poked him in the ribs. "Was she a lot more energetic? More flexible, maybe?" She grinned.

"No one, I repeat, no one is as flexible as you." He lowered his head and kissed her on the swell of her breast.

"So, when do you plan to meet her again?"

"I don't know. I'll be tied up with film promotion in LA for the whole of next month."

"It doesn't matter where you are. You can do this from anywhere."

"It's not a question of place, but of time."

A smile played on Jen's lips. "No time to time travel, Chris?"

He kissed the softness of her neck. "I'll make the time."

###

Afterward, as they lay curled together on the bed, she ran her finger in circles around his navel.

"Hey, can't I go meet you in this timeline?"

Chris turned to her. "No, Jen. You can't. We've discussed this."

192

She sat up. "Why not? It just seems so unfair! We're meant for each other so what's the problem if we meet a little earlier than expected?"

"I told you – it could affect timelines, alter the future. You can see that as well as I do."

"It's just so...wrong!"

She writhed free from his arms and left the bed.

The anomaly scan showed no anomalies. Chris stared at the photos of the tiny little beings growing inside his wife.

Jen served him breakfast in bed. "What's wrong?" she asked, as she poured him a cup of espresso.

That was the thing about finding one's soulmate. Jen always sensed the presence of something niggling at the back of his mind.

He slotted the pictures back into the envelope. "She keeps asking to meet him...I mean me."

"Oh." Jen set her cup down. "She wants to meet her Chris?"

"Yes. But why? Until they meet in their world, she can have her fun with me."

Jen smiled. "It's not just fun for her. It's her future. She must be excited to meet you in her world. I know I would be."

"It's just...annoying."

Jen fell into thought. "Do you want me to talk to her?"

"No, it's okay."

A flash of silver glinted on her nightstand.

"What's that?" Chris asked.

"What?" She followed his gaze. "Oh, that's just my forgetonator. Mitch sent it to me. He's crazy – he thinks I might want to become a Whizzer too!"

"You can if you want to?"

"No way! Look at me!"

Chris happily complied. She hadn't started showing yet. A stranger might figure out her condition only if she wore tight clothes.

"You can visit...me."

She laughed. "I can, and maybe I will. But not now."

He smiled. "Okay, whenever you're ready."

"So, we go with standard royal blue for the nursery?"

One night, he returned to find his wife sitting up in bed, sniffing.

193

"Chris, where were you?"

He rushed to her side. "What happened, Jen?"

"I've been in pain. Mitch had to drive me to the hospital. He told the staff you were at a shoot and unreachable."

"What did the doctor say?"

She sighed. "Nothing. It was a false alarm, must've been just indigestion or something. The doctor said she might advise me bedrest from the eighth month onwards."

He took in her appearance. Even in tears, she looked beautiful. She had thrown on a shapeless black top that tried but failed to conceal the burgeoning of her breasts and her stomach.

He sat next to her on the bed and heaved her gently onto his lap. "I'm sorry. I won't leave you again at this time."

She sucked in her breath. "Just, tell me before leaving, so that we can fix up an excuse."

"No, no. I just won't go."

"Chris, this was my idea. I don't want to have proposed it and then guilted you out of it. Besides, at least 'young me' is having fun."

She flashed a teary smile. He planted a kiss on her neckline.

On the flight back from shooting the last scene of a comedic caper, it dawned on Chris that time traveling had made the days fly past. In less than a month he'd become a proud father of twins.

Jen was waiting for him, serving up the roast chicken and vegetables that the housekeeper had rustled up for dinner. She had heeded the doctor's advice and taken to her bed from the eighth month.

After dinner, he stacked the plates in the sink. Jen idly flipped through a magazine for a few minutes before dozing off.

Chris watched her chest rise and fall under her nightgown. He bestowed a small kiss on her forehead, before shrugging into his topcoat and beckoning the travel coach. He tucked the forgetonator in an inside pocket.

As the coach whirled through space, through wormholes and time warps that put a distance between himself and his wife-to-be, a sense of magnanimity overcame him. He would allow Jen to visit his younger self, perhaps a few months after she had given birth and the doctor had officially granted her permission to have sex. In fact, he wouldn't just allow it, he would positively insist. Why should she not indulge herself in the pleasures that his young body could provide?

Would Jen be surprised when he presented her the chance? Would she throw her arms around him and kiss him, happy that he had thought of it? A small part of him wished she would refuse his offer. He couldn't imagine her wanting to frolic with a young version of himself the way he had with young Jen.

He gripped a bouquet of orchids in one hand. Young Jen adored them, but his wife didn't. In recent years, she had grown to love the scents of gladioli and petunias.

The policy did not recommend the carrying of gifts. Most time traveling visitors never toted any presents for those mired in the past.

The coach pulled up outside the balcony as usual. But this time, she wasn't there. He loved watching her shuffle through the door.

"Wait here," he instructed the driver.

He clutched the bouquet tight and tiptoed on the balcony. A slight gap in the sliding door afforded him enough leeway to open it and step in.

He crept inside the living room. From somewhere the vague sounds of hushed murmurs came to him. He imagined her talking to someone in the bedroom, the phone wedged between her shoulder and her ear. He could still surprise her. He would plant a light kiss on her shoulder as she stood with her back to him. She would whirl around and kiss him back, the phone slipping from her hand as fast as the clothes slipped from her body.

He tiptoed towards the bedroom. Strangely, the door was closed. Why would she close it? He paused just outside the threshold. Then, as if someone had turned up the volume, the noise filled his ears. A man's harsh grunts and a woman's breathless panting. He tightened his grip around the bouquet.

He pushed open the door. For a few seconds, everything appeared black. His eyes adjusted to the darkness, and the picture before him came into focus.

On the bed, two bodies lay intertwined, writhing and grinding. They were kissing deeply, so deep into their kiss that they didn't even sense him standing there.

Who was this man? And why did she need him? Wasn't he enough? He satisfied her every need, so why did she have to wrap her legs around this stranger?

The word escaped his lips in one breath before he could even stop himself. "Jen."

They sprung apart. She gasped at the sight of him. Even as he stood there loathing her with every molecule of his being, he couldn't help but admire the curves of her body. Sweat glistened on her skin.

Something made him turn towards her partner. The man gazed back at Chris, his icy blue eyes betraying guilt. Chris recoiled, staggering backward. For almost four decades Chris had seen that face every day in the mirror, and every time he couldn't help but think that the depth of his blue eyes revealed all the secrets carved deep in his heart. What man was this, who lay cowering in the arms of his woman, sporting repulsive sideburns that went out of fashion centuries ago?

Chris threw down the flowers and burst into laughter. "Oh Jen, why did you do this?"

He bent over her, stretched a hand out under her mattress, and drew out the knife.

"Chris, please don't!"

It was a sturdy device, butchers always carved up their turkeys using just such a specimen. Its smooth sharp edge was ideal for chopping meat into pieces.

He raised his hand.

"Chris, wait!"

"Stop talking."

"Chris, if you kill me now your wife dies and so do your twins. You know that, please. I'm begging you."

He smiled. "We don't know that for sure."

She lowered her voice to a whisper. "Do you really want to take that risk?"

His younger self spoke. "Please, we love each other. You know that."

You know that. Three words he found it impossible to argue with.

He plunged the knife into the man's heart.

"Chris, no! No! How could you do this?"

196

Blood seeped into the sheets. Pain surged through his left arm. His legs threatened to give way, but he hauled himself up and ran out of the bedroom, to the balcony and inside the coach.

The journey back home passed in a blur. The coach ricocheted and rattled through space. Chris ran the scene over and over in his mind. He wrapped his arms tight around himself and rocked back and forth in his seat. Only one word echoed in his mind – Jen, Jen, Jen.

At home he found his wife sleeping. Their bedroom bore an eerie resemblance to the one he had just visited. The blinds were drawn, a line of light from outside casting shadows on the white sheets. Jen lay fast asleep on her back, breathing softly.

He threw off his coat and the rest of his clothes on the floor and slid into bed beside her. Sleep evaded him. He admired her lips, which pouted even in sleep. He leaned towards her, planted a soft kiss on her face, and placed a soft hand on her belly.

###

She stirred awake.

"Hey," she said sleepily, her voice hoarse from sleep.

He was sitting up on the bed, pillows propped up behind him, long legs stretched out in front of him. Jen heaved herself up and placed a hand on his bicep. "What happened? Is something wrong?"

He turned to her. The first prickle of tears had sprung to his eyes. "Why did she do this to me, Jen? I thought she loved me. We're meant for each other."

"What did she do? Tell me. Should I talk to her?"

He lowered his head onto her ample chest.

"They were fucking like maniacs. Didn't she alter timelines or something by meeting him earlier than she was supposed to?"

His deep blue eyes pierced her heart.

Her voice faltered a little. "Maybe. I don't know."

A deep scar ran down his shoulder, from the clavicle to his upper arm. She reached out and brushed her fingers over his biceps. "How did this happen?"

He shook his head and buried his nose in her chest. They stayed with their arms wrapped around each other in the darkness. Somewhere far away a dog was barking. Drunkards were staggering home from the bar, kicking lampposts and cars randomly.

Much later he fell asleep. She shifted onto her side and opened the drawer of the table by her nightstand. The forgetonator lay in a corner, gathering dust. It was a useful device. She had traveled only once, but had never used it.

###

Gargi Mehra works in IT and moonlights as a creative writer. Her work has appeared in numerous literary magazines, including Crannog, The Forge Literary Magazine, The Writer, and others. She lives in Pune, India with her husband and two children. She blogs at www.gargimehra.com

RODENT'S INDEPENDENCE DAY

Christopher Blinn

"Hey, Grandpa, who was Punxsutawney Phil?" Gino, the youngest rat asked.

"Who was Punxsutawney Phil?" The grandfather gasped. "Don't they teach you pups anything in school?"

"We're not pups anymore, Grandpa." One of the children said. "Pups are baby rats and other rodents, we're all grown up."

"Yeah, now can we get ice cream like you promised?" Gino's older brother Vinnie piped in.

Grandfather promised the kids ice cream after the annual parade celebrating Rodent Independence. He stared at the ten-foot statue of Punxsutawney Phil, one of the heroes of the war. "Alright, let's go, but I have a story to tell you on the way."

"I like your stories, Grampy," Gino said.

"Thank you, but you better pay attention because when we get to the ice cream shop, I'm gonna ask you a couple of questions, and if you can't answer them." He paused. "No ice cream."

The kids carried on as they walked.

"I'm getting rotten vanilla with moldy cheese sprinkles," Vinnie announced.

"Cup or cone?" His cousin Sean asked.

"Hmmm." Vinnie thought. "A filthy cup I think."

"I'm getting a spoiled fish twist with extra scales in a stale cone," Sean said.

The grandfather stopped. "I'm serious gang. Wrong answers. No ice cream."

"Okay, okay, okay." They appeased, knowing he was bluffing.

Grampy eyed each child and began. "A long time ago there was a rat named Marshall. Marshall was a prisoner at a human army base and subjected to horrifying experiments…

1968 Camp Hero, Montauk, NY

"This one keeps coming back fine." A man in a white coat said and opened an oblong pod. He removed the top half releasing a hiss from the fogged glass capsule. He unstrapped a snow-white rat, scooped it, placed it on his shoulder, and ran a hand down its back. "What's so special about you?" He spoke in a baby voice. He petted it again and dumped it into a cage.

"Any idea why that one keeps coming back in one piece?" A second white coat asked.

"I was hoping you would tell me."

"No, idea. Blood tests are the same as the others in the group that we've sent through only he comes back healthy, and well you've seen how some of the others have come back." He thought of the unimaginable combinations some of the subjects returned in. "If they come back at all."

The pair moved to a long table and sat. The first man held his head in his hands. "You know Colonel Conroy is gonna have a fit if we don't have solid answers for him soon."

"I know." The man said flipping through a binder. He ran a finger down columns and across rows trying to find anything to help solve their dilemma. "We'll keep working. It's all we can do."

Present

Talk of the army in their grandfather's story caught the kid's attention. "Where were they sending them?"

"Where were they sending them? Excellent question." Grampy was happy to see his audience was following. "The question is not only where were they sending Marshall but when."

"When?" The kids looked puzzled.

"The army doctors had been assigned a project to help them win what the humans called the 'Cold War'. They were working on spying on their enemies remotely, concentrating using their thoughts alone when they accidentally stumbled upon a possible means of time travel."

"No way." Gino squeaked.

"Yeah, way." Grampy volleyed. "After several failures, the scientists thought they had discovered a way to send someone forward in time. They didn't want to risk the lives of any of their soldiers so." Grandpa stopped and spread his hands. "They began using rats."

"And then?" The kids begged.

"And then after a series of successes with our poor ancestors..."

1968 Camp Hero

"How long before we can send a man through?" Colonel Conroy demanded.

"We need a few more…"

The senior doctor cut off his colleague. "What Doctor Jones is trying to say is we are ready to go anytime."

The first doctor protested again but was stifled by his superior.

"Fantastic news Doctor Penn." Conroy's tone communicated the meeting was over. "Monday 0-six-hundred. See you then gentlemen." The door clanged shut behind him.

"You fool," Jones challenged Penn. "You're risking the life of whatever poor soul volunteers for this insanity."

Marshall listened from his cage. He had lost count of the number of times they had sent him through. The experimenters were surprised by his heartiness. But it was what they didn't know that would have really shocked them. Marshall had grown and learned in his travels. Things he had seen, no one would ever believe. The world of the future was run by rodents. Rats, squirrels, mice, guinea pigs, hamsters and hundreds more. They had won their freedom from the humans. The rulers of the future had come to power by gradually gaining intelligence. They garnered the support of some humans who saw animal testing as unethical. No longer would they be subject to experimentation, poisoned like nuisances in human cities, or caged as pets. They tried to negotiate a way to share the planet. But the humans scoffed at the newly intelligent rodent leaders. It was eventually only through conflict that Order Rodentia became victorious.

Marshall could speak, write, and think rationally. He taught his fellow captives as much as they could learn, but they were not yet on his level. He had the advantage of time. After what had to have been his hundredth journey, he found a way to manipulate the flow. He would return in what the doctors thought were mere minutes when he had been gone for days, weeks even months. Reading, learning, and training with his fellow rodents in their timeline.

And it was why he knew that this latest development was bad news. Doctor Penn's insistence that they were ready to push up the date of the experiment was all wrong. Marshall knew the test they were going to conduct was not supposed to happen for another two years, Groundhog Day 1970 to be exact. He needed to make a trip to the future to be sure the timeline wouldn't be changed by the doctor's actions and discover what steps he'd have to take to ensure the future world of the rodents.

Present

"Wait Grampa, what does this have to do with Punxsutawney Phil?"

"Patience my little ones. I'm getting there."

"You'd better hurry. The ice cream parlor is getting close." Gino pointed out.

"Alright, Marshall learned a lot as I've told you including how to use the machine to transport himself forward. His plan was to keep things as they were in the future where rodents lived side by side in peace just as we do today. Where everyone has what they need and helps those who don't. The same night when the doctors left, Marshall gave the orders. With the help of his captive friends working the controls of the complicated machine, he would make a trip to the future. The others stood by, their job was to cause a distraction if the mission was interrupted. Marshall instructed them to run amok as if they had all escaped their cages."

When Marshall returned, he was whiter than when he left. What he'd seen was horrifying and what he needed to do, to prevent the outcome, was even scarier.

"What did he see Grampa?" The gang pushed.

"Well, the doctors went ahead with their plans. The test was a success. The soldier came back unharmed. Whisked away and questioned endlessly, he told the tale of the rodent-ruled future."

"C'mon, what happened next?"

"What happened next would change the world forever."

1968 Camp Hero

"We have to send him back." Colonel Conroy pounded his desk.

"But we don't know if it's..." Doctor Jones was cut off again by his associate.

"Yes, Colonel. We can be ready to go again as soon as tomorrow," Doctor Penn offered.

"We need to confirm his reports, and intervene if necessary." The colonel showed no emotion. "The future of mankind may depend on it."

"Where...I mean when do we need to send your man?" The soldier's briefing had not been clear.

"Groundhog Day 1970," Conroy answered. "Some protesters set events into motion that day, winning the support of others against the unethical treatment of animals." He spit the last words. "Leading to a great conflict between us," the colonel hissed. "And them."

"We will be ready, Sir," Penn promised.

"You'd better be," Conroy's face was grim. "If we fail tomorrow humanity is doomed."

Marshall overheard the doctors when they returned to the lab. The news was worse than he thought. He figured he would have a few days to put together a plan to prevent the soldier's presence from disrupting the future, but tomorrow would be too soon. He'd have to go through and improvise.

Present

Grampy scanned his audience. Ice cream seemed all but forgotten.

"C'mon Gramps. What happens next?"

"It was almost two years to the day that the doctors needed to send the man. Groundhog Day 1970, you remember."

The kids nodded.

"The soldier had been given orders by the colonel...

1968 Camp Hero

"Private Thompson, the protesters must not reach the festivities. Do whatever it takes." Conroy barked.

"Yes sir," the soldier snapped a salute.

Doctor Penn led the man to the time pod. He wished the young soldier good luck and secured the cylinder.

Conroy nodded at the scientist, and the soldier was on his way.

They had no idea Marshall had snuck into the pod with their man.

Present

"The two time travelers arrived in a brilliant flash," Grandpa said. "Marshall scooted away unseen by the soldier. Choosing a geographic site was still a bit of a guessing game for the scientists, but they'd improved their accuracy to within three miles."

"You mean they figured out the when but not the where?" Gino asked.

"Precisely." Grampa petted his grandson's head. "They arrived in 1970 at the side of a road. Marshall scurried off into the grass while Private Thompson checked his map and compass. They were less than a mile away from the planned interception point. Thompson prepared his trap."

The kids waited. "What did he do, Grampy? C'mon!"

"Double checking his coordinates, the soldier opened his pack and pulled out a long rubber roll. Only this rubber had hundreds of sharp spikes in it. The plan was to roll the spikes across the road the protestors would be traveling on causing a blowout so they wouldn't reach the celebration."

"Did it work?" Sean pressed.

"Almost..."

1970 Punxsutawney

Private Thompson moved with practiced efficiency. He made a brief effort to camouflage the strip and dashed into the bushes. A light brown van was the target vehicle. To disable the wrong vehicle, the strip was to be activated by a cord. A quick tug by the soldier and the spikes would flip their pointy side up and bam, shredded tires. The hope was to keep the protestors away without causing any injuries. Of course, Colonel Conroy had authorized his man to use any means necessary to complete his mission.

Marshall watched as the soldier kept out of sight. He knew the car that the group was driving and there it was kicking up a trail of dust.

The soldier tensed.

Marshall moved into position. When he saw the soldier ready himself, Marshall struck.

Present

"Did Marshall stop him?"

"You bet he did," Grampa pumped a paw. "But the fight wasn't over yet. The soldier jumped up when he saw his trap had failed. He cursed at Marshall who took off at top speed, caught up with the van, and leaped onto its bumper. The soldier shook his fist at Marshall as the van sped away. It was time for plan B."

"Plan B," the kids were excited.

"Yes, plan B."

1970 Punxsutawney

Private Thompson humped it into town. He checked his watch. He still had time to make it to the town common and intercept the trouble makers but this time he couldn't afford to be gentle. Things could get ugly.

Marshall hopped off the van as soon as it stopped. The gang parked and opened the rear doors taking out homemade signs and a bullhorn. Marshall zipped underneath. He had to stay close to the group to do whatever it took to keep the soldier from altering history.

"Captivity will kill, Punxsutawney Phil." The protesters walked in a circle chanting. An officer politely herded the group away from the gazebo where the mayor would do the honors while still allowing them to exercise their rights. Marshall stayed as close as he could without being spotted. He checked the time on the clock in the center of the square. Two minutes until the danger would pass and the future would be on the right course. No sign of the private. Marshall relaxed.

"Gotcha, you little rascal." Thompson snatched Marshall.

This hadn't happened in any of the scenarios Marshall saw in his travels. The soldier was prepared to do anything to save his race Marshall knew. But how far would he go?

Marshall got his answer immediately.

"There's only one way this can end now." Thompson gripped his captive and pulled his pistol. "Too bad, I really didn't want to hurt anyone."

The crowd cheered as the mayor took the mic and opened Phil's cage. The famous groundhog emerged.

Present

"The army guy didn't kill anyone, did he?" Sean put his arms around his younger cousins.

"Not so fast kids," Grampy built the tension. "You see Punxsutawney Phil was no longer the ordinary groundhog he once was. Marshall, knowing he may need some help, made friends with Phil during his journeys and when he was ready, he told him about the potential disaster. 'When the day comes, you must be ready to act' he told him. Phil moved from his cage with a gait that onlookers would later describe as odd. Marshall knew he had to act quickly. The soldier raised his weapon."

205

Punxsutawney 1970

Private Thompson closed one eye and took aim. The crowd cheered when Phil appeared distracting the soldier for an instant. It was all Marshall needed. He chomped down on Thompson's thumb.

"Sonnuva…" The private dropped his prisoner.

Marshall ran.

Thompson fumed. Discipline forgotten, he chased his prey. The mission was compromised.

Marshall knew his job was done here but he still had some loose ends to tie up back in his present. Until that work was complete, the rodent future would not be set. The town common was huge, he dodged trees and bushes with Thompson on his tail. He needed to make a break for a bordering sewer to escape the infuriated private. Another cheer went up. Marshall decided a straight line towards the gutter was his best chance. He looked over his shoulder and ran headfirst into a hydrant. When he came to his senses, he was staring down the barrel of Thompson's pistol.

Present

"No, no, no," The kids cried. "Marshall can't get killed."

The grandfather crossed his arms. "War is a terrible thing, sometimes heroes give all they have to save others."

"No Grampy, Marshall just can't die."

"I know, buddy." The grandfather mussed Gino's fur. "Listen now…

1970 Punxsutawney

"Gotcha, ya varmint," Thompson scowled. He still hadn't recognized he'd blown his mission.

Marshall was still stunned from his collision with the hydrant. His head spun. No balance. He was a goner.

"Say your prayers rat."

Marshall heard the crack of the gunshot. He closed his eyes and waited to feel the burn of the slug. A second passed but no pain. People were screaming. Marshall patted himself down checking for injuries when he saw his friend Phil motionless at the edge of the park. Phil had jumped in front of Marshall at the last second taking the bullet for him. He lay injured on the grass. Marshall scampered to his friend's side. A police officer tackled Thompson.

"Ph, Phil." Marshall stammered.

206

"It's okay." The groundhog reassured his friend. "This is how it was meant to be." He gasped.

"No. It can't be." Marshall sobbed.

Onlookers rushed to the aid of the wounded groundhog.

"You have to go." Phil breathed. "You have much work to do."

"But…" Marshall knew his friend was right.

A man kneeled next to the stricken animal.

"Goodbye," Marshall said and took off.

Present

"Phil died?" Sean swallowed the rock in his throat.

"Marshall had to get back to the arrival point, back to the portal before it closed or he wouldn't be able to return to his time."

"Yeah, yeah but what about Phil?"

"Well, history says Marshall never saw Phil again." The grandfather delivered the ending. "That is who Punxsutawney Phil was and why we have a statue in his honor."

The kids were all silent absorbing the impact of their grandfather's history lesson.

"And what about the humans?" Vinnie broke the silence.

"The humans." The Grandfather started. "The humans, as smart as they were, never learned from their own past. The war with our ancestors was only the latest one they found themselves in and this time, unfortunately for them, it was the last one. Gone the way of the dodo as they say."

The kids sighed exhausted by the weight of what they'd learned. "What's a Dodo?" Gino asked.

"That's a story for another time." The grandfather rubbed his paws together. "Now who wants ice cream?"

Christopher Blinn lives in Marshfield MA with his with his three sons where he has worked for the Massachusetts Bay Transportation Authority for the past twenty-five years. He is the author of many short stories including entries in Hellbound Books 'Toilet Zone', Demonic Medicine from 4horsemen Publications and most recently Knight's Writing Press 'What Really Happened?'

DAYS OF FUTURE PAST

By Steven Streeter

I shot myself. Twice.

Good shots, too.

The first was right in the middle of the chest, then a second in the eye. Made a right mess of me, but it had to be done.

Well, maybe not, but I couldn't bring myself to kill my own son, and that meant the next best thing was to kill myself.

So, I did. Because I was expecting it, I didn't put up a fight.

###

I was born in 1973.

My father was a used car salesman who ran off in 1981 with a blonde bimbo who appeared in his TV ads when my brother was five and my sister was three. Then he came back into our lives in 1999. By then I didn't care and Aretha and I were not in a great place.

I maybe should have shot him instead, but then that whole grandfather paradox comes into play, so it sort of becomes impossible. But that's life.

My first memory is from February 1959. It wasn't Buddy Holly's death that affected me, but Richie Valens. I was four when my father told me about the plane crash so I watched the plane take off and carry the three stars away to their doom. I knew about Buddy Holly's music and the Big Bopper's 'Chantilly Lace' was great, but it was this young guy on the cusp of immortality that affected me the most. So young, his potential was just being realized, and yet he was gone. Even at age four, after listening to my dad – a Buddy Holly fanatic – tell the story, I knew this was a sad waste. I couldn't believe it. Then I saw it.

If only he'd had the opportunities I did.

My next clear memory is from when I was maybe five years old. My brother was a toddler and my sister was not even born yet. I walked outside when Mum was struggling with the pregnancy and my brother's urinary tract infection. I didn't like the way home felt, so I went for a walk.

It always felt like I went for a walk.

There were so many people gathered around that day. Smoke hung in the air like a bushfire. The people were rushing around

208

crazily. They were in tears, crying and weeping loudly. The police were everywhere. Hardly anyone seemed to notice a five-year-old wandering around as though he had every right to be there.

A teenager stared at me. I stared back. I knew him. He shook his head, but it was not directed at me. I thought he looked sad.

I didn't understand. Not then, anyway.

There were ambulances and fire engines and police and screaming. I didn't recognize the building – it was enormous, built into a hill with a huge flagpole on top, but things soon became way too hectic. I was just too young.

My third memory is from 1989. It happened to me only a month or so after that crowded scene, so I was still five. I was in Adelaide, on the grounds of the university. It was almost empty, so it must have been a holiday break, or the semester had begun. Maybe it was a weekend.

She looked at me from across the grassed area and came straight to me. She was alone. "Are you lost, little boy?" she asked.

"You're beautiful," I said. "You're beautifuller than my mum."

She smiled and blushed. I saw the book in her hand. The word on its cover didn't mean anything to me. Not then, anyway. Again, not then. An older man watched from halfway up a long flight of brick steps. He could have been the father of the teenage boy at the ambulance and police scene I'd seen a month earlier. I think he took me from the girl. He said something. It didn't make sense.

But at that stage of my life, absolutely nothing made sense.

I think she lied to me. It wasn't a faulty condom or that one percent chance that the Pill didn't work – she wanted a kid so desperately, and her biological clock was ticking, so she made sure she fell pregnant.

By then I knew the truth and I really didn't want kids. I didn't want that future that I knew was coming. But she was so desperate for a child that I couldn't protest. I was thirty-five, and she was thirty-seven. How could I tell her, that in eighteen years the child she was carrying would shake Australia to its very core? Just like, how could I tell her I'd spent my whole life, since I was five years old, in love with her? She never knew about me and the way I went for walks.

I hope now she'll never know about our son who will never be.

###

My brother was hit by a car and died when he was ten years old. Eleven years later he married the woman who would become his first wife of three before he admitted to himself that he was gay.

I knew, of course. I'd seen him with his partner looking old and happy.

My brother's death was when I learned about the grandfather paradox. I was there. I was eight. I knew what I had to do. I watched the fifteen-year-old me try to save him, but fail.

The thirteen-year-old me up in a tree screamed but to no avail. But he already knew what was coming, because I was only eight, I could grab my brother's pants and pull him out of the way. To the thirteen-year-old me it was a memory he was now watching from a different angle. But the fifteen-year-old me was powerless.

You see, you can't go backward and change the past. You can only go forward and change the future. No grandfathers affected, just grandchildren. The future is always mutable.

I remember futures that never happened because I changed them. When I was seven, I watched my ten-year-old younger brother die and saw my fifteen-year-old self fail to stop it while my thirteen-year-old self screamed. So, when I was eight, I knew what I had to do and I did it.

And yet, when I was thirteen, sitting in that tree, I knew what I'd see. But I didn't see the fifteen-year-old me. Just the seven-year-old watching and the eight-year-old pulling my brother back by the pants. By the time I was fifteen and my brother was still there I didn't need to go back. I remember something that never happened.

I read a newspaper a week after the whole tragedy at Parliament House in Canberra in 2026.

My name was there, father of the man who had committed not only the largest mass killing in Australia's history – taking that unwanted mantle away from Martin Bryant – but also the first assassination of a sitting Prime Minister. Of course, the PM wasn't the only person killed, but that was essentially what changed the country.

I had to stop it.

I already knew I had to act before November 11, 2026.

On November the tenth I aimed a gun at him, but couldn't do it. Not my own son.

210

Instead, I watched the carnage unfold. Again.

I watched it nine different times. Nine members of that crowd were me. Only two of them haven't seen it yet, because it's now 2016 and I'm forty-three, and the forty-eight-year-old me and the fifty-year-old me haven't existed yet. The fifty-three-year-old me is at home dreading this day when his son will destroy the country.

By 2031 Australia had fallen rather easily under military rule, and it was all my son's fault. Those deaths caused the government to collapse. Someone had to step in. The people wanted to feel safe in a world that had gone crazy. Until then, the craziness had existed elsewhere in the world, but not in Australia. Giving control to the armed forces made comforting sense.

Letting them keep control made life easier.

Letting them take full control just followed on.

Australia would never be the same again. And it was all my fault.

Aretha's parents named her after Aretha Franklin. But how a mousy little white girl, quietly spoken, with long straight hair and blue eyes magnified by her glasses could remind anyone of the undisputed Queen of Soul is anyone's guess.

I didn't know her name when I first met her in January of 1989, but eleven years later in February of 1989, my first day at Adelaide University as a precocious sixteen-year-old, I found her. She was in her second year. I'd never forgotten her, and she was easy enough for me to find. She was sitting by herself at the edge of the grassed area.

I stared at her. She looked up at me. Her expression became strange. "Do I know you?" she asked.

"I was going to ask you the same thing."

"No, seriously," she went on. "I feel like we've met somewhere before."

"Yeah, I know. Me too."

"So have we?"

"I'm not sure." I grinned sheepishly. "Can I meet you now?"

She smiled and introduced herself. Her laughter was like music. I fell in love with her all over again.

I knew Aretha was going to be with me for life, and she was going to be the mother of my son. I could have stopped everything then and there and changed the future by not going to meet her, but I had

211

to find her. I couldn't see a future without her. This philosophy major who took me under her wing like a mother hen, married me a year later, after my own graduation.

I couldn't help myself. I'd been in love with her for over a decade. I couldn't not be with her when I had the chance.

But really, I still didn't know what the future held.

For the first time since I was five, I went back to Canberra. Aretha and I had been together for over a year, with me a second-year student and she a third year who was acting as my sort of de facto tutor.

In a class on morality and ethics, we were discussing regrets and how they could cloud too much of our lives. Very deep for second-year students, but that was our lecturer, an old hippy who I'm sure still thought it was 1967.

Like most of the rest of the class, I started to think about the past and my own regrets. I didn't have many; I'd changed my choices where I could, so I had these unreal memories, but it meant I knew how life would turn out.

That huge memory of the future, I'd seen as a five-year-old started to dominate my thinking, a memory yet to pass.

I went for a walk.

It was as hectic as it had been when I was a five-year-old. People were everywhere. But I now recognized the building. It was only two years old as I knew it, opened in 1988 – the new Parliament House in Canberra.

I looked around at the chaos and felt a wave of guilt, though I had no idea why.

My eyes met those of a five-year-old child I knew all too well. I shook my head at him helplessly.

This still didn't make any sense. Not yet.

People will occasionally ask older people where they were when certain historic events happened. Where were you when JFK was shot, when Nixon resigned when the Twin Towers were felled on September 11? Well, the one I actually like to think about is when man first walked on the moon.

I was nineteen years old and I sat in a classroom at Adelaide University. All those students of 1969 ignored me, more interested in watching on a black and white screen those grainy first steps of Neil Armstrong. That occasion filled me with such optimistic hope, even if I knew it would be over all too soon and space exploration would take a back seat to nearly every other facet of scientific endeavor.

And I can tell you where I was when the Berlin Wall fell as well. Aretha and I were watching it on TV with a heap of her university friends, smiling from ear to ear. Even as a sixteen-year-old, I understood what it all meant and how this was a good thing.

As a fourteen-year-old, standing on the Western side, I didn't understand, but I could feel a sense of euphoria wash over me with the absolute joy in the air.

As a twenty-three-year-old, standing on the Eastern side, it was relief and a true sense of freedom that hit me. I even ran at the open gates and pressed through, as though I'd been living in Berlin my whole life.

As a thirty-seven-year-old I watched it from a distance, knowing that the future this would lead to was something none of these people could ever imagine.

I can also tell you that VE day in London scared me when I was twenty-one, and in 1969, Woodstock was amazing beyond words, but Bessie Smith was the best singer I'd ever heard live.

But my worst day ever was the day my son blew up Parliament House while it was still in session.

The past is better experienced as the present. But that's not an option for everyone.

Apparently just for me.

I still don't really know why my son did what he did. I know where he got the explosives and how, as an intern for one of our state senators, he got access to the chamber. I know how he set it off, and how he was caught only five minutes later walking down towards old Parliament House without a care in the world.

But the big "why" question hangs over it all.

It eludes me.

Was it my fault?

I must have known it was coming. How could I not?

I put up no resistance at all.

I just stared at me.

213

The first bullet hit and I did nothing. The second bullet hit and I fell.

Then I walked and I knew what was going to happen to me in three months.

I was ready.

1999, and the second book Aretha and I had written together – Terretics: A New Philosophy For Twenty-First Century Western Life – was doing very well, especially in Europe. That was when my father decided to make himself known again.

But I knew he would.

Somewhere in this house, my seventeen-year-old self was watching events unfold. And though I didn't know it then, my thirty-seven-year-old self was also reminiscing, but that self wouldn't be around for much longer if everything went according to plan.

My father simply turned up on our doorstep, hoping that our fame had turned into some sort of financial windfall, I know.

He never got inside.

I didn't need him.

But I knew he'd die in 2015, and at that moment I'd be there and we'd reconcile at his death-bed. But I also knew that I wouldn't make it to 2015; I'd be dead long before then, at my own hand. I was effectively shutting him out of my life for good.

I just didn't need him in 1999; I felt like I didn't need him ever.

Aretha and I were in the middle of a personal crisis. She wanted kids and I didn't. I was putting her off, trying to change the future. She felt I was being selfish. Things were rapidly coming to a head between us, which would only be calmed by a world tour for the book in the New Year and a piece of tragic news. At least I cared and tried to give her what she wanted.

And then my father turned up.

Talk about bad timing.

We got into a screaming match. Well, my father screamed and I acted all stoic and cold. He left in tears.

I went for a walk.

I watched him yell at my mother, saying she was cold and unfeeling and that he wanted love and beauty, and not saying that he was feeling old and wanted to be with a pretty young thing so that he could try to recapture his youth. My mum didn't raise her voice,

214

but she cried. Neither knew that three young kids were huddled together, pretending to watch cartoons on the television but listening to their parents fighting.

I couldn't stay there, so I went for another walk, back to 1999.

Aretha was waiting for me. She comforted me. She didn't know where I'd gone, and she didn't ask, but she was there for me.

Three months later she miscarried. And because we'd had that attempt at a child, things got better between us. For a while.

My name was in the newspapers after the massacre at Parliament House. The story had changed.

I'd died before he was born. But it still occurred anyway.

That was impossible, wasn't it? What happened to my timing?

It's 2007 and I'm aiming at myself, my three-month older self. The gun is shaking in my hand. I can do this, I know I can. I've effectively done it already. Hidden around here are so many different versions of me watching this death scene that I have already seen and will see again for a very long time.

My death is a part of me. I am expecting it.

"Don't."

I look. My victim me looks.

I'm older again and I'm approaching us.

"Go for a walk," he says. "Shoot us and go for a walk."

I do. The two bullets hit. I don't remember the person being there before. The dead me is on the floor. The older me is now gone. I go for a walk.

Nothing has changed.

The Prime Minister, the deputy Prime Minister, the leader of the Opposition, the Speaker of the House, twenty-five others are all dead, dozens more injured. The structure is still damaged. Australia is still plunged into darkness.

But how?

I return. This time I don't shoot.

"Honey, I've got some news."

I stare at Aretha. She is smiling nervously.

"You're pregnant," I say. "It's going to be a boy, by the way." I show no emotion at all. No, that's not quite true; I think there's some anger there.

Her smile is gone. "It must have been an accident," she says. "The Pill isn't a hundred percent, the condom could have leaked, anything."

"I'm not the father."

"How can you say that?" She is on the verge of hysteria already.

I take her hands. "It's my fault," I say. "I didn't give you what you wanted so desperately, so you went to Kevin Larwood. I know. It was only functional. He tried to say no, but you insisted. Still, you refused to kiss him at all. It took three tries, but you're pregnant."

"How can you know this?"

I shrug.

Her lower lip quivers, but she cannot say anything. She cannot understand how I know and yet how I can be so calm.

Then I say, "I am begging you, please get rid of the child and I will give you a child of our own. I've been selfish. You deserve better."

She doesn't answer. I am asking a lot.

My son is seventeen in 2026. He's not in Canberra. He's in his last year of high school in Adelaide. We love him. Australia is safe.

Aretha has never forgiven me for what I made her do in 2007. The son that would have been born in 2008 was never born.

Our lives are colder.

It's my fault.

But I did it for the right reasons.

It's 2016. I went for a walk this morning.

I watched a five-year-old in 1989 tell a girl he never knew that she was prettier than his mother. I watched from a distance, from halfway up a long flight of brick steps.

I did something I didn't think I could do.

I changed the future from the future.

The new memories bombarded me like bullets from a machine gun.

The pretty girl led the boy towards the administration area. I went across to them. I called him by name. He looked at me curiously. He knew me instinctively and came to me.

216

I think I hinted to Aretha I was his father. She must have seen the resemblance as she accepted it and kissed him on the head.

"The boy in 2026 isn't yours," I said to my childhood self. "Just do what's natural. Don't worry about the future."

Young me looked at me strangely.

It's 2016 now. I listened to myself. Maybe I didn't understand it then, but I still listened.

These memories I have now don't correlate with what I know was supposed to happen, and what I remember happening. My son is already fifteen. My twin daughters are twelve.

My son wasn't born in 2008 or 2009. He won't kill members of parliament and he wasn't born when Aretha and I were too old, to make up for a reluctantly terminated child that wasn't mine. She was thirty when he came into the world. She's happy. We're happy.

I didn't reconcile with my father on his deathbed. I reached out to him when the girls were born. He's an all-right grandfather, but at least he's there this time. Mum can even handle being around him. She is a fantastic grandmother, by the way, and Aretha's parents are also pretty cool.

We have a family.

###

I went for a walk yesterday.

Richie ignored me and got on the plane anyway.

Maybe I didn't change the future after all. Maybe I set the future to rights. Maybe it was the way it always should have been. Maybe I had to correct a mistake.

Maybe I should stop going for a walk. Maybe I should just let the future happen.

Maybe…

But not until after I see how everything is going in ten years.

Things are different from the way they were last time I was there, I'm sure of it.

The future just isn't what it used to be.

###

Steven Streeter is from rural Australia and has been writing since childhood. He is a former professional wrestler, with two children, and has recently completed his third university degree. An unabashed fan of pulp fiction and escapist entertainment, he has had

217

a number of short stories published in various anthologies and magazines, the most recent being 'The Leader Of The Pack' in Vinyl Cuts (Scary Dairy Press, 2024). He has also had a young adult horror novella published (Under Ground, Black Hare Press), and two adult horror novels (Patch of Green, Little Demon Books; Invasive Species, Am Ink/AM Dark).

THE NOSTRADAMUS PROJECT

By Martin Klubeck

Captain Renatus and Dr. Vida took the elevator down to sub-level 12. Renatus made an attempt at small talk. He wasn't good at small talk.

"How long have you been doing this?" he asked.

She was looking through his paperwork for the third time. Renatus had been thoroughly vetted, tested, prodded, pricked, and poked. Capable staff had done a complete workup of his pulmonary, endocrine, circulatory, and nervous systems. It included X-rays for his skeletal system and MRIs for his muscular system.

They chose very few for the program and Captain Renatus was next up.

But she checked everything again anyway.

"I came on board mid-way in the project," she gave him a brief glance. "Five years now."

Like Renatus, she understood the concept of small talk, and also like him, she had never been good at it. She also realized that travelers were always nervous. Some fought their anxiety by talking. She preferred the ones who bottled it up inside.

He said, "I'm number 26, is that right?"

"Yes," she didn't make eye contact. Instead, she flipped to the last page in his file. No living relatives, no next of kin. "Everything appears in order, Captain," she said with a satisfied sigh.

"Thanks, ma'am. Must admit I'm a little nervous."

No kidding, Vida thought. "It's quite normal. In fact, if you weren't nervous, we'd be worried. I'd probably have to wash you out and call up the next candidate." Her smile didn't quite say she was joking. Because she wasn't.

"Good to know."

Vida caught something in his tone and glanced at his face. It was a little red. An Air Force pilot, a test pilot, was blushing, and apparently nervous. There was a boyish, 'gee whiz' quality to the man she found endearing.

"Do you get nervous before a test flight?" She asked this so earnestly, he wondered if it was part of the pre-flight evaluation.

"Always."

219

She gave him a real smile.

It helped his nerves. Renatus smiled back.

They laughed together. Not a back-slapping, side-splitting laugh. They were like two old friends sharing a private joke.

"Twenty-five times without a hitch so far, right?"

"Except for the last one. He didn't come back, well, altogether," she said looking down.

She waited a bit and then looked up, a mischievous grin on her face.

"Sorry, I couldn't resist," she said.

They shared another smile, and her's was wider this time, his a little more forced.

Renatus found her surprisingly attractive. Unlike the women he had dated (few and far between due to his job), Vida didn't wear make-up. No lipstick, eye shadow, or eyeliner. Nothing. For some reason, he found the absence of cosmetics enticing. He wondered if she was a naturalist.

She wasn't.

Vida never saw a reason for cosmetics. No reason to spend money on them, no reason to go through the time to apply them. She had always been too busy to bother with mating games.

The elevator passed the 4th sub-level.

"We've never lost a traveler and we've never had any complications," she said, no smile this time. No teasing.

"But we can only go once, right?"

"Yes. We don't want to take any risks with your health. Once is enough. We've been monitoring each traveler since we began. We want to ensure there are no long-..." she noticed his face and added, "...or short-term adverse effects."

His shoulders relaxed a little and a sigh escaped his lips. He closed his eyes and took in a deep breath. He kept them closed and breathed in three more times.

She watched, assessing his calming ritual. Some talked, and some meditated. One actually slept standing up. She found that everyone dealt with stress in their own way.

They passed the 8th sub-level.

220

They finished the ride down to the 12th in silence.

When the doors opened, they walked out onto a platform. It had a protective railing and a staircase wound down and around the expansive room. He looked up. It was his first time in the chamber.

"This is the portal chamber. It's the size of a football field if you rolled it into a large sphere." Most travelers did better with sports-related analogies than metric measurements.

"Wow."

She smiled. She had been half-expecting his schoolboy response to the chamber.

"The stairs we're taking run around the chamber, down to the ground floor. What you're seeing is the outer portal, suspended within the chamber."

There was an enormous golf ball structure suspended by hundreds of wires. It seemed to float within the round cavernous space. The ball was semi-translucent so he could make out another, smaller sphere inside.

As they went around and down, she continued her speech.

"There are a lot of scientific reasons we used a sphere made up of multi-planar surfaces."

"You mean dimples?"

She looked at him and then back to the chamber.

"Like a golf ball?" he asked.

"I guess."

"Why?" he asked.

"Why what?"

"Why is it like a golf ball?"

She looked at the chamber.

"I'm not sure." She seemed puzzled at her own lack of knowledge. "But that's not important. What's important is you remember your task, what you need to do."

He nodded, looking around the chamber as they descended. At many locations, he could see individuals with hard hats, white lab coats, and clipboards. They stood in openings along the wall of the chamber. They seemed to be examining the sphere.

She noticed his gaze, "I'm guessing this is like your preflight checks?"

221

"I guess. We don't use clipboards, but we do have checklists. Lots and lots of checklists."

She gave him another smile. For a talker, he wasn't bad.

"You know, I never thought about it, but you're right. We have a lot of clipboards!" she said, getting another smile out of him.

She wondered if this was what a first date was like.

Why this guy?

She had ushered the last five travelers to the pod, and nothing like this had ever happened before.

She spent the rest of the descent explaining in layman's terms how the portal functioned. He had read all about it and received a lecture from the lead scientist himself. He'd also watched a video explaining everything, but he was happy to hear her go over it.

It calmed him. And he liked her voice. He also liked watching her walk ahead of him. It kept his mind off of the trip. A trip in which his molecules would disassemble, travel through a man-made wormhole, and reassemble at the other end. All to have it done again for his return trip.

Like no other test flight he'd ever flown.

When they reached the bottom, they walked to the center of the chamber. There was an escalator-like ladder that went up twenty feet into the portal. She pulled a small remote control out of her pocket and depressed one of five buttons. The steps started climbing up into the pod. They were on an oval track so that while they would go up, others could be coming down the other side.

"Step on and grab hold."

She didn't state the obvious, be careful. Getting injured now would be a serious fail.

She stepped onto a slow-moving rung while grabbing one a little higher than her head. She rode up into the sphere.

He followed easily.

Inside, she waited for him a few feet back from the egress point. He stepped off gracefully.

"Follow me." She led him down a short corridor. "Do you have any questions regarding what you have to do when you arrive?"

They had also drilled that into him over the last week. Every day they tested him and reviewed his mission. Their thoroughness

222

impressed him. He thought it rivaled what he went through with the test of a new airframe.

"No, I can recite it in my sleep."

She stopped and turned to him.

"What! You want to test me?" he grinned.

"Sure. If you get it right, I'll give you a prize when you return. But you can't leave out anything and you can't get them in the wrong order. Nothing added, nothing left out."

"Challenge accepted."

He looked up and to his left. He started reciting the litany they made him memorize:

"1. Upon arrival, calm myself - the journey can be rough.

2. Check the surroundings - get my bearings."

They had shown him maps and a video of the island. It was a small private island, owned by the project.

"How'd you afford an island without government funding?"

"You failed," she said.

"Wait, what? You asked if I had any questions,"

"Time for questions was earlier. That's not in the steps. You failed."

She brought his file up and opened it. She pulled her pen from her lab coat pocket.

"What? You're going to write that on my record?"

"Yup."

"What, that I asked a question?"

"No, that you have a sense of humor," she said and spun on her heel, turning away from him. She continued down the corridor.

"Hey!" he called a little too loud.

He hesitated, letting her get a few more feet ahead of him before following.

His mission wasn't as complicated as a test flight. He wasn't worried. First, make sure he was all in one piece, literally. Then make sure the island is in one piece. There could be any type of weather when he arrived. Granted it was a tropical island, but there was always the risk of hurricanes. Once he was sure it was safe, find his way to the house. It was a beautiful, ranch-style chateau built by the first owner, and renovated by the project. There was an outdoor and an indoor pool. He thought it was a bit of overkill when the ocean was only two hundred yards away.

When he got to the house, he would find clothes, and he should pick out ones that fit. Then he had to go to the basement and turn on the generator, a gas-powered contraption. A family living on a nearby, well-populated island handled the maintenance. They came to the island on a predetermined schedule. They fueled the generator (if necessary) and ensured it was in good working order. They also refreshed the food and water stores.

After his return trip, the caretakers would ensure he had shut down all the electronics. They would clean up and prepare the house for the next traveler. This was a quarterly ritual. Every three months, a new traveler would arrive, carry out the same tasks, and then leave.

The tasks were the important part. Not the traveler.

Once the generator was up and running, he should drink at least 32 ounces of water and eat. The trip could mess with his metabolism and make him disoriented. He needed to stay focused.

So far this should take no more than 90 minutes.

Next, he was to turn on the hardened NeuraLink Systems computer. It would take another 30 minutes to run through its diagnostics and come alive. During that time, he should continue eating and drinking. There was also supposed to be a stack of newspapers on the large table in the living room. He was to check each paper. The caretakers delivered and stacked them. Information was compartmentalized, so all they knew about Project Nostradamus was their role in it.

If they knew more, they may not have agreed to the premise.

He had to check the news for the last three months and identify, then memorize any significant events. He had to search for catastrophes, atrocities, and disasters. He would have to skim the papers and then check the internet using a satellite uplink from the NeuraLink computer.

Remembering the checklist was easy. Remembering exact events, dates, and times was harder. Although a good memory was a prerequisite, they taught him new recall techniques. These improved his ability to memorize dates, times, and locations.

224

He wondered if those techniques came from one of the team's doctoral research papers. He wondered if Dr. Vida, his guide, was the one who formulated them.

After digesting any and all critical information, he had to walk to the top of the only mountain on the island. A long-dormant, actually dead, volcano. The trek wouldn't be high or difficult. At the top, he would find another portal, but a much, much smaller version. He would have to climb in, shut the hatch, and wait.

Hurry up and wait.

The hardened NeuraLink ran the preprogrammed return trip. The countdown started when he turned on the system. A signal would be sent to a satellite and the program would start. Eighteen hours after that, the program would activate the return portal. He had to make sure he shut everything down in the house, all within the time constraints. This included the computers, the breakers, and the generator. Then he had to make it to the return pod before the exit window. The return trip triggered an E1-type electromagnetic pulse, which would likely fry any functioning electronics.

He asked, "So why do we shut everything down?" He knew the answer. It was in the briefing Dr. Vida's father had given. Her father had been the lead on the project since its inception.

"The E1 EMP will destroy all active fuses and systems. Pretty expensive to get everything set up again."

When they reached the stairs up to the next inner chamber, she let him go first. He climbed the five steps (no escalator here) and came out in the middle of a minor chaos. Lab coats with scientists in them were speed walking in every direction. There were more clipboards, hard hats, pens, and eyeglasses than he could count.

"Dad, here's your next victim," she said as her father, the other Dr. Vida, walked up to them.

"Captain Renatus, congratulations. You're about to make the future," her father said as he extended his hand.

"Thanks, Sir, but don't you mean to make history?"

"No, no. That was done on the first trip. You will be changing the future!"

Renatus looked for his guide, but she had rushed off, lost amongst the swarm of white lab coats.

225

The story of the first traveler was legendary within the project. Since only organic material could time travel, no robots or cameras had been allowed. The traveler would have to go from the landing point to the house. They would have to boot the system and repair it if necessary. That meant they had to have an intelligent test pilot. They never entertained the lesser primate monkey option.

So they had to find someone with a near death-wish. The logic had been worked out. The hypothesis was tested, at least mathematically. The best computers ran the model over a thousand times. Each time the computers removed more and more variances. They couldn't make it 0%, but they were able to limit them to an acceptable level.

The first traveler had no idea if it would actually work. No one knew with certainty that he would arrive when and where they predicted. They didn't know if he would survive the trip or if he did, if he'd be able to return. They couldn't predict his physical or mental condition upon arrival, and they didn't know for sure if the return pod would even function. Although the Quantum Models showed it should work, they had doubts. They knew anything, and everything could go wrong. So, being the first required a traveler who was almost certifiable.

Even Test Pilots want the machine they're flying to follow proven aerodynamic principles. There were no proven principles for time travel.

Being the first might attract a few daredevils. The fame and glory would be worth risking life and limb. But in this case, that honor would be a very quiet one. Only members of the project would know. At least until well after the travelers were dead and buried. It could be centuries before the project was declassified. It likely would not happen in their lifetime, or their children's, or their grandchildren's.

The problem was, it was too dangerous.

If the world knew time travel was actually possible, there would be a new arms race.

Every time the impossible was proven possible, others achieved it quickly; for example, powered flight, artificial intelligence, and nuclear power. It seemed everyone was able to achieve a 4-minute mile after Sir Bannister did. Now it was commonplace. The only way to ensure no one else achieved time travel was for no one to ever know it was possible.

The first traveler was Lieutenant Michael Corben. He had no family, no fear, and little common sense. He left and returned without incident. Upon his return, they tested him relentlessly. They didn't know what to expect. They took an MRI to measure everything. If there was any physical deviation, they were determined to find it. They ran every test again (four times), comparing pre and post-travel results. He spent over three months in observation.

They also tested his memory, which worked fine. But he only had to bring back one piece of information. He memorized the Mega Jackpot winning numbers. The jackpot had reached a trillion dollars for the first time in history.

With the funding issue resolved, the project was able to move forward. They returned over twenty million dollars, all the money that had been invested (and spent). They apologized that the project ended up being untenable. Investors, some altruistic philanthropists, were disappointed but appreciated their honesty.

They also appreciated getting their money back.

###

"What would Ben Franklin say about this?" Captain Renatus asked.

"About time travel? He'd probably say it was science fiction. But he had an excellent mind and by that, I mean, for a scientific mind, he had a great imagination," Dr. Vida said.

"I actually meant the secrecy."

"Are you testing me, Captain? He would undoubtedly say it was impossible to keep this project a secret."

Captain Renatus smiled.

"And yes," she went on, "I know the quote. Three people can keep a secret if two of them are dead. But we have safeguards in place."

"The non-disclosure agreement?"

"Other things also. No need to go into that. But I will say, you are the first to make that your topic of discussion. Most ask about the quantum analysis or what really happens and how it works."

"I've heard rumors about trouble."

Dr. Vida raised an eyebrow and waited.

"And I wouldn't understand the science stuff anyway."

Dr. Vida wasn't sure if the captain was being modest or if he was being honest. In either case, the rumors had bothered him too.

"Yes, there seems to be a leak. One that will have to be fixed."

"So nothing to worry about..." the young captain said, without conviction.

"Nothing to worry about," Dr. Vida agreed.

"I understand the premise of the project. I go forward in time, to an isolated location where we have zero chance of affecting the future. Then I comb the news for the previous four months looking for major events."

"Yes. So, we can save lives and avert catastrophes."

"Why not do it once a year? Or even once a decade?"

"We predicted news sources would continue to decline. We expected only the latest and biggest news stories would make it into mainstream media. And we were right. Less and less is documented, so we need to query the future on a more regular basis. Checking every four months works pretty well."

"And have we averted anything yet? Saved any lives?"

"No, not yet. We started looking a few years into the future to start, one decade to be exact. But we've recorded everything so in a few years we'll be able to start taking advantage of our predictions."

"What about the trouble?"

"The zealots who learned a little about our project call us false prophets."

"And that's a cause for concern?" the captain asked.

"All prophets end up killed by the people they try to save. They even killed Christ for warning the people about the future."

"Wait, you're a Christian?"

"I'm a scientist and a realist," he said as if that answered the question. "People don't like hearing what's going to happen before it happens. Especially when they learn they are screwing up. We're screwing up the environment and killing each other in an endless string of wars. We're heading toward self-annihilation at a record-setting pace."

"So, you're going to change the future? Kill Hitler when he was a child?"

The doctor smiled pleasantly.

"No, but we plan to save as many lives as we can. The idea is to lessen the negative impact of coming catastrophes."

"And the fanatics? They don't want you saving lives?"

"It isn't that simple."

"Do they think you're messing with God's master plan?"

"If they do, they don't truly believe. If there is a God with a capital G, we can only do what we're doing with His permission."

"So you're doing God's work?"

"As much as Jonas Salk, Edward Jenning, or Alexander Fleming." Dr. Vida used their full names, not deigning to equate himself on the same level as his predecessors.

"Salk invented the polio vaccine, but who were the other two?"

"Smallpox and penicillin respectively. Together they saved millions of lives."

"And still counting," Renatus added.

"Yes, and they didn't worry about saving the life of a future Hitler or a future Van Gogh. Not our job, our calling."

"You save them all and let God work out the details," Renatus said.

"You really want to know about my faith, don't you?" Dr. Vida asked.

Renatus smiled. "Well, you never answered the question. In the military, we're not allowed to ask. If you don't want to answer, that's okay with me."

"Yes, yes I'm a Christian."

They had arrived at the prep station. Another person, a woman, in a white lab coat held open a large bag. It had the captain's name and rank on it.

He started to disrobe. "Can't you tell the fanatics that you're one of them? I mean a Christian, not a fanatic."

"That won't work. If you believe in God, you have to believe in the devil. They claim we are the devil's workforce."

Captain Renatus placed each item into the bag. First his shoes, then his shirt, then his belt and pants. "Because you are predicting the future," he offered.

"Because we will eventually predict The Second Coming."

"Do you mean Judgement Day?"

"Yes, and God clearly stated that no one will know the day or the time of that event."

The woman collecting his clothes smiled.

"They claim that if we were to identify the day and time of the rapture before it occurred, we'd be breaking God's covenant, or some such nonsense."

"Why is it nonsense?" Renatus asked.

"If God said no one will know the day or time, no one will. If they actually believed, they would not be afraid that anyone could do what God said was not possible. They have no faith."

Renatus finished undressing. He felt uncomfortable standing naked in front of everyone. The discomfort lasted only a short time since no one seemed to notice his nudity or care about his discomfort.

"Let's get this done before you catch a cold." Her voice from right behind him made the captain jump. He turned and saw it was the other Dr. Vida. She, like everyone else, had a clipboard in her hand. He turned away again before she could see his smile.

Too late.

She stepped up beside him and noticed he was blushing again.

"You know that isn't how catching a cold works, right?" he asked.

She smiled and pointed to the ladder, the third and last one.

When he climbed the ladder and closed the hatch behind him, he heard a voice over the speakers wishing him luck. He was glad it was the young Dr. Vida. Just because it had worked 25 times didn't mean it would work this time. If it were to go wrong, he wanted the last voice he heard to be hers. He gave a thumbs up.

A blue, thick, warm liquid filled the chamber. He counted to three.

"Another successful send off," the Doctor said to his daughter.

His daughter didn't respond. She had a lot to do. She set about her work, but before she could finish, things changed. Until that moment, thirty minutes after launch, everything had been normal. It mimicked the routine she had participated in every time since she joined the project. It was the same as the inaugural event. But everything after that moment was a gross deviation from the norm.

Scientists don't like deviations. The more radical the variance, the worse the consequences.

###

Alarms sounded throughout the facility. It would later be learned that the alarms were triggered much later than they should have been. Terrorists (what else could they be called?) had breached the complex's security in a violent attack. Overwhelming numbers had swarmed the facility, killing more than ten guards. The attack was aided by excellent intel. There was definitely an informant within the ranks of guards or scientists.

The attackers tried to disable the warning systems and had almost succeeded. One valiant guard, tased and shot three times, was able to trigger the manual alarm. She would never receive the medal she deserved.

Nothing would ever be confirmed. The deaths of security, terrorists, and scientists would never reach the public.

Nothing would be documented. None of the heroic deeds of the security guards would ever be shared. The fanatical determination of the terrorists would spawn no martyrs. None of the attempts by the scientists to save their work would be noted.

The treachery of the insider would go unpunished.

No one would know of Dr. Vida's quick actions to save what he cherished most.

When the alarms sounded, he rushed to the video board. Each screen displayed four different views of the chaos. It engulfed the upper levels of the facility.

His mind, one of the quickest and best in the world, calculated the risks and likely outcome. It took him less than a second.

"Prep the pod. Now!" he yelled. He never yelled. In his adult life, he had never raised his voice.

"Move, damn it!" He had also never cursed.

Those in shock rebooted their mental processing units and started hurrying about. They flushed the pod. The sound of it was clear above the din of the firefight.

He ran to his daughter. "You have to go."

"Go where?"

"You have to tell Captain Renatus that he needs to wait to return. Wait for at least 90 days. Give me that much time to ensure everything is online and functioning. Otherwise…"

He didn't need to finish; she had caught up.

"You should go. The knowledge you carry is the most valuable thing here," she said. "You're the only one who could fix whatever gets broken!"

"Then I have to be here or no one will fix it to bring me back. And I can't go anyway." He pointed to his chest, to the pacemaker beneath. He would have been one of the first to travel if he could have. Unfortunately, he had a mechanical (non-biological) device buried in his chest. The pacemaker ensured his heart worked properly. It also ensured he would never experience time travel.

"You know as much as I do," he said. "You can fix anything at that end that needs it. And you can even recreate this if necessary."

The sounds filling the floors above gave her no time to argue. She knew her father was right from an empirically logical standpoint. She started stripping. She felt no shame in undressing in front of her father. Or the other scientists. She handed him her necklace, a plain silver chain with a locket, and St. Christopher's medal. The locket contained a picture of her mother. The medal had been hers.

He looked at the tightly cut afro. No pins, or clips in her hair.

His daughter climbed the ladder and shut the hatch.

She imagined her father wishing her luck or telling her he loved her. But she knew he wouldn't do any of those things. She thought, right then, at that moment, he was all scientist and working to resolve a crisis the best way he knew how.

Of course, she was wrong. Right then he was all father, doing everything he could to ensure his daughter was safe.

But he didn't wish her luck, or tell her he loved her.

Instead, he initiated the transport.

The chamber filled and she counted to three.

When she opened her eyes, she was face down in a field of grass.

She felt the warmth of the sun on her back, a cool breeze ran across her skin, brushing the grass against her sides.

She very slowly rolled over and even more slowly sat up. She knew there was the possibility of motion sickness. She breathed slowly, deeply. She concentrated on her breathing, looking at her feet. She felt good. No vertigo. No problems.

Okay.

She looked around. She was in a large natural clearing. It seemed to match the descriptions (and photos) she'd seen of the arrival zone. But something was amiss.

She could feel it. She looked around for Captain Renatus although she didn't expect to see him. He would have headed off to the main house over an hour ago.

She knew what time it was. They always sent the traveler with an arrival time of ten hundred hours. The position of the sun was easily predicted. They didn't need a time machine for that. Direction finding would be easy. The time of day ensured a mild temperature regardless of weather conditions.

She was sent an hour later, eleven hundred hours.

No clouds. The sun was where it was supposed to be and so she turned 45 degrees to her right.

She couldn't see the trail. There should have been a well-maintained dirt trail leading to the main house. Could she have her bearings wrong?

She waited. No reason to rush off. No reason to panic.

She double-checked. She remembered that there was supposed to be a marker on a tree at the edge of the clearing.

She walked to the tree line, to where she was sure the trail should be. To where the marker should be.

Nothing.

But she did see a shape moving in the shadowed woods. It was coming toward her. He was coming toward her.

"Renatus?" she shouted in a whisper.

She didn't know why she was being cautious. No one should be on the island. No one except the Captain. As the figure came nearer, she was sure it was a person, a man.

"Doc?"

It was Renatus.

"What are you doing here?" he asked. He came into the light of the clearing. Still nude. "Is this some elaborate joke? A new reality TV show?" He seemed upset.

"What are you talking about?"

"Well, nothing is the way I was told it would be. No trail, no markers, no house, nothing. And now you're here. Naked."

It was as if she just realized. She wanted to cover herself, but resisted the urge.

"No, this is not a joke. Something's wrong."

"You're telling me? I've checked in every direction. The main house was supposed to be within 300 yards of the clearing. Even if I got the direction wrong, even if the markers had been removed...there is no house. In any direction!"

She wanted to say, that's not possible, but as a scientist she had never uttered that phrase, and she wouldn't start now. She also wanted to ask if he was sure, but she had read his dossier multiple times. He was thorough, smart, and very detail oriented. She could trust his assessment.

Instead of asking useless questions, she worked on the problem.

"How about the exit pod?" she asked.

"I haven't checked that yet."

They looked up toward the small mountain, visible from where they were.

"Let's go," she said.

Her scientist's brain, the brain she had relied on most of her life, was calmly trying to tell her something.

Climbing up the mountain was a waste of energy and time.

Why would there be anything there if the house wasn't where it was supposed to be?

How could the house not be where it was supposed to be?

But she needed something to do and she wanted more data.

Discuss the possibilities.

From the top, they'd likely find nothing, no equipment or evidence of a human presence. But they'd also have a clear view of where the house should be.

"Could we be on the wrong island?" he asked.

She took a deep breath and then another. She had to keep panic from taking over. If she became irritated, angry, or impatient, panic would be that much closer.

"No, that is unlikely," she finally said.

"But it's possible?"

"Anything is possible." They trekked out of the woods and started the climb. But there was no road. There definitely used to be a dirt road that ran up the side of the mountain—or at least there should have been. It had been there for decades.

"If someone with clearance and the necessary knowledge gained access to the system."

"Uh-huh," he added a nod to his words.

"...and they were able to make changes without anyone noticing..." More nods.

"...and they overrode the pre-programmed failsafes..."

"So definitely possible," he said.

"...and found an exact duplicate of our island, minus any signs of human life."

"Or they could have created a clone of the island." He turned and looked at her.

They stood there staring at each other, daring the other to break first.

She won. At first, it was a small grin, then his face spread into a full, ear to ear smile. When she smiled back, he started laughing in loud, healthy guffaws.

She joined him.

She couldn't remember the last time she laughed as hard.

A much better reaction to the situation than panic.

For a reason, unknown to them at the time, they both became a little self-conscious about their lack of clothes. It hadn't bothered them until the laughter. Perhaps it was the pause in their conversation or that they weren't worrying any longer.

The pressing problem seemed more distant.

And they noticed.

That's a little unfair actually. They both noticed when they first saw each other in the clearing. Renatus worked very hard not to show how much he liked her body. It was a good body. Firm and healthy, she worked out regularly. She wasn't an extremist, but she believed a healthy mind required a healthy body. She ate well, exercised, and made sure she got enough sleep, not what most people thought she would be like. They thought anyone with three doctorates must be someone who slept barely at all, did nothing but read, and had never seen a gym. All wrong assumptions.

Conversely, her assumptions about him were near-perfect. She knew his physical and mental status. She knew his military and personal history. She had read his psych evals. She knew that he also worked out regularly. Being a test pilot required him to be extremely fit, and he was. But both of them had done their best to look each other in the eyes only. They didn't let their view drift below the mouth. At least not much.

"We should get going," she said, laughter subsiding to giggles.

"Okay. We'll be able to see the whole island, right?"

"Yes, as well as check on the return pod."

He didn't say what he was thinking, *if there's a return pod.*

He tried again to engage her in conversation. He liked her voice, it calmed him. For her part, she knew talking was a coping mechanism for him, but she didn't mind. It was working for her also. She looked down at her wrist, wanting to check her heart rate on her smartwatch. Of course, she had left that behind along with everything else.

"Why are you here?" he asked again.

"There were...complications."

"Complications? What kind of complications? You mean you knew about this?" He gestured to their surroundings.

"No, no, we had no idea. I still have no idea what's going on here."

He let that sink in a little before getting back to his question. He noted that she had not answered it, and he was pretty sure he knew why.

"What were the complications?"

"There was an attack on the facility." She exhaled the breath she had been holding.

"What type of attack?" He imagined everything from a special forces' infiltration to a small tactical nuke.

"Terrorist, I think. There was a lot of noise, gunfire, and explosions."

Now he understood her reluctance to discuss it.

"Is your father all right?"

"I don't know. I hope so."

They climbed on in silence for a while.

"Again: why are you here?" he asked for the third time.

"We had to warn you not to try and come back until we found a way to let you know it was safe."

He nodded. "He'll be okay," he said, with little reason to believe it.

"If not, the program may be dead. There are still parts of it only in my father's head. And if the facility is destroyed..." She didn't finish the thought.

"Couldn't they use one of the other facilities?"

"What other facilities?"

"Aren't there other sites?"

She shook her head.

"No, only one. Why would you think there were others?"

"The pod was named Genesis I. So, there must be a II and maybe a III, and IV, right? You don't name something I unless there's a II. The first Die Hard movie wasn't Die Hard I. The Fast and The Furious wasn't a one. Even Star Wars wasn't numbered."

"Star Wars was episode IV," she said, proud that she knew a little pop culture.

"Actually, it hit theaters in 1977, and was titled Star Wars. Four years later in the re-release, they added Episode IV to the title."

She was going to break every stereotype. Nerds were supposed to know trivia.

"No, that was my father's superstitions. He numbered it 'One' so he didn't jinx the possibility of others."

"Superstitious?"

"More stereotypes. They were nerds. They didn't believe in magic or miracles (although they played D&D). But no, definitely not superstitious.

"Rarely does the first effort succeed. The attempt went off without any problems, which was statistically a miracle. The fact that our first efforts had been a success were..."

"Unrealistic?"

"Improbable may be a better word," she offered.

"Impossible?"

She gave it some thought. "No one would have predicted it would work. There was no reason to believe we could travel through time."

"And space."

"Space?" she asked.

"Yes, you not only send people into the future, but you send them to a different location."

She nodded. He was smarter than she thought, and realized she had brought some preconceived notions, herself. She was not immune to stereotyping.

"That was the only facility, the only time machine? No prototypes? No failed tests?"

She nodded. "Impossible really. But nothing is truly impossible. Most things are improbable, but nothing is truly impossible."

"Nothing?"

"Nothing. If you believe something is impossible, you'll never figure out how to make it happen. If time travel were impossible, no one would ever do it."

"That's why your father keeps it a secret," he said.

She nodded. "If people believed it was possible, they'd achieve it eventually...and it could be a very bad thing for the world."

Renatus understood evil. He had seen it in atrocities carried out against other humans across the world. He had joined the Air Force because of them. He wanted to make the world a safer place.

"I understand," he said, "but people did find out."

"No, I don't think so. The terrorists, whoever they were, can't have known. Or can't have believed it. I think they only knew we were able to predict the future."

"That would be enough, according to your father."

Mention of her father made her remember he was back there or back then, and he was likely hurt or dead. They finished the climb in silence.

When they reached the top, it was nearly thirteen hundred hours in the afternoon. The sun was high in the sky. The further they got from the ocean-cooled breezes the hotter it felt. They'd worked up a sweat on the climb.

Now at the top of the small mountain, they at least had a breeze due to the higher altitude.

Looking around they found a natural plateau at the top. It wasn't high enough that their breathing was labored. It wasn't large enough that they couldn't see across the entire space. The surface was covered in naturally short grass.

No pod.

No equipment.

Not even a bare patch of grass where the pod would have been. They looked out across the island. They could see the clearing where they had come from. They could see the shorelines on all three sides. They jogged to the other side of the mountain and peered down. It was a sheer cliff on this side as it had been for the last 100 thousand years. They walked back to the side they'd just climbed.

No house. Where the house should have been, there were trees and grass. It looked like there had never been a house, a shed, or even a satellite dish. There were no roads leading to or away from where the house should have been. On the shore, the dock was gone. There was no sign this island had ever been stepped on.

"Could we have gone the wrong direction?" he asked.

"The island's pretty small."

"I meant the wrong direction in time. Could we have gone back in time?"

"Well, the island was known for centuries to the Fijians. It has been inhabited off and on since 1612. When the island was discovered, the first and only structure built was the dock. So, we'd have to be before 1612."

He took a deep breath. Then another. He breathed in with his nose, smelling the air.

"It smells new." He wasn't sure what he meant by that, but the words spilled out.

She took a deep breath and nodded.

"It tastes clean. But it probably always did. It is a tropical island."

"I've done training in the ocean, mostly for crash and recovery exercises, and I've never smelled or tasted air like this."

She thought about that for a moment and said, "Not only would the settings have to be way off in the computer, but it would have had to be off twice. And exactly the same to send me to the same time as you."

She sat down in the grass. It was soft.

He didn't like her eyes being level with his waist so he sat down next to her. Not too close.

She finally decided she could tell him.

"We definitely didn't go in the wrong direction. It's not possible."

He smiled at that. "I thought you said nothing was impossible."

"True. Let's say the possibility is higher that you will polymorph into a blue dragon in the next five seconds."

She actually waited for five seconds.

"How do you know?"

"We haven't been able to figure out how to travel back in time. Only forward. Time travel into the past is still not possible. Who knows, someday it may be, but we haven't figured that out yet."

It was his time to think. "So how do we use the return pod? Isn't that traveling back in time?"

"Yes and no. You return to the same place and general time you left. Whatever amount of time you spend here is how far from the time you left you'll return. If you're here for three hours and return, you'll come back three hours after you left."

"And no deviations?"

"None yet."

"Okay, so if we didn't travel back in time, how do you explain this?" and he waved his hand over the island below them.

"I can't."

They sat thinking. Finally, he laid back, put his hands behind his head, and looked up at the sky.

"Could we be on a different island?"

"No."

"How about an alternate universe?"

"No."

"But all of these things are possible."

"They're not impossible."

More thinking.

"How about..." but he couldn't think of any other possibilities, no matter how ludicrous.

They spent another hour on the hill.

"So, what do we do?"

"I think we'll have to survive. There is plenty of edible vegetation. The weather on this island is temperate year-round, so we shouldn't freeze. We'll need shelter for any inclement weather. We'll also want some form of clothes."

He wasn't sure he agreed with her on that part. "So we're stuck here for the foreseeable future. Just us?" he asked.

"Unless they send someone else. But, yes, we should proceed with the assumption that we're on our own."

"Well Doc, what's first?"

"How about you stop calling me Doc?"

"Okay, but I don't know your first name," he said.

"It's Evelyn."

"Hi Evelyn, I'm Adam," he said, sitting up and offering his hand. "I know," she said.

Marty struggles daily to balance his work, passions, and family life. At the best of times, the three converge. Marty is an Expert chess player, a sports enthusiast, public speaker, life coach, streamer (Tiberian64), and a perpetual student. He loves playing, competing, teaching, learning, and living.

Martin has six business non-fiction books in print, with his book, "Metrics: How to Improve Key Business Results" being his most critical success.

And now Martin has entered the fiction writing world. His latest work is a compilation of his six novellas, The Adventures of Sir Locke the Gnome. It is now available as an Audiobook, read by Bob Feifar. Writing Sir Locke the Gnome mysteries has become a great way for Martin to share his love of both Sherlock Holmes and Dungeons & Dragons. He wrote his first novel, The Time Warp King, with his daughter. It's a YA novel set in two worlds and two times. Marty is happy to announce that this book is also available as an audiobook!

You can find his short stories in three anthologies from Critical Blast Publishing. The Monster Next Door in the anthology of related horror stories (Aug 2023), Serial Killer in The Devil You Know Best (Mar 2024) and Comfort Food in The Fables Next Door (June 2024).

ON THE PRACTICAL APPLICATION OF TIME TRAVEL

By Ann Tjelmeland

We've all done it. We've stood in the shower, driven down the road, or lain in bed and asked ourselves the same question, "If I could go back to my younger body and relive my life knowing then what I know now, would I? Would I really want to live it differently?" Then we shrug and forget it. After all, it's a silly question. It's not like it's ever going to be possible.

###

I pulled my old car into the parking lot, set the break, grabbed my purse, and headed to the lecture hall across the campus. I have to admit I'm nervous, no scratch that, I'm as giddy as a schoolgirl, which is absolutely ridiculous. Here I am a grown woman of 60. I'm a well-established woman, getting ready to retire, and happy with what I've accomplished in life. My son Luke, is a fine man. He has his little family and we live close enough for me to spend time with the grandkids. His wife, Sarah, is a treasure, she's everything a mother could want for her son. I'm content. So why am I here? Why am I practically skipping? I'll tell you why, it's because I'm going to see him. You know, HIM!

We've all got a HIM or a HER in our past. Someone we met in our youth, briefly connected with, had a short but amazing moment and then they were gone. Whether they went away to school, joined the army, or took a job on the other side of the world; all too quickly they were gone. It doesn't matter why, something beyond our control caused us to separate before either was ready. We each went on with our lives, we each lived our lives. But there was always that little space in our hearts reserved for that one special love.

God, I feel stupid, chasing after this man, I bet he won't even recognize me.

###

I had been at my desk, wasting time reading my old alma mater's newsletter and current events, when I noticed a lecture being given, entitled, "On the Practical Application of Time Travel." I laughed out loud, then I read the name of the presenter. My insides clutched, my mouth was dry and I felt dizzy. It was him. We had lost track of each other years ago. I already knew that I would attend. Oh, I tried to pretend that I wouldn't, that it didn't matter, but it did matter, it mattered terribly.

I splurged on all the "girl" things, I had a manicure and a pedicure. I had my hair styled and added some blond, to tone down the silvery-white that my hair had become. I went shopping and bought a new outfit, shoes, and a purse. Hell, I'd even considered trading in my old car. I could certainly afford it. Luckily, I came to my senses, and besides, I like my car. I'm like that, I start to get carried away, then get a grip and back off. That's the story of my life, which makes me wonder if I'd given into my impulse and offered to go with him when he'd left the state to finish school, would we still be together? Ahh, there's no use asking that question, the past is the past, and we can't change it, can we?

I arrived at the lecture hall and I sat in the front row. I watched as he gave his lecture, not hearing a word. Gorgeous as ever, but sad. Wonder why? A few seconds later, his hour-long lecture was over. I still have no clue what he said. I had watched him move. I had seen that little half-smile that used to turn me to jelly. I stayed in my seat, and he walked towards my side of the stage. Our eyes met, and he flashed a brilliant smile at me. *Did he truly recognize me?* Yes, he did, he leaned down and asked me to wait, His voice was firm, "We need to talk! Won't be more than half an hour." I sat and waited.

Finally, he was packed up and ready to go. He asked where we could grab a cup of coffee. I'd forgotten that he loves his coffee. I'm a tea drinker. I offered my house. I keep coffee for Luke when he visits. He followed me in his car.

I was nervous. We headed to the kitchen. He began asking me about my life as I prepared coffee. I told him about my first marriage which had ended in divorce and my second one which had left me a widow. He told me that he hadn't married until his late thirties but was now a widower. We commiserated on how difficult it is to lose someone you love. He looked into my eyes, "But we both already knew about that particular loss, didn't we?"

I blushed like a schoolgirl, surprised by my embarrassment, I held his gaze and whispered, "Yes, yes we did."

Silence reigned and we sat gazing into our drinks. He said, "Don't you have anything stronger?"

I broke out the scotch. We moved to the couch. He started a cozy little fire and we talked for hours. He asked what I thought of the lecture. I admitted that I wasn't paying much attention. "In truth, I hadn't heard a word."

He laughed and said he was glad he didn't see me until the end, he might have forgotten why he was there. Then he became serious and asked if I knew why he'd spent the last 30 years working on time travel.

I admitted I had no clue. He said, "Because I could never forget us."

My head spun and not because of the scotch. I could hardly breathe. He continued speaking and explained that we can't physically travel back, but he can send our consciousness back to our younger bodies. It's my fantasy come true. Suddenly, all the implications rushed me at once. If I do this, Luke won't be born, and my grandkids will be nonexistent. I am suddenly violently ill. I can't possibly, I can't kill my child…

After weeks and months of getting reacquainted. It became clear that he offered me the chance to go back and live my life again, this time with him. After much soul-searching, I finally agreed. I realized that going back would create another timeline. My son and grandkids will still exist in this timeline. I would live in our new one, and there would never be a chance to see them again. I agonized over the loss. Mentally, I could accept it, but emotionally it was all but impossible. What mother can willingly leave her child? Finally, we'd said everything there was to say. Neither of us wanted to separate again. We longed for the time we'd lost. We forged our plans.

Everything was ready. We'd explained it as best we could to Luke. He has accepted that I'm leaving, I don't think he bought the whole "time travel" story, but it doesn't matter. I've sold the business and transferred the house title to Luke and Sarah.

I was in my old car again. I drove to his lab and knocked on the door. His assistant answered. She cringed and wouldn't meet my eyes. She explains that there has been an accident. While he was setting things up in the transfer chamber, the lab mascot, a cat, jumped on the console and landed on the toggle that activated the transfer. In an instant, my beloved was gone. She and the rest of the team tracked him, he was in his body, but living in the past, years after we had originally separated. I asked them to send me to him, for many reasons that I don't fully understand, I'm told it's impossible. It has something to do with weeks of calculations and predicting the location of Earth in time and space, new dimensions having been created, and the entropy of our lives at the time of arrival, all of it is gibberish to me. What I do understand is that the answer is, "No". I'm shocked. Staggering to the parking lot, I can't believe it's over, again. We're over again. I cried, I screamed, I wanted to collapse but grief and rage kept me on my feet. Ultimately, there was nothing for me to do but climb into my car and drive home. I felt shaky, my vision blurred, and my head spun. The last time this happened it was from joy, not grief. What in the world am I going to do now?

There's a strange car in my driveway. I pull to a stop next to it and wonder if Luke is already showing the house to prospective renters. My head pounds, it's a searing, throbbing pain, and I can't see. I practically crawl from the car. Now I'm being carried and someone tucks me into bed. There is a cool cloth on my head. Gentle hands push my hair to the side. A voice says, "There, there, it's almost over. The temporal shock wave really kicked the shit out of you, but your memories will adjust."

I opened one eye, only to realize that my vision was messed up, there were streaks of light and halos in rippling effects as if I were viewing the world from underwater. But I recognize his voice, he gently says, "Amid all our planning I came to a point where I realized exactly what you were sacrificing for me. How could I say that I loved you and let you give up everything that matters in your life? I decided to go back alone.

I hope you weren't too angry with Snuggles, he's a good cat, if a bit needy. Perhaps, I should have told you, but I didn't, I knew you would argue. You wouldn't want me to give up my life either. But in truth, you were always the love of my life and it was empty without you. I knew that you had to give birth to Luke and get divorced. I couldn't take him from you. I knew you understood that he would be alive in an alternate timeline, but in our new timeline, you would be

245

without your family. I didn't want you to give up your son and grandkids for me. How could I ask that? I had such guilt."

"Yesterday morning, it occurred to me that there was a better way. I spent all day and night in the lab and recalibrated, modifying my arrival to be shortly after your divorce. I intended to tell you all about it when you arrived. But that blasted cat. When I saw him leap, I knew what would happen."

"After I arrived, I was relieved that my memories remained. I suspected that they would but wasn't certain. I still knew how to construct the machine. This time I thought better and decided that it could wait. Then I moved close to you, I have to admit I felt a bit stalkerish, but I had to know if you had remarried, and found that you hadn't."

"It took me weeks to decide how to arrange to bump into you. We dated for a few months, then married and we've been together for nineteen years."

With a soft chuckle at the irony, he said, "Just give it time and everything will fall into place, you'll remember us."

Ann retired not long ago. Her career as an international pastry chef was cut short after a tragic skydiving incident; involving top-secret information, escaped lab hamsters, and a baklava. (Don't ask!) To take up her time while in recovery, and give herself something to do besides throw knives at the walls she has barricaded herself in her attic and begun to write. Incidentally, this vexes her three, ball-addicted, golden retrievers, who have no compunction about breaking the door down and lovingly dragging her down the stairs and into the yard to play fetch. All things considered; it's not going well; the world should be concerned.

Made in the USA
Columbia, SC
13 November 2024

46394623R00152